W9-CDM-914

TAKE ONE
FOR THE TEAM

Dear Reader:

After Thomas Slater's *No More Time-Outs*, which was a mind-blowing read, we are now treated to its sequel, *Take One for the Team*.

We continue to follow one son, Wisdom Jones, who is determined to rescue his family members from their destructive lifestyles: from his pastor father who is a nightmare to his profession to a sister trapped in an affair with a thug to a drug-addicted brother.

Meanwhile, Wisdom deals with the fact that the only kidney donor for his dying mother is an old enemy, Highnoon. The storyline and characters make for an adventurous tale that leads readers to question what would they do if in the same situation.

As always, we appreciate your support of all of the Strebor Books authors and we strive to bring you powerful, cutting-edge literature from the most vibrant voices on the current literary scene. Please check out Slater's first novel, *Show Stoppah*, as well as *No More Time-Outs*. Under the pen name Tecori Sheldon, he also penned an urban fiction novel, *When Truth is Gangsta*.

You can follow me online at www.facebook.com/AuthorZane or on Twitter@planetzane.

Blessings,

Zane

Publisher
Strebor Books International
www.simonandschuster.com

ZANE PRESENTS

TAKE ONE
FOR THE TEAM

A NOVEL

THOMAS SLATER

SBI

STREBOR BOOKS

NEW YORK LONDON TORONTO SYDNEY

SBI

Strebor Books
P.O. Box 6505
Largo, MD 20792
http://www.streborbooks.com

ISBN 978-1-59309-438-6
ISBN 978-1-4516-7807-9 (e-book)
LCCN 2012933943

First Strebor Books trade paperback edition November 2012

Cover design: www.mariondesigns.com
Cover photograph: © Keith Saunders/Keith Saunders Photos

10 9 8 7 6 5 4 3 2 1

Manufactured in the United States of America

For information regarding special discounts for bulk purchases,
please contact Simon & Schuster Special Sales at 1-866-506-1949
or business@simonandschuster.com

The Simon & Schuster Speakers Bureau can bring authors to your
live event. For more information or to book an event, contact the
Simon & Schuster Speakers Bureau at 1-866-248-3049 or visit our
website at www.simonspeakers.com.

WISDOM

FRIDAY...

I sat outside on the bleachers of a neighborhood park that the locals had nicknamed "The Hole." It wasn't too cold out, but my knee was singing me the blues rendition of the National Anthem. Cornflake-sized snowflakes gathered around the shoulders of my gray uniform jacket. The last two months of my life were replaying inside my dome like some ghetto version of a Shakespearean tragedy. Tyler Perry would've been tossing Bentley Coupes through my bedroom window for an opportunity at the option of transforming my dys-functional family drama into one of his record-breaking, box-office smashes.

To recap: My mother was dying from kidney complications and needed a donor—like yesterday. When out of nowhere, this gold-tooth-wearing serpent, Highnoon, slithered from my past with a sleazy proposition. Somehow, he'd found out about my mother's condition and wanted to help. It turned out that he was the exact match for a donor. There was a deadly catch to it. His generosity had been spawned by revenge. And I was the closest living relative to the one responsible for his pain. The proposition was sickening. He would give my mother a kidney if I surrendered my life to him for his sick, twisted pleasures in quenching his thirst for revenge. There was nothing that was too special for my mother, so I agreed by signing Highnoon's contract. We were in his version of The House of Pain, and I was about to fulfill my end of the bargain when he asked me *the* question: Did I have one last thing to say? It was something to that effect. He was at my left eye with something that looked like a blow torch when I answered. "Yeah. I wish that I could have one week to put my family right with the Lord, and each other." Highnoon turned off his machine of torture and gave me seven days, one whole week, to restore my wayward family to its place of purity in God's eyes.

Somehow, I had to manage to corral four wayward souls and force them back on the path of righteousness. Indeed, it would be a tall order, and I would be working with only seven days to get it done. My sister, Tempest, would need major convincing to keep her legs closed to the offers from others, and finally open her heart up to her husband. I had to find my crackhead baby brother again, Jordan, before he got himself smoked by a cop hell-bent on revenge. The last time I'd gone chasing him through the ghetto for some intervention, my partner, Rico, and I, were staring down the barrel belonging to two crack-pushing BéBé's Kids. Reverend Poppa Jones, my father, the pastor at Infinite Baptist Church, couldn't keep his pecker out of the women in his congregation, and my big brother, Yazoo, would prove to be my toughest battle. He wanted to be a gangsta—except the Negro ain't never had street nowhere in his DNA. Seven days to turn their lives around—I had seven friggin' days.

But now, I was among fifteen chumps who occupied seats on cold bleachers waiting patiently for a turn to get into a pick-up game in progress. Over the years, The Hole had gotten its fair share of bad press, a virtual media feeding frenzy. Almost every other month, it was nothing to turn on the local news and see coroners dragging bodies from the place. There, the possibility of a pick-up game ending in gunfire was more common than hemorrhoid flare-ups. But regardless of its brutal nature, some of the biggest stars in the NBA once battled on its blacktop. Young, hood-hopping hopefuls still flocked to the park to mix it up with the old-heads in the glorious pursuit of that next level reputation.

Light snowfall made conditions on the court slick as flakes melted upon surface contact. It did very little to stop the action on the court as play heated up. A punk named Pogo was showing his ass. He went baseline and threw one down on some tall, lanky guy named Alex. The park exploded with "oohs" and "aahs" as Pogo landed, offering a double bicep pose, feeling himself. This Negro and I had history. Bad blood that dated back to my injury. The jerk had been the one responsible for me shredding my ACL. And knowing it, I couldn't explain what type of madness had drawn me back there, to the same place where my knee and basketball career had been shattered. For me, The Hole was a place where my dreams had ended and my nightmares had begun.

I could no longer fool myself. My reason for today's visit was pure evil solely sponsored by Satan. Inadvertently, Highnoon had turned me into a monster with the proposition. I could do anything to anybody and wouldn't have to worry about consequences from the laws that governed man. Pogo was about to feel my wrath. The Bible stated that revenge belonged to the Lord, but I couldn't go to my grave knowing that the fool responsible for costing me an NBA career was still serving up Negroes on the basketball court. Of course, Pogo had given me a song-and-dance about it being accidental, a case where his athleticism had taken a backseat to his passion for aggressive play. Of course I never believed the shit, not for one moment. From day one, Pogo had been a jealous-hearted bastard with a nasty reputation for being a dirty player. He hated on my game, ups, handle, and the fact that my career was taking off, while his was flying way below the NBA radar.

I sat back, knee throbbing, going over a violent list of things I'd planned for my old enemy, when Pogo got into the passing lane and intercepted the basketball. The anticipation of a highlight reel dunk captured attention. Pogo exploded down the court, beating defenders, getting his steps together, and launched himself from the free throw line—like MJ. I wasn't hating on the brother or nothing, but the Negro's sneakers were player eye level as he floated by and two-handed monster dunked.

"Game, nigga!" Pogo shouted, cold smoke escaping his mouth as he hung from the rim. "Get the next set of victims out on this bitch!" The nine other guys walked off the court, dressed appropriately for the weather in sweats, hoodies, and sneakers, to grab a seat or hydrate.

"Good game, my nigga," a sloppy-looking cat said to Pogo.

"I don't know why yo' ass didn't go pro," said another chump with a big nose, sloping forehead, and rocking a unibrow.

Victim was right, I thought. Because after today, Pogo was going to need the assistance of a pogo stick to ever reach his vertical-leaping maximum again. He saw me and immediately walked his cornrowed, R-Kelly-looking ass over like he'd never robbed me of a golden opportunity at gracing a cover of *Sports Illustrated* magazine.

"What up doe, kinfolk?" He fist-bumped me. The schmuck was about six-two and wearing a hoodie that boasted a *Just Do It* slogan across the chest, a skull hat and some crusty, water-soaked Olympic 6 Air Jordans. I had to hand it to him. Pogo had a huge set of grapefruits.

"I see that you haven't lost a step. Nice game."

"Thanks, kinfolk! You know these young cats come up in here to make a name. They'll never style on my watch."

I removed my jacket and placed it on the aluminum,

exposing my gray uniform shirt. Under any other circumstances, I would've never worn jeans with black work boots to get it in.

"I hear you."

"I ain't seen you around here in a minute, not since the evening of the accident."

My temper was on boil. I couldn't believe that this trout-mouth little punk was still tagging his jealous rage as an accident. But I stayed cool.

"Damn, Wisdom, I don't see how you could come back here anymore. Me personally, I would've put a pistol up to my head years ago and pulled the trigger. It would've been too much for me to lose all the money and fame that came with the NBA." He glanced in the lot where my mail van was parked. "I guess I ain't as strong as you are."

I hadn't missed Pogo's cute little diss. It was all good, though.

Normally, I would've conducted a thorough evaluation, skimming the sidelines for talent before I made my selection. But I didn't have winning on my mind. So I randomly selected four nobodies from the side.

The moment that the ball was inbounded, I was all business. My knee was screaming bloody murder the first trip down the court. Being back in the saddle had me feeling like I was invincible. I had to check myself. I wasn't there for the thrill of the game. And Pogo found that out the moment he lost his man and tried to go all

Michael Jordan with it. An alley-oop was tossed and Pogo catapulted himself off the ground to grab it. If it had been an NBA game, the flashbulbs would've been blinding in an effort at capturing his effortless flight, and the roar of the fans would've been deafening. But it wasn't the NBA and Pogo wasn't Kobe Bryant.

Much in the same manner, I lowered my shoulder like he'd done years ago and delivered a nasty undercut. I would like to say that time stood still to watch Pogo suffer the same fate he had given me on the evening of the NBA draft. I stood erect and took great pleasure in watching his wiry body do a somersault over my six-six frame like a propeller that had busted away from the hub of a plane while crashing through thick trees. Pogo tumbled to the cold, unforgiving ground, landing flat on his face. I'd been saving that undercut for quite some time. It was executed perfectly, but I wasn't aware to what degree the idiot had been injured.

Pogo lay there perfectly still. I thought I might've killed his ass until he groggily rolled over onto his back. In the place where his face had lain, there was a pool of crimson-red blood mixed with a small puddle of water. I thought that I hadn't done enough, until he cringed, opening his mouth. I was satisfied; his once healthy smile had been vandalized by a mouth filled with bloody, jagged stumps. And although I was filled with pleasure resulting in the rising pain on his face, I somehow knew that it would never equal out to the millions I would've earned in the NBA. Seeing him gag on his own blood and spit out teeth fragments was priceless.

My job was done.

Nobody said shit to me as I walked off to the side and slid on my jacket. I didn't have to offer an excuse for my actions. A few of those cats were around when Pogo had taken away my NBA opportunity and a chance to give my family a better life. They knew the deal. It was the big payback.

The others probably looked at it as though it was a senseless cheap shot. There were a couple of bums from his team trying to help Pogo to his feet. But every time they tried, he sank back to the asphalt. I'd completely fronted on my team in pursuit of my own brand of justice. I was pumped and ready to take on those that had the nuts to step up and play Captain Save-A-Hoe. Other than a few stares, like I'd lost my damn mind, everybody else was fixated on the carnage left behind on the court. I was cold but I wasn't completely heartless. So I went into my pocket to fetch my MetroPCS. I was about to dial nine-one-one when I heard somebody yelling from a distance using a familiar tone. I turned slowly but with the uncertainty of somebody caught between running like a coward and mannin' up. Walking across the snow-covered grass in the distance, maybe fifteen to twenty guys were coming my way.

That was about the time when I figured out coming to that part of town by myself had been baptized in stupidity. The newcomers had walked on the court and watched as two of Pogo's teammates dragged his worthless carcass away. I'd won a small victory, but something told me that the army was there to win the war.

I recognized the leader. He was a small dude with an extra-large mole on the chin, clutching a pistol in his right hand. The barrel was about the size of one of my extra-large feet. Most of the guys that had been there before these fools rolled up had taken flight at the sight of the pistol.

"So, Sasquatch," Molechin said with all the disrespect one could muster. "We meet again, but this time"—he looked around at his crew—"instead of your big mouth boy getting the drop on us, we got you."

It was one of the BéBé's Kids that Rico and I had rolled up on the night we were searching the ghetto for Jordan.

"You still pissed at my boy for taking your strap that night and telling you to get your ass back in school?"

Moleman brought his weapon into full view as if experiencing an orgasm at the sight of it. "No worries. I got a replacement here. We 'bout to cause you some serious brain damage, nigga."

None of his soldiers said a word. It was as if they were awaiting his command. All were dressed in black Timbos, same color Dickies, and Carhartt jackets. Stone-faced killers. I cursed myself for being so stupid by putting myself in the line of fire. High-noon's contract would be worthless if I didn't make it back. And Momma would most certainly die.

It surprised me that a few morons had stayed behind to

see how this would play out. But it didn't come as a total shocker that one of the spectators was Pogo. The Negro was livid. Whatever the color of the towel that he'd been using to absorb the blood leaking from his mouth, it had turned completely red.

Moleman raised his piece. "Nigga, this is gonna be nice. I'd been hoping to run back into you. I've been dreaming about putting yo' ass in the dirt for so long that my dick itches."

"The pharmacy has creams for conditions like yours." The first thing that came to my mind was the night that I'd beaten the brakes off Paco and his goons in Southwest Detroit. But Jack had my mouth quick with the insults that night. I was completely sober at the moment. This time I didn't quite know where the insult had come from, but it triggered life from his soldiers.

"You niggas, chill!" The mole-chinned little schmuck commanded his troops. "I got this one."

He closed the distance between us but stayed out of my reach. In dramatic fashion, he yanked back the slide on the pistol and turned it to the side like the Black modern-day gangstas in the movies. "After I do you, I'm gonna find yo' crackhead brother, Jordan, and send him to see you. That bitch owes me money." He laughed like he was holding all the cards. "Oh, and what's the other nigga's name?" Molechin asked a soldier near him wearing dark shades.

"Name's Rico, boss."

Molechin arrogantly laughed at the fear displayed by my eyes. Apparently, the creep had been doing a little street research.

"Yep, Lace and his crew are out tracking yo' boy as we speak. You didn't think that we would let you and yo' mans get away with styling on us, did you? The shit cost us our jobs, homeboy, and now you gots to pay."

The little runt was about to squeeze the trigger when five black Hummers appeared out of nowhere. The powerful trucks dominated the snowy terrain as they drove across the grass with urgency, fully maneuvering like they had driven right off of the big screen and out of a Michael Bay action movie. Everybody froze as the trucks came to a stop, blocking off every possible route of escape. The doors opened on four of the vehicles and out jumped cats who were dressed in army fatigues and combat boots, baldheads, and packing some serious heat. Nothing but AR-15s surrounded Moleman and his crew. Where the little chump's troops once stood with the ferocious posture and stone-faced resolve of glorified killers, their faces were now animated by sheer terror.

Once the area was locked down, the driver from the last Hummer walked to the back door and opened it. Highnoon stepped out dressed like his small militia and smoking a Cuban cigar.

"Wisdom, Wisdom, Wisdom." Highnoon sang my name in his usual, flat, irritating cadence. "You didn't think I'd let you out without bodyguards, now did you?"

Over the years I'd built up a tough reputation on the streets as a man who could hold his own when it came to watching his back. And I could've ridden that wave of pride, but it would've been total bullshit. I was inwardly smiling and trying hard to hide the look of relief on my face. For once, I was pleased to see Highnoon's gold-toothed grill.

"Wisdom, go and take care of your business." Highnoon stared at his men. They raised their weapons, all trained on Moleman and his crew. "I'll finish cleaning up here."

Without words, I walked to the mail van. I didn't owe him a damn thing, not even a thank you card. I saw the save as him protecting his investments, looking after his portfolio.

Before I could close my door all the way, Highnoon said, "Seven days. Don't waste them. The clock's ticking."

Giving light to this new situation, I was gonna need a little longer. The look on Molechin's dumb little face let me know that Lace had a hit on Rico. My trip to the Great Beyond would have to be postponed. I would need two additional days. Unbeknownst to the both of us, chasing Jordan through the ghetto that night and embarrassing the hell out of Molechin and his boy, Lace, would come back in the form of bounties on our heads. I felt like the entire thing was my fault. I had to warn my boy. I didn't know Lace's reputation, but a baby gangsta with his toes stepped on would be up for putting in the work to restore his standings with the homies, even if it meant murder.

"Highnoon," I said. "I'm gonna need you to add two more days on top of the seven you've already given me."

Highnoon glanced at Molechin and his partners. He removed his cigar from his lips and disrespectfully blew smoke in Molechin's grill, shaking his head. "I'm feeling generous today—tell you what, you got two more days. You're a rich man now—you have nine days total. God created the world in six and on the seventh day, He rested. Get it done."

"I'm not God," I said.

"No, but after these nine days"—he glanced over the firepower pointed at Molechin and crew—"you'll be with Him." The big ape dismissively turned his head.

Regardless of all the insidious players that were involved inside this high-stakes game of life and death, I had to pull out the win. My mother's life absolutely depended on it. There was no turning back. In front of me the game had begun. This was that last-second, heroic shot that every little kid around the world dreamed of making. I would go into battle armed with the knowledge that I had no more time-outs left to successfully take one for the team.

NOWHERE TO RUN, BITCH

Tempest shot up from the bed with her right hand covering her mouth to stifle a scream, and her left over her racing heart. Sweat beaded her brow, just enough to saturate the rim of her colorful, flower-printed headscarf. The nightmares of being arrested for trying to smuggle drugs into prison had started biweekly at first, but now they were a regular nighttime theater of horror, less the price of admission. Tears fell from Tempest's eyes and her chest heaved as she desperately tried to get a grip on her breathing. She was in trouble and seriously doubted if anyone could help. Geechie was the real-fucking deal and had become a menacing presence in Tempest's day-time hours. Now, he was a terrifying, diabolical force inside her dream world where the young thug acted as head devil in charge.

In the early morning sunrays that managed to navigate and penetrate the cracks of the vertical blinds inside her bedroom, Tempest brought her knees up to her chest. As she hugged herself, tears of frustration, grief, shame and anger rained down, but did little to wash away the filth and guilt of her adulterous moments with Geechie.

Her extramarital affair with the homicidal maniac had connected her in a way that left her powerless to free herself. One of their late-night, bump-and-grind sessions had somehow wound up on a DVD that was in Geechie's possession. He was trying to use it to exploit Tempest into being his mule to transport drugs into prisons. It was typical blackmailing procedure. Do the deed or else. The *else* would be complimentary copies mailed out to the hubby, her family and every gossiping hair-stylist who worked in her shop. Not to mention some YouTube exposure. Geechie had promised after he was finished with distribution, she would have her own reality television series with the Kardashians trying to keep up with her.

Tempest didn't want to do it, but she had no choice. Her marriage and businesses she'd worked so hard to build would implode from the scandal. The embarrassment from the fallout would be enough to drive her to the brink of insanity. There was no other way. Tempest rocked back and forth as if to release tension from her body and not let it grow into the kind of debilitating stress that would require medical attention. Poor Darrius, her beloved husband, would be devastated. He would probably file for an immediate divorce.

On paper, she would be the perfect mule for the job. Nobody would ever suspect a prominent businesswoman like her to haul dope into the penal system.

No criminal history. Not even a single parking ticket. Tempest had heard Geechie brag a few times about how he would make tons of cash by supplying prisons with his product. She had let the devil get between her legs and now he was trying to screw her for life. The bad part was that there was absolutely nobody she could confide in. Everybody inside her family was busy fending off their own demons. Her oldest brother, Yazoo, had gone ape at the family meeting and punched out her lights. In the midst of all the chaos, Jordan, her cracked-out baby brother, had somehow managed to five-finger Reverend Poppa Jones' Rolex watch from his study and vanish into thin air. Her father was far too busy whoring from the pulpit to advise her. The stress alone of a confession of this magnitude would be enough to finish her critically ill mother. She wasn't even about to go there. Wisdom was the only one she could depend on, but she couldn't bring herself to tell him. At that moment, she felt like the dirtiest whore on a planet where dirty whores reigned supreme. Telling Wisdom about her indiscretions would draw serious judgment. Sure, he would sympathize with her and suggest a way out, but she wouldn't be able to live with his silent opinion of her.

It was five minutes to seven. She reached over and switched off the alarm before the thing could start ring-ing at seven o'clock, her usual time to rise and shine. Friday was one of the busiest days of the week for the shop. Since she couldn't trust—nor would she burden one of her irresponsible, ghetto stylists—not one of her employees to collect booth rent, Tempest hesitantly crawled from the California king and headed for the shower in her master bathroom.

She caught a glimpse of her haggard image in the huge mirror over the double-sink vanity while trading in a headscarf for a shower cap. Tempest immediately looked away. She didn't like what she had become, a female version of her father. For many years, she'd watched as the good reverend's well-known affairs with women in his congregation reduced her mother from a proud, healthy woman to an emaciated, brokenhearted carcass within inches of a homegoing celebration. Now, she was doing the same thing to her husband, and with common street trash—somebody who wasn't worthy to sniff the blossoming fragrance from her nectar of love.

Tempest turned on the shower and let it run until steam clouded her vision. She tucked a few rebellious strands of hair under her cap and brought the nightgown up over her head. She stepped in and let the warm water wash over her body.

A drug mule, she thought. Someone of her status, reduced to such a lowly, law-breaking role. Rage immediately followed her thought. She wished, for one moment, that God had endowed her with the power to temporarily change genders. The man that she would become would beat the living hell out of Geechie's woman-beating ass. Not just for herself, but for women around the world who were bullied by shit like Geechie. Inside of a man's body, Tempest would serve Geechie an ass-whopping so severe that the Negro would be plead-ing with her to kill him. It would be nothing compared to stripping the gangster bare-butt, booty-naked while forcing the kingpin to tuck his genitalia between his legs and walk—knock-kneed—down a main street at rush hour.

Tempest's giggles ballooned into full-blown laughter. She laughed at the pathetic image until she started coughing. The crap was so funny. Tempest hadn't laughed like this in a long time. She grabbed a loofah from the shower caddy and soaked it with body scrub scented with coconut and lime.

She had had an extremely difficult childhood. Besides her father's demons, she had managed to stay clear of all the teenage, ghetto pitfalls that had claimed her peers: drugs, teenage pregnancy and abortions. She couldn't take all the credit though. Her parents were so strict on her that Tempest didn't have her first date until senior prom—even then she had been told to be in by midnight. Blaming her parents would've been the easy way out.

As she lathered and rinsed off, Tempest admitted to herself that she was the only one to blame—not her father or mother. They hadn't forced her down on Geechie's dick. The truth was raw and shocking. And it felt re-energizing, like a man on *Maury* who'd just found out that he was not the baby's father.

Tempest turned off the shower and grabbed a hanging bath towel. She quickly dabbed dry and wrapped it around her torso. Lately, she had found herself reading the Bible. There was a scripture that resonated with her: "Train up a child in the way he should go: and when he is old, he will not depart from it" (Proverbs 22:6). Her parents had trained and brought her up by using the powerful Word of God.

Tempest moved to the front of the sink nearest the bathroom door looking out into the hallway. Yeah, she had strayed. She had parted her legs for a sorry ass, mangy, stray mutt and was now scratching from a flea infestation of misery. There was a digital clock sitting on the vanity in the corner by her husband's sink. Trying to figure shit out had placed her way behind schedule. Normally by this time, she would be finishing up breakfast and getting ready to walk out of the house. She brushed her teeth, thinking it was a good thing not having to be bothered with putting on a face. Tempest was a natural beauty and thanked God for His blessings.

She moved back into her bedroom and walked right in her spacious walk-in closet, having realized the error of her ways would put her back in God's Grace. He alone would be able to deal with Satan's closest son. Tempest had gone on a few runs with Geechie and seen firsthand how he brutally dealt with those who opposed his will. Goosebumps chilled her flesh as she thought about the man known as NiggaWhat—there had been so much blood.

Tempest selected a tan pantsuit, leopard-print shell and caramel leather Michael Kors shoes. She took a seat on the comfortable cushion of the bed bench, desperately trying to fight down the horrifying images of a very badly beaten, bloody NiggaWhat after Geechie had done a number on the poor man's head with a simple tire iron.

In a rush, she began moisturizing her flesh with body cream. Tempest slipped into her bra and panties, somehow managing to suppress the graphic, mental photos of death. She wasn't so lucky to escape the sounds made by a dying man that had been recorded and periodically played in her head like old forty-five records. It was a deep, throaty gurgle. Some type of rattle. Tempest couldn't help the feeling of guilt that washed over her body. She'd witnessed a murder. Geechie had put her front and center. The entire unpleasant experience had been nothing but a mere warning to her. He wanted her to know that he wouldn't hesitate to kill her. There was nothing she could've done for the dying man. Going to the police wouldn't have been the intelligent thing to do. She feared ending up like NiggaWhat.

Geechie was dangerous and probably borderline psychotic, but she was determined not to let fear hold her in captivity. Nobody was going to control her. Yeah, the maniac wouldn't hesitate to shoot her, but she couldn't be afraid of her own death. God was the true ace up her sleeve and her life belonged to Him—not Geechie, but her Lord and Savior.

Tempest pulled on her pants, pulled over the shell, and slipped into her shoes. She walked back into the bathroom.

Silly her.

With all the worrying, she'd forgotten to remove her shower cap. Her long mane fell around her shoulders. With a rat tail comb, Tempest stared into the mirror while straightening her hair. If she didn't get a move on soon, her stylists would be blowing up her cell and trippin' about not being able to get into the shop. There were a few decent girls who worked for her, but none she trusted enough to give keys.

Final touches belonged to lip gloss and eyeliner. She grabbed her jacket and made her way down one of two spiral staircases. Tempest's heels echoed as she walked across a huge marble foyer, headed toward the front entrance.

She'd become a creature of habit. Almost every morning she would enjoy reading the *Detroit Free Press* while eating breakfast. It was clockwork, like her going out at the same time in the morning to retrieve the paper from the front porch. But today, there wasn't any time for a bite to eat. Her plans were to simply grab the paper off the porch and stop at the Tim Hortons around the corner from her West Bloomfield home for a bagel and coffee. Tempest fetched a cuir-colored ostrich Gucci bag with light gold hardware and car keys from a sofa table.

She was halfway to the double doors when her cell vibrated inside her handbag. Tempest stopped to remove her phone. It was a text. Couldn't have been from her husband—not this early. Darrius was away on a business trip and never called at this time of morning.

Probably one of the girls from the shop, she thought.

Tempest retrieved the text. The fine hairs on her neck stood up and an Arctic chill ripped through her body when she read Geechie's text:

You can't hide, bitch.

Panic gripped her. But this shit had to stop here. She had to let the asshole know that she was determined to stand her ground. The Lord would suffer her not to be moved. She texted back two words: **Fuck you!**

Just like that, she had declared war on a man who practically hungered for bloody situations. Tempest didn't know how this thing was going to turn out. She would dig in her heels and pray for some kind of divine intervention. Nothing short of a miracle would save her in dealing with a monster that lived on death and destruction.

Tempest hit a button on the keypad and heard that old familiar sound of the garage door creaking open. She had intended on just stepping out, grabbing the paper but leaving through the garage attachment. But when she opened one of the colossal mahogany doors, the sight of Geechie and his bodyguard, Flash—who was built like the Himalayan Mountains—caused her to freeze.

The chocolate-complexioned creep even had the nerve to smile as he held on to her *Detroit Free Press* paper. Geechie brought his phone into view.

"Naw, Ma, you got shit twisted." He dropped the paper. "Fuck *you!*"

Geechie rushed through—his man-mountain on his heels. Instinct caused Tempest to sling her seven-thousand-dollar handbag at his head. The flying bag knocked his ass senseless. The lull was all she needed. Through the living room and into the kitchen, Tempest was moving as fast as her six-inch heels could take her.

"I'm coming for you, bitch!" Geechie maniacally taunted.

His voice sounded like he was still at the front door. There was a room between them—or so she had thought, because when Tempest went to open the garage door attachment, a strong pair of hands almost snatched her out of her clothes.

"Somebody help!" Tempest screamed, trying to wiggle free.

Geechie's bodyguard, Flash—as big as he was—was having a tough time trying to hold on. Geechie walked up as his boy struggled with Tempest and immediately backhanded the shit out of her. The blow did little to stop her from struggling and yelling for help. Tempest watched in horror as Geechie removed a pistol from his waist. She screamed for help even louder.

She didn't shut up until he pointed the thing in her face.

This is it, she told herself. She made peace with her Maker. Geechie was about to send her to a place where NiggaWhat was probably waiting on her. When she saw the blood dripping from the corners of his mouth, Tempest realized that she had fucked up—royally. The purse hadn't missed after all. Geechie's mouth had caught the full brunt of her swing.

The Negro was beyond pissed.

He tasted his warm blood. "Damn, Ma, I ain't tasted my blood in a long time." Geechie grabbed a handful of Tempest's hair and yanked it back, placing the barrel under her chin. "Almost taste like your pussy." He dabbed his blood with an index finger, offering it to her. "Taste it."

She pleaded, "Please don't kill me."

"You comin' with me, Ma. I ain't gonna kill yo' ass. Not until I fuck you one last time." Geechie turned the gun until he was holding the barrel. "This will teach you to do what the fuck I say." He raised the weapon high and brought the butt down hard across her forehead.

JORDAN

Robbery was a way of life now. Crack was a master that demanded to be served first and before all others—which explained the reason why Jordan was concealed in the shadows and observing the parking lot of an all-night liquor store.

Desperation had caused Jordan to abandon his normal method of operation. He normally didn't work at night, but the heat from his crime spree had pushed him to take risks. Elderly women—his normal prey items—had been warned by the media to stay off the streets until local authorities could apprehend the purse-snatcher. With almost every old broad heeding the warning, he had to give the SSI crowd a break. Middle-aged women still possessed that fighting spirit to put up a tussle in order to keep their belongings. And since meals had been few and far between for him, Jordan didn't carry around enough weight to go toe-to-toe with some of the bigger sisters. Evolution had caused him to step his game up. These days, he carried around a .38 revolver. The ever-dangerous detective named Popeye was still hot on his trail and had forced Jordan to seek shelter in abandoned homes.

Two nights prior, freezing temperatures had caused him to break into a rundown two-family flat. Scrounging around he'd managed to find a blood-covered .38 Smith & Wesson. There were only three bullets left in the chamber—more than enough to get his point across. It wasn't lost on him that the thing had probably been used in a murder, but he welcomed the protection. He'd wiped the weapon down and had it tucked into his waistband, crouched down in the shadows, and hid on the side of an all-night liquor store.

His world was quickly closing in on him and he needed to have a conversation with his little white god. He needed to score some crack and only knew of one way to come up with the loot that would enable him to reach his destination. Jordan wanted to get high and reach the stratosphere—tonight. Sobriety had proven to be a head-cracking adversary and he could no longer live with the guilt of knowing that he'd put his girl-friend, Monique, in Popeye's crosshairs. In order to locate Jordan, Popeye had found Monique and brutalized her to extract Jordan's whereabouts. The rogue cop's mother had been one of Jordan's many victims. Once he found out that Jordan had been responsible, Popeye had been tossing the neighborhood trying to flush him to the surface.

The gun had given Jordan the courage to come back to his old hunting grounds. He wasn't afraid anymore. The three bullets would be enough. If Popeye continued beating the brush for snakes, he would indeed find one.

Jordan would be the copperhead who would bear Smith & Wesson-like fangs to deliver a lethal, hot, penetrating lead dosage of venom that would put Popeye flat on his damn back.

The side of the store where Jordan stood was in an alley with a commanding view of the parking lot. Everybody knew the storeowner to be a cheap bastard who neglected little things like surveillance cameras. There would be no grainy footage of him sticking the gun into the face of his victim to hand over to the police. A bigboned sister had gotten out of an older-model Cadillac Escalade a few minutes ago and was now inside the store. Jordan stood watching for other visible occupants inside the SUV, but the lady seemed to have come alone. He reasoned that the dark-skinned, heavyset lady was probably packing heat. These days everybody and their mamas who lived in the state of Michigan were running around and flossing CCW permits. Jordan knew most women to keep the weapons in their purses—which made owning one useless. It would make getting the drop on the lady a piece of cake. He planned on having his piece up to the fat broad's head before she could do anything.

Jordan figured she'd be in the store for a few moments, so he had time to chill and reflect on his family. His father wasn't shit—matter of fact, the good Reverend Poppa Jones, in his estimation, was a piece of shit. The old bastard, and his inability to keep his dick out of the old hags in his congregation, was the sole reason why his family was so fucked up today. This stood to reason why Jordan had started smoking crack in the first place.

It was the lake.

He was trying to escape from the lake. His oldest brother, Yazoo, had had a different father from the rest of them. All the children in the family had affectionately come to know him as Daddy Frank. Daddy Frank had been an avid outdoorsman. He loved to fish, hunt and sometimes go camping in the woods. When Jordan's mother, Wilma, had ended her relationship with Frank and moved on to marry Reverend Poppa Jones, Frank never shied away from the commitment to his son, Yazoo. Eventually, the reverend and Wilma had produced more kids, and as the family grew, Daddy Frank always involved all of the kids in his many outdoor excursions.

One in particular stood out from the rest in Jordan's mind. The memory was enough to catch in his throat, causing him to cough a few times. His stomach felt queasy and a lonely teardrop slid from the corner of his left eye.

The lake.

He was back at the lake. On that day, he'd somehow accidentally fallen into the cold water. His brothers had desperately tried to fish him out, but to no avail. Wisdom had become alarmed as he witnessed the current sweep Jordan out of their reach. Jordan couldn't remember what happened next. For the life of him, he couldn't figure out what had kept him afloat. Some unknown explanation had caused him to remain calm. He didn't splash around as the current took him farther and farther away from shore. Jordan didn't have much memory after seeing his people grow smaller as he drifted from the bank. He closed his eyes and floated. Then out of nowhere, he could hear the sound of water violently splashing about and Daddy Frank screaming his name. Hands. He felt Daddy Frank's hands close around his narrow shoulders, and with one mighty push, Jordan was propelled back toward the shore. What happened after that was a complete blank. The next time he'd seen Daddy Frank, the man looked to have been asleep in a box with flowers all around.

Ever since then, Jordan had been on a personal crusade to stay away from the truth. Crack had become his chief coping mechanism. Naturally, he blamed himself for Frank's death, but when he got high, he could not give a flying fuck. In his opinion, the wrong man had died that day. And if he would've been granted a life or death choice about who got to stay and who shipped out, Reverend Poppa Jones would've been the nigga tapping at St. Peter's pearly gates. The shit was pretty deep; a man with no biological commitment to his father's family had been the one providing the emotional stability.

Now their lives were in complete anarchy, with every last family member battling with demons. His brother, Wisdom, a once promising NBA prospect, was now stuck at a go-nowhere job and tied to an ungrateful bitch by his unborn child. It would kill Tempest to know that he'd seen her a few times driving around town with some gangster named Geechie in the passenger seat of her SUV, the one her husband was making the payment on. Yazoo, his oldest brother, had a pure hatred for God and was determined to challenge the Holy Divine at every given opportunity. Jordan had also seen him around town with Geechie. His poor mother had one foot in the grave and the other on black ice. On top of it all lurked the good reverend, who didn't hesitate to stick his book of revelation in every nasty hole that wore a skirt and heels.

Jordan had to put all of his family's skeletons back into the closet and seal the door super-tight. The fat broad was hoofing her way out of the store holding a plastic bag held by the handle in both hands. The strap to her purse was around her left shoulder. The woman looked like she bore the strength of an elephant. A simple run-and-grab wouldn't work in this case. He wouldn't be able to generate the momentum needed to snatch and keep on moving. Sure, he'd calculated the lady to be carrying a gat in her purse, but wondered if he was wrong and she would come from under her thick jacket with the smoke. Jordan's back would be exposed and she wouldn't hesitate to shoot the shit out of him.

Standing there brooding over possibilities had seriously thrown off his timing. The mistake was letting her get near her truck before he started out after her. Jordan almost slid on snow-covered ice as he sprinted behind her with the half-emptied .38 out in front. Instinct must have caused the lady to turn her head, but she didn't panic. She kept on stepping toward her vehicle.

"Stop, you bitch!" Jordan yelled as he drew near his victim.

The lady was amazingly calm for somebody who had a gun-wielding crackhead chasing her down. Showing no fear, she dropped the bags and took a few more steps toward the Escalade.

The bitch had enough nerve to smile, Jordan thought as he watched her raise a remote keypad to unlock the door. Jordan wasn't ready for what happened next. He saw it coming and tried to hit the brakes, but black ice got involved. Jordan slipped and went down hard. From his back, he saw her open the back passenger door.

"I got yo' bitch, you crackhead mothafucka!" she screamed back at Jordan. The lady turned her attention back to the open door. "Sic him, boy!" she commanded.

The humongous, snarling Rottweiler leapt from the truck and ran straight for Jordan. Adrenaline pushed Jordan to his feet, but before he could turn to run, the heavy beast pounced on him, sending Jordan and the animal freefalling to the frozen ground. The dog latched onto Jordan's left forearm and started shaking it like a rag doll. It was a good thing that Jordan had found the old crusty overcoat in the house where he had discovered the weapon. The coat was two sizes too big and worked like an airbag to prevent the canine from sinking teeth into his flesh. Jordan struggled to free his arm, and with both hands, he held onto the dog's neck for dear life.

"Get him, boy!" Jordan could hear the owner encouraging the dog from somewhere above the action. "Kill his thieving, crackhead ass, Cujo!"

The dog viciously tore at Jordan's clothing—ripping and shredding it—in an attempt to get a lock on some vital part of his body. The Rottweiler had him pinned underneath its large body and grew more aggressive as the woman urged the dog to kill. Every foul thing Jordan had ever done white water rafted through his mind. This was it. God was fed up with his shit, and was now in the process of calling his black ass home.

The mutt was strong, but Jordan fought like hell to keep the dog from his throat. As the Rottweiler thrashed and flailed about, Jordan was able to slip his left forearm underneath the dog's throat.

With his right—that was it! His right hand still held the revolver, tucked in his hand, pressed against the dog's throat. In all the confusion and fighting for his life, he'd totally forgotten about the .38 with three bullets. Jordan could feel his left arm giving away under the dog's strength. He wasn't gonna be able to keep the animal away from his throat much longer. Jordan had to make a move, and make one fast if he was planning on walking away from this thing with any life left inside his cracked-out body. The two struggled for control, with the dog's teeth so close to Jordan's throat that he could feel and smell the animal's hot breath. There was no way to get off a shot—not without removing his gun hand from the dog's neck and risk having his throat ripped out. But something had to be done. He didn't have the stamina to tussle with the beast too much longer. Anything more than a few seconds would count as dinner for the pooch. The Rottweiler had to be put down, even if another part of Jordan's body was sacrificed to accomplish the objective. The damn thing had to die, and whatever bullets were left, the owner would probably catch a hot one for having this much security.

Whatever brain cells he had left from his many crack binges were enough to quickly devise a strategy. Before Jordan could think anymore, he rolled his entire body over to the left. The move surprised the dog and freed Jordan's gun hand. The chink in the armor of the plan was that the dog grabbed hold of his left hand, and clamped down on the hand with so much force that Jordan screamed as if the animal had castrated him. The dog tugged, snarled, and tried to rip Jordan's hand clean off his arm. Warm blood dripped to the frozen ground and mixed with a pool of slush water they'd rolled into. With all the power in his 140-pound body, Jordan placed the pistol to the dog's right temple.

"Don't shoot my…"

Boom!

Brain and skull fragments sprayed out of the left side of the dog's head. The beast dropped instantly. It took a moment for the owner to process the scene. Her pride turned into rage after grim reality set in. Without warning, she charged Jordan. He shed himself of the dog quickly. There were two more rounds left, and he used one of them to try and take her head off. Luckily for her, the lady slipped in a small pool of her dog's blood. The bullet missed her, but shattered the windshield of her SUV.

"You sonofabitch!" she screamed, splashing around in an effort at gaining her footing.

Jordan was surprised that no one was out at this time of night. The street was clear. The storeowner had to have heard the shots and was probably calling the police. Jordan willed his small frame to a vertical base. He allowed his injured hand to dangle, blood sliding between his fingers and dotting the ground. The closest urgent care center was at least twenty minutes away by foot.

The woman's loud screaming over her dog was sure to warrant a few lights in the surrounding houses to switch on. Jordan tucked the gun and staggered off down the street.

The staff at the urgent care center took one look at Jordan's injuries and immediately rushed him into a trauma ward to wait for transportation to a local hospital. The amount of tissue damage was extensive. Jordan had torn ligaments and minor muscle damage. He figured somebody must've been praying for his stupid behind.

The dog had come within a canine tooth of severing a nerve and nicking an artery.

The doctor attending to Jordan's wound didn't hesitate to remind him, once or twice, about how lucky he'd been. But Jordan knew the difference between *luck* and a flat-out blessing. Once again, he'd nearly escaped the Grim Reaper. It could've been tragic, with him bleeding out on the walk over to the clinic. The injuries were beyond the small clinic's capabilities.

The doctor wasn't sure, but he informed Jordan that minor surgery might be required. He did what he could, but to receive proper medical treatment, Jordan would have to be transported to Detroit Receiving Hospital, the state's first Level I Trauma Center.

After his wound had been cleaned and wrapped, a fat and dumpy-looking white woman, wearing an outfit that suggested homelessness, walked into his ward with paperwork to fill out. Jordan wasn't sweating a damn thing. He was homeless and without health insurance. What more could she want from him? He was lying on a gurney with his hand looking like the mangled meat version of a Rubik's Cube and didn't have time for formality. His left hand was out of commission and would be useless for a while. Survival on the street depended on strong hands. Snatching aluminum siding off of abandoned houses took strength, speed and accuracy. It was a formula that couldn't afford any of those missing components. A fella could find himself tossed in jail, or worse, getting his eyebrows kicked in by some ambitious, young, tough dude with a club looking to get his picture in the hero section of the newspaper.

The broad in the homeless getup wouldn't let him loose unless he properly filled out the forms. Jordan thought, *fuck it*, and indulged her. Tupelo Harrison was the name he gave. The address of a local McDonald's went down on the line as his home address. Jordan had the restaurant's address committed to memory. He'd stood in front of the joint enough and bummed spare change. If it weren't for the sharp pain in his left hand, he would've been laughing his ass off. The lousy pain meds they offered did little to smother the steadily growing, pulsating pain. His tolerance to the weak meds was largely due to his addiction. A few milligrams weren't shit to him. Jordan needed crack. There was nothing like his little white god to put his mind at ease.

Ms. Trailer Trash offered a few more forms and walked off saying something slick.

Boy, Jordan thought, *if only I hadn't ditched the pistol in a safe hiding spot.* The doctors would've been picking his last bullet out of her ass. He'd allowed himself to slip up. *What in the hell was I thinking?* He hadn't been thinking at all. His victims were usually old and feeble. Popeye's mother had been the only one that he'd gone hard on. The old bitch wouldn't give up the goods, so he had to show her the cost of resisting a guy like him, and that explained why Popeye was all over his ass. He'd had another close call an hour ago. Jordan hadn't prayed in a long time, but he was silently thanking God for not allowing him to shoot and kill that lady. He didn't know what had come over him. This new fool that was taking over seemed to have little or no remorse about hurting people. The crack had taken his soul and was now pressuring him to go to the extreme in obtaining the rock.

The woman's mutt had managed to pull one last act of loyalty from above the grave. If it wasn't for the dog's blood, the owner would've been in the morgue and Jordan would be looking down the smoking barrel of a murder case right now.

But now, he was screwed. His injured hand would be a bona fide weakness. Most of the jobs he'd done in the past involved two hands. The crackhead was the ultimate predator. The only other predator that presented any fear was another crackhead. Jordan knew this to be true because he'd broken it off on a rival for trying to jack him out of a few packages a week ago. He couldn't do it with the mauled hand, though. He would be like a wounded fish in the ocean of the ghetto, waiting for a shark to come along and do him dirty. He had one bullet left. Maybe that would be all he needed. Stick a gun into somebody's face and they wouldn't hesitate to give up the goods. Nobody belonging to a sane mind would ask for a bullet count. He needed to get high. Ghosts were haunting upstairs in his attic and the crack rock was the only Ghostbuster that he could call.

An EMT unit arrived for pickup. Jordan watched as

two huge, beefy, uniformed black men pushed him through the clean, white hallways and out into bitter cold temperatures. Within seconds, he was loaded and on his way to Detroit Receiving Hospital.

On the ride over, he didn't give up any information to one of the nosey-ass EMTs who repeatedly questioned him about the incident. Jordan might've been a smoked-out fool, but he wasn't a fool by nature. Not only had he set out to commit an armed robbery, but in the process, he'd killed a dog and tried to smoke the owner. Assault with a deadly weapon carried close to life behind bars. It was a stretch that would see him dangling from the ceiling of his cell with a sheet tied around his neck before he'd do that type of time.

The two paramedics unloaded and wheeled him into a huge waiting area. It was Friday night and the hospital was jumping. The hallways were lined with gurneys belonging to the sick and assaulted. The way gunshot and stab victims who had been flat-out bludgeoned to the brink of death, were wheeled through the emergency room doors, made Jordan think that Detroit's neighborhoods had become like assembly lines, but instead of cars, the city was producing death and destruction.

Jordan watched as the thicker paramedic joked and yucked it up with a dark chocolate, fine-ass nurse wearing navy blue scrubs, while handing over his paperwork. Doctors and nurses were everywhere. There was definitely no shortage of orderlies pushing patients in wheelchairs.

Jordan's hand was killing him, but there was a greater chance of a Twinkie surviving on the set of *Biggest Loser* after the cameras stopped rolling than for him to be seen immediately without health insurance.

An extremely obese male orderly, with a gigantic, nappy Afro, rolled Jordan through a secured door. Sweat trickled down his brow as he labored to push the gurney. He parked it against the wall, breathing like he had been walking while trying to lug around, on his shoulders, one of his plus-sized brethren—and his breath! Jordan had smelled fresher breath belonging to crackheads with halitosis. He was grateful that Acid Breath walked off without saying a word.

The hallway was long and narrow. Poor lighting didn't stop Jordan from raising his head to view his position. It came as no surprise that he was at the end of a long line of stretchers. The frail and emaciated-looking elderly gentleman parked in front of him was clowning. He was balled up in the fetal position and loudly moaning as if hospital staff gave a damn. The old dude was bellyaching so tough that Jordan couldn't hear himself think. And if it wasn't for his mangled hand, he would've gotten up and pushed the geezer farther down the hallway.

Jordan's hand was throbbing as if the Rottweiler had somehow found a way to reattach itself from the other side. He cursed himself for being so careless. Now he might need surgery behind this fiasco. The *surgery* he could handle. It was the rabies shots that almost had him pissing his pants. The quack over at the urgent care clinic had warned him about the possibility of contracting the rabies virus. And since there was no way of knowing if the dog had had vaccinations, Jordan would have to undergo several rounds of painful injections in the navel. He cringed at the thought.

The double doors down the hall swung open and a middle-aged white man dressed in gray scrubs pushed through a brown-skinned younger man in a wheelchair. The young guy in the chair didn't seem to have any visible signs of trauma, but seeing the tall, light-complexioned, uniformed police officer walking behind the orderly sent shockwaves of fear sweeping through Jordan's body.

Paranoia was trying to urge him to get up and bust a Harrison Ford-style, Dr. Richard Kimble *Fugitive* move in the opposite direction. The only thing that was on his mind was the thought that the dog-owning bitch had probably given the police a description of her attacker. If *The First 48* had taught him anything, it was that in cases involving fleeing and wounded suspects, police usually coordinated with area hospitals to furnish a description of the perpetrator. Jordan tried to keep calm. Fighting back the adrenaline belonging to the fight-or-flight reflex was a different beast. Failure of any kind could quite possibly end with his booty belonging to an inhuman-sized homo-thug for the next fifteen to twenty years in prison.

As the officer drew near, Jordan took a page from the book of the old man lying in front of him. He slowly turned his entire body away from the aisle, faced the wall, and curled into the fetal position. He moaned like his hemorrhoids were subject to explode at any moment. Only when Jordan felt the breeze from the trio walking past did he ease his foot off the accelerator of anxiety. He positioned his body enough so that he could size up the situation. It turned out that the cop was merely overseeing his prisoner. The dude was handcuffed to the left arm of the wheelchair.

Jordan didn't know how much more drama he could take. His night had started off with the simple desire to get high. Now, a dead dog, an angry dog owner and one mutilated hand later, he still was no closer to firing up his crack pipe. And to add nuts on top of the sundae, Dragon Breath was back, but this time he spoke.

"We have a bed for you in Room 7—" was all he said. His funky breath hung in the air like the stench left behind by an old batch of collard greens. Although the three-minute trip was hell on his sinuses, Jordan was relieved to be out of the hallway. The County Jail was only a few miles from Detroit Receiving Hospital. Prisoners were sometimes transported there to receive treatment. The last thing he wanted was for a police officer to identify his face.

It turned out that Room 7 was an enormous room made up of tiny, curtain-enclosed beds.

"Get undressed and put this on." Stink Breath ordered, tossing a hospital gown onto Jordan's lap. Jordan looked at the man like his forehead had turned into a paper check for one million dollars. He wasn't about to put on shit. He was determined to keep his clothes on until the very moment the surgeon started cutting—in case he had to bust a move. If he was going to jail, it would be in the dignity gear he was wearing. The last thing he needed was trying to escape wearing a hospital gown with his ass hanging out the back.

As he watched T-Rex Breath and his thunder thighs walk away, his coat was the only article of clothing that Jordan removed. The left forearm of the area had been ripped to shreds.

Jordan was tired, and far too exhausted to get up and close the private curtains around his space. He was irritable, cranky, and in too much pain to worry about nosey-ass people looking in on him like he was some type of crackhead zoo exhibit.

Jordan thought about how life would've turned out if he'd stayed home that day. Daddy Frank would still be alive to provide mentoring services to him and his brothers. Yazoo wouldn't be trying to prove himself. Wisdom would have completed rehab by now and been posterizing Dwight Howard. Tempest would probably be a better wife to her husband—although he seriously doubted if anything could be done about his mom and Reverend Slynuts. But Daddy Frank's leadership and guidance would have been enough to insulate him and his siblings from the wrath of Reverend Poppa Jones' demons.

He laid the old, mangy-looking wool topcoat over an armchair next to his gurney. He hated hospitals. His mother had been in and out of them for the last four years. Jordan always had that feeling of helplessness. She was dying and there wasn't a damn thing that he could do. He looked around his tiny enclosure. Instruments hung from the wall behind his bed. He didn't know any by proper name. Blood pressure cup, the light used to examine ears, noses and throats—he knew those.

At the moment, his mind shifted gears and Monique was featured. He couldn't shake her. It had been the only reason why he was at the liquor store in the first place— to turn a stickup. Get money so that he could smoke until he felt nothing. She was his best friend, and now…

A lonely tear slowly slid from his right eye. He was the one responsible for her being beaten beyond recognition. Jordan hadn't been able to conjure the nerve to go see his girl, but the crackhead community was like the cracked-out version of CNN. Word of what Popeye had done traveled through the neighborhood like a brush fire. The message was out: The cop wanted revenge, and anybody caught with Jordan would suffer the same fate as Monique. He had become a social pariah—an outcast. But it was all right. Once he was fixed up, Jordan had plans of putting the old neighborhood in his rear-view mirror.

He lay back and tried to relax. The doctors at the hospital were effective, but slow on making their rounds. It was something to midnight when Jordan closed his eyes. His hand wasn't gonna let him get much sleep, but at least he was warm and had fresh sheets. Jordan was asking himself how in the hell was he going to survive on the street with one hand when he heard the voice. It was barely audible at first and seemed to be coming from another room. He trained his ears to ignore everything except for the voice. The owner seemed to be headed in his direction—and fuck, his curtain was open.

He heard it again, but this time, the voice was confirmed. The deep pitch belonged to a Detroit Police harbinger of death. Jordan's blood ran cold. He quickly swung his legs over the side of the gurney. When the voice boomed with laughter, Jordan stood to his feet and threw on his overcoat, easing his injured hand through the sleeve. The surgery would have to be temporarily postponed. Healthy hands wouldn't do him any good if the rest of him were lying on a slab in the city morgue, looking like a pulverized side of beef. There was a supply cabinet right underneath the blood pressure cup. He quickly stuffed stretch wrap and gauze packages into huge coat pockets.

Jordan's heart was pumping Kool-Aid and his bowels were begging for the opportunity to evacuate the vicinity. Terrified, he slowly took steps to peer around the corner of the curtain. The butterflies in his stomach didn't let up at the sight of the coast being clear. It could've been a trap to lure him out into the main hallway, and then beat the brakes off of his monkey ass.

The old, gray-haired, dusty-looking white lady across from him rose from her gurney and had the nerve to pull the sheet up to her chin. Jordan gave the lady a "Bitch, please! Don't nobody want to see yo' old wrinkled titties" look.

The voice seemed to be traveling in the opposite direction, like the person was moving away from Jordan's location. It did little to calm his nerves. He forced his feet to walk, expecting to be gang-tackled once he stepped outside of the area.

In walked a nurse, about mid-to-late thirties, a barrel-shaped body and bushy weave down to her waist. The heifer eyed Jordan suspiciously. Tabatha was the name on her nametag. To Jordan, she didn't look like a Tabatha—more like a Laquisha.

"Excuse me?" the nurse asked with attitude. She looked at his bandaged hand and funky-looking coat. "Can I help you?"

Jordan thought it would be best not to say a word. The broad looked to be confrontational and he didn't need her noise factor right now—nothing that would attract attention. He moved right past her, stopping at the entrance of the pod. Carefully, he stole a peek around the corner.

Yup, it was him all right—Popeye! He had his back turned and was talking with the officer that Jordan had seen earlier with the young brother cuffed to the left arm of the wheelchair. His heart fluttered and it felt like he had to take a nervous piss. The nurse looked at Jordan like she was about to scream for help. It was either now or never. He pushed himself into the corridor and quickly put his back to Popeye. Jordan pulled the collar of his moth-eaten coat up around his neck and tried his best to act natural. The way that his heart was pounding in his chest, Jordan thought that the organ would burst from his ribcage, sprout legs and arms, and start hauling ass.

The door was within reaching distance. It was automatic and opened by the soft push of a stainless steel, square button mounted to the wall. With his right hand, Jordan pushed the button, half-expecting to receive a bullet in the back. The door opened and he walked out without creating a newsworthy moment. But his ordeal was far from over. He still needed medical attention—just not in this hospital.

Preferably, one in the suburbs.

He didn't know how he was going to manage getting out there, but being a crackhead automatically made him one helluva persuasion artist. He would find a way.

The next step was getting the hell outta Detroit. Hell, he had family in New York. Yeah, that was it. He would wait to see if he needed surgery, and then he would be on his way to the Big Apple…provided he stayed alive that long.

REVEREND POPPA JONES

My nice leatherback Bible and unfinished sermon lay on the table where I was sitting. My many unscrupulous exploits had me traveling way outside of the city to enjoy a simple cup of Starbucks coffee. No one knew of my questionable reputation in Grand Blanc, Michigan—at least not anyone that I knew about. I was involved in so much unholy mischief that it was a miracle I was still standing on this side of the dirt. And being the pastor at Infinite Baptist, one of the largest churches in the city, had placed a bull's eye on my back in the form of critics and media vultures, just circling, waiting for an opportunity to peck a scandalous story from the bones of the many skeletons that were happily dancing out of my closet. Call it *paranoia*, but I felt like my every move was being shadowed.

It was the same feeling that was always present whenever I was over to Sister Walker's expensive home in Sterling Heights. The sister used to be one of the wealthiest members of my church until the untimely death of her husband. The Negro had left me with his grieving widow and not much else. But everything started when she'd asked me over a few times for personal Bible Study. This had become a service that I rendered to those who were financial boosters, folks who God had called to seriously share with my ministry, through tithes and offerings from their six- and seven-figure incomes.

On one of my many trips over to the sister's house, she'd confided in me about her horrible marriage. Her husband had never attended church. I had begun to think that a marriage to this Brother Walker was all in her head. I'd never seen this man, not one time, while visiting Sister Walker—and no wedding photos. But the money to afford her such a fabulous home and ritzy life-style was coming from somewhere. She often told me that Brother Walker was always in South America on business. So one night, she was distressed, and as usual, I tried to comfort her through scripture. Fifteen minutes later we were both undressed and going at it like two horny teenagers.

I'd spent countless butt-naked nights in this man's house playing a very dangerous game of "Guess whose penis your wife is sitting on?"—the pastor's edition. A few months later, in my office in the church, I'd discovered that Brother Walker was more than a whacked-out figment of Sister Walker's imagination. In fact, through snot and tears, I'd learned that Wellington Walker owned a security firm in some Latin American city. Somehow, the brother had gotten lost in a jungle and was killed by an animal. The story was a little hard for me to swallow, but I doubted if she could make something like that up. Maybe my paranoia was attributed to the fact that Wellington's game was in security—which meant investigation—depending which way I chose to look at it. I didn't feel safe with that information.

While sipping on strong black with one Equal, I sat facing the door like I was some type of cowboy desperado who'd run afoul of the law, collecting enemies on both sides of the U.S. Marshal star. I'd raised so much hell inside the city limits with different women that there was no telling what angry boyfriend or husband would jump out of the shadows and deliver unto me a shotgun eulogy. Slydale, my former deacon chairman, was leading the charge among a growing and colorful list of enemies who would had me whacked for an extra wafer and grape juice on Communion Sunday.

One should always wait on the Lord, but in Slydale's case, I had to get that Negro removed from office before he stumbled upon solid proof of my many indiscretions. So I went old school—or better yet, Old Testament, and beat the ugly rascal at his own game of "eye for an eye" justice. All it took was an endless supply of alcohol, a hooker, her friends, one greedy security guard, a rented hotel boardroom—which I was careful to pay for in cash—Slydale, and his entire posse of evil, troublemaking deacons. It all produced one hardcore, hooker-on-deacon, XXX DVD of hallelujah horniness. I would never forget the look on Slydale's face when I presented and played my tell-all DVD at the last meeting with the deacon board. Of course, there was denial and crying, but I definitely wasn't counting on Slydale's right-hand man, Deacon Kelly, to suffer a subsequent heart attack. And when words were useless, Slydale lost control of his mental faculties and tried to attack me. It was a good thing that God jumped in the way—in the form of a big, young, corn-fed deacon who looked like a Hummer wearing a suit. Deacon Braxton snatched up Slydale before he could get to me and planted the disposed chairman/porn star on his back.

While I should've been feeling remorse about not letting things naturally run their course, I was feeling powerful; a kind of power only wielded by those who were missing something in their lives. For me, I was completely out of alignment with God. I was stumbling around in the muck and mire with a weak declaration for repentance. Satan had me by the nose and dancing to his song—a dangerous party anthem of adultery, lust and lies. It would automatically end with me being pulled up like a weed and tossed into the fiery furnace, where there would be weeping and gnashing of the teeth if I didn't reform my ways.

Outside the window, snow was falling in huge flakes, and as dusk settled over the strip mall, the approaching darkness seemed to force the evening commuters through the doors in search of that expensive cup of liquid high. I took a drink from my beverage, thinking about the heavy burdens of running a mega-church. My many obligations to the church kept me on the run. I seldom ran across a chance to relax and chill. Even right now, I was putting the finishing touches on my Sunday sermon. I'd turned off my cell phone, because out here, I could unwind—decompress.

I could people watch.

I sipped from my cup and watched as two young, gorgeous blondes dressed in green aprons professionally greeted each customer. The two women were an absolute joy to watch. Aside from being pleasant, the young tenders were delightfully engaging, charming and treated every customer like they truly understood the meaning of excellent customer care. They laughed, made jokes, and while one masterfully blended delicious drinks, the other retrieved cookies or pastries from a huge see-through display case of assorted sugary treats. Every now and then, I would receive a crotch-arousing, flirtatious stare from the shorter one who reminded me of a young, blonde version of Kate Beckinsale.

May God forgive me—I was entertaining the thought of lying between the legs of my very first white woman—when a tall black man entered the store. The place almost fell silent at the powerful presence of this man, who could pass for a shorter version of the actor Leon. The Negro looked to be early 30s, full beard that connected to a shaved mustache, keen features, but his eyes—the eyes looked sinister. All I could say was that the brother had impeccable taste in fashion. I could tell that simply by his expensive, chocolate brown cashmere topcoat. The same color, finely cut Italian suit was sharp. Next to knowing Jesus, I was omniscient in my knowledge of high-end fashion. I knew enough about prices to know that the Negro had paid about five thousand dollars for his tailor-made piece of wearing pleasure, with tote-covered, two-tone Italian shoes. The brother might've stepped off the cover of *GQ*, but the vibe he gave off was pure evil. It was almost like Satan had gone on an expensive shopping spree, dressed, and was now passing himself off in the form of man, standing in line for a delicious cup of Starbucks' hellish goodness.

He attracted attention the moment he walked through the door. White folks were naturally suspicious of blacks, so the ones that sat around me probably held their camera phones underneath the table, itching to dial nine-one-one—or obtain some sensational YouTube footage—if he made one false move. But I knew better. Nobody who was dressed like him would be looking for chump change out of a cash register.

I, for one, wasn't caught up in judging a man by the shiftiness of his eyes, but the content of his heart—character. Besides, who was I to throw stones? I was a backsliding soul living in a glass house that was built on contaminated grounds. Besides, with all of the white folks leering at him like he was guilty of drug-dealing, pimping, sleeping with white women and sodomizing little white kids, he didn't need his own kind to put extra knots in the hangman's noose.

I had forced my focus back on God's work. But every time I tried to write, I had this feeling of being suffocated in a dark abyss.

I was up to my Holy Ghost in trouble.

No matter how hard I worked for the Lord, I couldn't shake my demons. Exorcism, prayer, holy water—none of those things seemed to defeat my strong, carnal appetite to be *the man* and have sex with multiple women. Sister Lawson, Sister Walker, my new piece, Paula—were just a few whose beds I found too irresistible to resist.

Despite all of my sinful shortcomings, God's tender mercy still covered my miserable hide, and my church was flourishing. If membership continued to rapidly increase, I was going to look into purchasing the old Pontiac Silverdome. If the good Lord had seen fit to bless Joel Osteen with the former Compaq Center as a lavish house of worship, the Silverdome would be a piece of cake.

But no matter how hard I tried to dress my mess up and call it success, my family was suffering. The fallout from my own personal battles had infected each of my children in ways that left them powerless against the destroyer. My baby boy, Jordan—God, it hurt me to my heart to say—but Jordan was a crack addict with a revenge-driven, psycho detective hot on his trail. I wasn't supposed to know that my daughter, Tempest, was running around on her husband with pure evil dressed up as a dangerous drug dealer. My stepson, Yazoo, had pledged his life to hating God and being a damning pestilence to the human race. The Negro had been blaming God for the accidental drowning death of his father. It was outright defiance, and a battle that his sorry tail would tragically lose.

The impression that would be indelibly seared in my mind was the night of the family meeting—the one I had been vehemently against. I could remember it like it was yesterday. Yazoo had punched Tempest in the mouth for disrespecting his dead father. Before I could grab the Negro, I was put on the seat of my trousers by a blinding right cross. When the police finally did show, they found my son, Wisdom, trying to choke his brother into going toward the light. Amidst all the chaos of my family trying to rip each other apart with their bare hands, Jordan had managed to creep into my study and steal one of my Rolex watches.

The fallout from the pandemonium that night left my daughter with a sprained neck and a concussion. Yazoo went to jail for the entire weekend. Wisdom hated me that much more. It didn't take a divine vision for me to know what had happened to Jordan. The boy had probably found a crack pusher and traded my watch for his little packages of rock-sized white devils.

I hadn't been sleeping much as of late. Whenever I did, nightmares were usually waiting. Ever since I'd walked out on my wife, Wilma, at the steakhouse a few weeks ago, after she'd crucified my character and embarrassed me in front of other dinner guests, I'd been experiencing reoccurring dreams about sickly, emaciated cows and pale white horses.

I might've been living my life on 666 Avenue, near the cross sections of Lust and Just Plain Sinful, but as a biblical scholar, I was a perfectionist. The symbolism behind my dreams was not—by any means—lost on me. I recognized warnings when I dreamt them. Sick cows brought the book of Genesis to mind— Chapter 41, to be exact. It tells the story about Joseph. Joseph was the son of Jacob, and the light of his father's eye. This light of favor wasn't lost on his brothers. Jealousy enraged them to the point of plotting his murder. Brother Rueben suggested no bloodshed, but opted for throwing Joseph in a pit inside the wilderness. Brother Judah came up with what he must've thought of, at the time, as the ultimate brainstorm—selling him. Why let Joseph waste away in a pit when they could make a little change? So, they sold their brother into slavery.

To make a long story short, Joseph found himself in Egypt, working as overseer in Potiphar's house—the commanding officer of Pharaoh's bodyguard. While there, he shunned the advances of Potiphar's wife. One day, while hot for Joseph's love, she grabbed him by the robe; he came out of it and ran for dear life. The guards rushed in and saw her holding the garment. She yelled rape and Joseph was thrown in jail. In prison, Joseph's amazing ability to interpret dreams quickly got back to the Pharaoh—who'd been having puzzling dreams of his own. Pharaoh called for Joseph to make sense of his bizarre dreams. To Joseph, Pharaoh spoke of standing on a riverbank and seeing seven healthy cows, followed by seven unhealthy, emaciated cows surfacing from the water. He then went on to tell—of the same dream—about seven healthy ears of corn and seven unhealthy. Joseph explained that the healthy cows and ears of corn meant that they would have seven years of plentiful harvests. The seven unhealthy cows and seven empty ears would be seven years of famine.

Judging by today's standards, famine to a person like me represented the poorhouse, but I was more concerned with the pale white horses. In the Book of Revelation, a rider mounted the top of a pale white horse. He was the harbinger of death. The Grim Reaper. God was trying to bring me back into the fold with the threat of poverty and death.

For all of my rallies, I couldn't tap into that part of me that housed the strength to bind temptation. I was a sinner—and worse, I was a sinner with no desire to stand up and throw down in the name of the Lord. Every time I tried to slip away, Satan baited the hook of his expensive fishing pole and heavy-duty line with Viagra, Sister Lawson, Sister Walker and Paula. The lure was too enticing not to bite.

Truthfully, locked deep down inside my subconscious,

I was angry with God. When my wife had taken sick, our marriage fell ill also. Suddenly, it was more about her and not us. Our condo had to be modified with special medical equipment. Our many nights of sleeping in the same bed were over. It left me sleeping in the guest bedroom with too much time to think. I wasn't totally blaming her kidney failure for my passionate love affair with extramarital vajayjay. Her biweekly dialysis visits had turned her into a bitter woman who snapped at me every time I tried to get close. A man gets lonely after too long. It was wrong, but I started looking to my flock for consolation, full of desperate churchwomen who viewed me like how I *should've been* looking to serve the good Lord.

Sister Lawson, Sister Walker, and my new piece, Paula, were there to pick up the pieces. Each one of those lovely ladies catered to my ego. Sister Lawson had gotten a seven-figure settlement from the city in the accidental but fatal police shooting and death of her husband. I was still enjoying the brand new Cadillac Escalade she'd cashed out for me. She had the bucks, and she damn sure had the booty. Sister Walker's lovin' was so good that it left me feeling like a king. Well, Paula—let's just say that she showered me with all three: booty, money and a place to lay my head. I needed all three after the steak-house, when I'd gone back home and packed up my belongings and left my wife. Paula owned a half-million-dollar home in Orchard Lake, one of the richest cities in Michigan. I'd met her when I was asked to preach at the tenth anniversary for a trio of ministers who called themselves The Mighty Warriors of Christ. Paula was a temporary solution until I could rid myself of the haunting lust that bubbled up at the sight of thin waists and big booties.

I hated the man that I had become, a regular biblical plague on society. A bootleg preacher who peddled hypocrisy. For many years, I watched with stomach-churning sickness as false prophets gave God's real soldiers a bad name. Now, I was one of them.

The night at the steakhouse, my wife had had enough of being disrespected and me using the Lord to cover up my acts of adultery. Coincidently, Sister Walker had picked the same restaurant to dine. Instead of the broad having her ass at home mourning the death of her husband, she had pranced through the door in the company of some pudgy white man. The heifer thought it was cute when sashayed her nice backside toward my table and exchanged pleasantries with my wife. The dumb broad thought that Wilma wasn't looking when she made a telephone receiver with her right hand and mouthed for me to call her. Wilma slowly stood from the table. Naw, the witch hit me in the forehead with a hard dinner roll, and *then* she stood from the table.

She addressed everybody in the room. Wilma played the "dying wife" card beautifully, all while damn near turning those rich, white dinner guests into an angry lynch mob by tearfully regaling them with my womanizing tales. After the job was done, every woman in the building was looking at me like I was the pastor version of Hugh Hefner. My wife had creatively assassinated my character. The only thing I could do to maintain a shred of dignity was to walk out. So, I turned my back and walked out on my dying wife. I didn't find out about Wilma's heart attack until a couple of days later. When I heard the news, all I could do was drop to my knees and pray for her. After what I'd done, how could I show my face at her bedside without my son Wisdom wanting to rip it off?

With my head bowed, I was so into my "woe is me" mantra that the person standing over me had to clear his throat twice to get my attention. I looked up and my blood instantly ran cold. His intense stare was on me— the fiendish eyes inside the face of a man who could've easily won the competition in one of those reality TV shows where they searched for aspiring models.

Smoke rose from his coffee cup as he pointed at the chair in front of me.

"Is this seat taken?"

I looked around at all the empty chairs while pinching the bridge of my nose. I wasn't in the mood for company. Being a man of God meant that every soul had a visiting purpose.

"I guess it was waiting on you," I said with a big smile. "Have a seat."

I didn't understand why I hadn't smelled the sweet fragrance of his cologne sooner. I recognized the distinctive aroma of Escada from any other. It was exclusive to Saks Fifth Avenue.

"Thank you." He set a napkin on the table and put his drink on top. The brother reached out his hand. "My name is Red, last name Rum."

I shook his hand.

"Like the alcohol drink? That's rather interesting," I respectfully said as I tried desperately to place his name. I'd heard it somewhere before.

He took a sip of his coffee. "Yeah. My old man originated from Haiti. He came to the United States, met and married my mother. I tried to research the name, but hit roadblocks. My parents both died in a car accident, and with not much family, I guess the name's origin will remain a mystery."

"I'm terribly sorry, Brother Rum." I tried not to be distracted by the strong, negative aura that emanated from his presence. I was a spiritual leader, one of God's people who didn't have time to fear. Fear was tormenting and he who feared was not made perfect in love. But something about this man wasn't right. "Well, where are my manners?" I said. "I didn't introduce myself. I'm Pastor Poppa Jones of Infinite Baptist Church."

"A reverend. One of God's boys, huh?" He blew on his coffee and scooted around in his seat to get comfortable. He looked around at everyone sitting near us. "I know that place. You got yourself a huge church, Pastor. You one of those television evangelists?"

"Not as of yet. But we're working on a few things."

"Hallelujah! Pastor, I knew coming into this particular Starbucks wasn't a coincidence. I had prayed all day that the Lord would deliver me a simple solution to my problem—and here you are."

I smiled politely. "So, Brother Rum, it's always a pleasure for me to serve the Lord by attending to the personal needs of His sheep." I closed my Bible and was about to tuck it and my sermon away in my black leather Gucci briefcase when the brother stopped me.

"Don't you dare put that weapon of God away! I believe we're going to need it."

I guess I should've been impressed with his level of enthusiasm for the Word. But I couldn't close my ears to the cynicism of the pitch of his voice. I thought the brother was creepy, but not too creepy to share in God's word.

I tried to hide the disturbance on my face with a smile. I opened the book. "Brother Rum, how can I be of service?"

He sat across from me and stared directly into my eyes. I'd seen some horrifying things in my day, but none were like his dissecting, penetrating gaze. It was like a snake that had locked onto its target and was getting ready to collect the prey in its strong coils and squeeze away life. The brother searched around until he could find the right words.

"I need you to talk me out of murdering the man who's sleeping with my wife."

Many things run through a man's mind when he thinks

that he's about to get a cell phone call from God. Was this my pale white horse? The harbinger of death?

Oh my Jesus, I thought. Out of the many sinful things that I'd expected to come out of his pie hole, this was beyond any of them. This was too close for comfort. I tried not to show my uneasiness. To mask my nerves, I kept a smile on my face while reaching in my pocket for mints. I brought out a couple and unwrapped one. I popped it into my mouth.

"Would you like one?" I politely asked.

"No, Pastor. I just need you to talk me off of this ledge." He was serious—no smile, just a deadly look.

I was panicking on the inside. I wasn't proud of it. I'd had sex with my fair share of married women, but I couldn't remember any with the last name *Rum*.

"Do you know this for certain?"

He turned up the intensity in his cold, reptilian eyes. These couldn't have been eyes that belonged to sanity.

"Pastor, I know what I saw."

"Brother, if you believe in God, then you believe in His Word: Thou shalt not kill. Look, you are obviously a man of God. The fact that you are seeking out a Godly solution means a lot. Apparently, you care enough about human life to seek counseling."

I paused for a moment. I didn't know if it was to collect my thoughts or pay attention to the clock hanging on the wall behind the cash register. More customers drifted in with the blowing snow. Our conversation blended in with the chatter of those sitting around us. Paula was expecting me home soon. But with a disgruntled husband sitting in front of me, God only knew if I would ever get to see home again—not to mention everyone else in Starbucks.

"Pastor, do you know what it's like to have your wife betray you?"

I said nothing. I sat there waiting on him to admit that he'd seen me creeping with his old lady, and whip out his cell phone with an incriminating video clip. The brother had my undivided attention.

"The pain is so intense. It hurts so bad that retribution is the only pill one can swallow to stop the pain." He looked around the room of white folks, like one of the men was guilty, and Brother Rum was about to deliver justice through gunfire. "I did some investigation. I found out that the guy is pretty wealthy—powerful, too. Pastor, you're familiar with the story of King David and Bathsheba?"

I nodded my head. I let him talk. I could basically tell the intention of a man by listening to word selection.

He went on. "There was this soldier name Uriah. He had a pretty wife; the Bible says that she was very beautiful to look upon. David was the mightiest man in the land—he had a harem of gorgeous wives. He could've had any woman in the land, but he picked Bathsheba, Uriah's wife—the wife of a poor, loyal soldier who just wanted to do his civic duty and fight proudly beside his brethren. But King David wanted his wife so badly that he used Uriah's loyalty against him. David wrote a letter to one of his superior officers and used Uriah's own hand to deliver it. The document revealed David's twisted plot to have Uriah murdered, and he used the enemy's hands to do the deed. The officer's duty was to have Uriah fight on the front lines. Up there was the bloodiest. The valiant soldiers who fought in that position always perished. When the deed was done, and Uriah was dead, David— we'll just say that King David was free to enjoy the spoils of adultery. The party didn't last too long because the prophet, Nathan, showed up. God had the prophet to deliver a parable to King David about a rich man who had everything and a poor man who had nothing but one sheep. The poor man didn't have much, but what did have, he shared with the sheep. He grew the animal only to have a rich man take it away."

I knew the parable well, and I also knew the foreboding consequences of using my power to gain what I wanted—even if it was coveting another man's wife. I was getting sick in the stomach at the possibility of this man reaching into his expensive coat, pulling out a gun, and sending me back to my Maker. I tried hard to conceal my fear.

At that moment, some bratty kid stole our attention by crying and pointing at a chocolate cookie on a full tray inside the display case.

"I feel like Uriah. This rich man is trying to steal my

sheep. She's the only thing that I have in this world, and I should make him suffer. Even David was punished when the Lord took his first baby born of him and Bathsheba." He looked at the door as a chilly gust of wind swept in behind more costumers. "What's the matter, Pastor?" the brother asked with a sneaky smile on his face. "I'm the one that needs the help, but the way that you are acting, I assume that you have something to hide." He took a sip of coffee. "Is that true, Pastor? Do you have something to hide? You wouldn't happen to be like King David—would you?"

"Brother Rum, I understand that you have a serious problem, but let's keep this in perspective. You're here because you believe our meeting is some type of divine intervention. And if that's the case, then this is about you—not me. Lean not to your own devices or understanding. Brother, these are destructive urges of the enemy, and if you act on them, then you won't only be running afoul with man's law, but with God's law also."

"That's some mighty fine preaching, Reverend. I can see—not talking about you—but now I can see why these preachers have more women open than Kmart still has doors open. You people can be real slick-talking with the Word. Hell, you almost got me with that one."

"Anger rests in the bosom of a fool. Don't fool yourself. Like Cain, the blood of your brother would be on your hands for life. There is no wiping it away. Don't do anything that's going to cause you to suffer pain."

He looked at me with a straight face and nodded his head like he was in agreement. The brother looked at his watch—which appeared to be a twenty-thousand-dollar Audemars Piguet. "Well, Pastor, it's been a blast, but I'm afraid I must be running. It appears that you have me at a stalemate. I think I'll go out of town to clear my head."

"Sometimes you must remove yourself from the situation to better understand the consequences of rash actions." I offered.

Brother Red Rum looked at me and smiled. "You have all the answers, don't you?" He drained the last of his coffee and stood to straighten out his coat. "There's one thing I want to leave you with because you also look to be troubled. 1 Samuel 3:13—For I have told him that I will judge his house forever for the iniquity which he knoweth."

Was my dirty laundry that apparent, staining my face for all to see? I didn't exactly know which hell this man had spewed up from, but he seemed to be in the same zip code as my wretchedness. The scripture left a blistering, cold chill traveling up my back. I could only assume that this was a warning from God for me to stop dancing around to Satan's hip-hop tunes of adultery, deceit and lies.

"Oh, Pastor, just in case my wife and I reconcile and want to get some counseling—would you happen to have a card?"

Only God knew I didn't want anything else to do with this man. And if it were up to me, I would get as far away as I could. But since it wasn't up to me, I took out my wallet and reluctantly handed the brother a card.

The look that he gave me was one I'd witnessed many times in those psychological thrillers where the killers looked deeply into his victim's eyes one last time before dishing out death.

He turned toward the door, but not before looking back at me. "I have a feeling that I will—well, my wife and I—will be seeing you real soon, Pastor."

Not even a flirtatious wink from the Starbucks version of Kate Beckinsale could pull me out of the fear that I was feeling. I had nothing. I didn't know the man, but I guess I didn't have to know somebody in order to feel threatened. My dirt was catching up with me, and it was only a matter of seconds before all hell broke loose.

I glanced at the clock. It was getting late, so I took out my cell and powered it on. After the smartphone finished booting, it rang. There was no number on the caller ID, so I assumed it was Paula. I answered.

"Hey, Preacher, remember me? Let me save you some time," the female caller said. "I'm the one that you knocked up and left like trash to blow in the winds on a ghetto street. It was about money in the beginning, but now, I want you to suffer. You have to deal with me. I'm not going away. I decided not to kill you, but I will embarrass and humiliate you to the point where your church membership will dwindle once your scandal hits the papers. I want you to squirm like the worm that you are, Poppa Jones. I want you to suffer like I will by carrying and delivering your bastard child. One day, you will look up and see my wrath." She ended the phone call.

As if I don't have enough trouble, I thought. It was the voice of the one who could bring down my house of cards. She was scorned and hell-bent on having her vengeance. They couldn't build a closet big enough to house all of my skeletons. My indiscretions were rising out of the darkness faster than the ascension of smoke from a burning building. I was floating atop a sea of sin, trying desperately to plug the holes in my life raft. No matter how many holes I was able to patch, more water kept springing up from new ones. And since I couldn't walk on water, I was doomed to be swallowed and live out my miserable existence inside the belly of the beast.

The voice was more than a threat. It was a promise. For the first time in my life, I was scared and didn't know if prayer could save this sinner.

WISDOM

SATURDAY NIGHT...

The world was cruel and unforgiving. It was a place where men killed and committed an assortment of heinous crimes to disguise the countless insecurities that made them appear weak, pathetic, and vulnerable. There were men like High-noon, who possessed the kind of juice to create politicians, but who was too weak to understand that his brother, Pat, was a worthless piece of trash who was destined to have his ticket punched. The tragedy was that Smoke, my cousin, was the ticket puncher. Many years ago, Pat had tried to make Smoke look weak to impress some of his homeboys. Smoke wasn't buying it. He and Pat had the kind of words that always led to blood-and-spit-flying brawls, ending with my cousin stomping the brakes off Pat. Like all cowards who lose at hand-to-hand combat, Pat went home and returned with a handgun. Smoke ran into an alley and grabbed a huge chunk of pipe, and before Pat could point the weapon, my cousin beat him to death.

Fast-forward some years later, and Highnoon still had

lust for vengeance and blood. My cousin, Smoke, had long since committed suicide in prison. But it still wasn't enough for Highnoon. The Big Kahuna had made me a unique proposition. He wanted a life for life. Since he couldn't get at Smoke, I would have to do. He had plans to torture me and inflict pain until he could no longer feel the suffering of losing his brother. Somehow, the big-headed, gold-tooth-wearing monkey had found out that my mother needed a kidney to stay alive. He happened to be her exact match for a donor. Wilma Jones meant the world to me. Instinctively, I took the offer. I almost thought that since our families had been so close at one time, Highnoon would call this shit off and give my mother the kidney without any strings attached. I was wrong. All the sucka had given me was seven days—with a two-day extension—to get my affairs in order.

But I had one stop to make before running with that seven-day challenge.

I was over at the house belonging to my best friend's mother. Everybody called the middle-aged woman Mama Lemon. Figgy "Rico" Lemon and I went all the way back to diapers, baby powder and sandboxes. I was there the morning that he stamped the mess out of a Puerto Rican bully named Rico. To further humiliate the Puerto Rican, Figgy assumed the bully's identity and started calling himself Rico. We were tight, with an unbreakable bond that was stronger than the one that I was supposed to have forged with my siblings. I still hadn't told him about Highnoon's offer. Being a former Golden Gloves champion, Rico was half-cocked and always down for the rough stuff. I wasn't sure how he'd respond to the proposition, and I couldn't have him mixing it up with Highnoon anytime soon—at least not until I got what I wanted. By that time, I was sure that the King Snake's demise would be moot to me.

A couple of weeks ago, while chasing my cracked-out brother through a rough area of Detroit nicknamed "The Cemetery," Rico and I tracked Jordan to a crack spot guarded by two heavily armed, pint-sized crack dealers who reminded me of the gangsta-version of Craig and Day-Day. We'd embarrassed the two death-dealing runts pretty badly before collecting Jordan and getting in the wind. It had totally slipped my mind until a few days ago when I'd gotten my revenge on Pogo for intentionally ending my NBA dreams. I was getting ready to step away from Pogo's crumpled-up carcass when one half of the Two Stooges showed up with his crew and pointed a gun.

It was the one that I had rightfully nicknamed Molechin. The creep had a mole on his chin that was almost the same size as an eyeball. Apparently, they hadn't forgotten about us and had been plotting revenge since that night. Molechin laughed in my face when he told me that he would kill me, and when I was dead, his other half, Lace, would make sure that Rico suffered the same fate. The Negro had aimed the pistol at my face and was getting ready to pull the trigger, too, when Highnoon showed up and foiled the plot. I still couldn't believe that Highnoon had been following me, but I guess his reason was legitimate. I wouldn't be any good to him dead.

I hadn't heard anything else about Molechin until this morning, with word of the police having fished his badly beaten corpse from the icy waters of the Detroit River. The killing had Highnoon's signature written all over it. His boy, Lace, would be sour behind the murder and want immediate retribution. A tip had revealed that Lace was supposed to rush the spot of Rico's mother at some point tonight.

There were a few of us hiding in the shadows around Mama Lemon's crib, waiting on the theatrics to pop off. The schmuck had picked the coldest night of the winter—thus far—to start tripping.

We had a great tactical advantage with the one-way street. Word from the grapevine was that Lace and his crew were nothing more than a bunch of filthy, stinking, drive-by shooters. They were punks and sissies—clowns who couldn't go toe-to-toe, so they hid behind triggers. Inside of a real man's world, it was like a boy hiding behind his mother's skirt. But we had something special planned for the bubblegum gangsters. Through some of Rico's back-channel connections, we even knew the type of vehicle they'd be using. We had a weasel-proof trap.

It was so sweet that it should've been illegal. Boxing in tournaments, Rico had gotten to know shady people in high positions of authority. Some were sprinkled in among our numbers who were standing by in tactical positions. The way we had it rigged, none of the enemies would be able to get off a shot. The move would afford Rico a chance to go one-on-one with Lace—providing he didn't send his goons to do his dirty work. But I doubted it; his boy had been erased. This shit was personal.

The temperature was in single digits and steadily dropping. Since the houses on the block did not have driveways, Rico and I were parked at the curve, in front of Mama Lemon's house, and sitting in a late-model Ford Focus. We were freezing our asses off. Because of the automatic lights, we couldn't turn the car on. It was a quarter to midnight and the street was desolate. An idling car, especially at that time of night, would have probably raised suspicions.

"Man, Rico," I said sincerely. "I didn't mean to bring this problem to Mama Lemon's front door."

Rico rubbed his hands together and blew on them at the same time. He tried desperately to get some blood circulating. Street-lights were few and far between. The moon was full—beautiful inside the night sky, and provided enough natural light to see the wisp of cold smoke escaping Rico's mouth.

My homeboy was ready for war. He was appropriately dressed in a thick Army jacket, combat boots and fatigues, with an army green bandanna tied around his head, looking like Tupac Shakur's character, Birdie, on *Above the Rim*.

"Wisdom, cut it out. You and I go back like throwbacks. We did what we had to do that night for family—feel me? If we ruffle some feathers, fuck 'em."

"You my dog and all, but dude, what's up with the *Birdie* look?"

"Don't front! You know I like channeling my inner Tupac before I take the field of battle."

"Fuck you, Birdie, old pickle-head muthafucka." I quoted a line from the movie and tried to sound exactly like Bernie Mac's character, Flip.

I was laughing so hard that I was in danger of straining an abdominal muscle. Rico was laughing so hard that he farted.

"I guess when this is over; you better go in the house and check your drawers, playa." I joked, and covered my nose from the awful aroma that smelled like air pollution. "Damn, Rico, I thought you ate healthy!"

We might've been yucking it up, but the situation was real and truly dangerous. I owed Rico my life. He'd been there on more than one hazardous occasion. Regardless of his nonchalant way of looking at it, my family drama could potentially bring death to his street.

"Man," Rico said from the driver's seat. "I'm still tripping on the way you told me that Yazoo nutted up at the family meeting. That fool ain't learned nothing, huh?"

"I don't think it's nothing for him to learn. I hate to say it, but the way he's going is gonna land him in jail or the grave."

Rico nodded his head. We were all tight, and had been that way since we were kids. Rico looked up to Yazoo like an older brother. Naturally, he didn't want anything to happen to him.

Despite the thought of knowing that in just a few moments, human blood could flow like a river, it felt good to laugh with my homeboy. So much had happened within the last few months that it had me weighed down and dragging ass while I tried to get to the finish line. I had so much pressure on me that it felt like the pipes of my sanity were about to burst. I wanted so badly to lift my burden by thoroughly confessing to Rico about all that I was going through. Out of all the contacts in my cell phone, there was absolutely nobody I could think of who could console me.

For the first time since we'd stepped inside the car, we were able to relax a little, and blow off some much-needed steam. I took the moment of silence and appreciated the snow-covered, wintry landscape of the ghetto. Mother Nature's fresh blanket of whiteness had the place looking peaceful—serene. Tamed. But underneath her frozen tundra lurked the sinister truth about my city. It was ugly, and a pus-filled eyesore that held graphic images of the carnage left behind by conquering figures on their march toward immortality. I'd struck up a deal with one, a bargain that would see me playing the role of a savior. Growing up in church, I was very familiar with the sacrifice of Jesus Christ—the torture and torment—all of it was so that I could have life, and have it more abundantly. I would never compare myself to the Savior, but I was getting ready to make a similar sacrifice so that my mother could live.

Highnoon wanted to see me beg and crawl for mercy. The prick actually believed that his offer was forged from charity. The cockroach even tried to sound convincing, like he was doing me a favor—like he was an honorable man who lived by a set of principles that didn't include whacking out an ex-friend without first coming to his aid, and asking permission in the form of an outlandish life-swap agreement. The way I saw it was that I was going down for Smoke's sins regardless, whether I agreed or not. I was always on his radar for termination. The whole thing was twisted, and no matter how I tried to understand it, the shit didn't make a damn bit of sense. He was a ghetto, eccentric asshole with power and not the slightest idea of how to effectively use it.

I managed to get past the tormenting questions of *how* and *why*. I tried to focus on how I was going to inject heavy milligrams of change inside the corrupted lives of four lost souls who were seriously in need of a Holy Ghost makeover. With only seven days to work and execute the plan, I didn't have a clue as to how in the hell I was gonna scare Yazoo, Tempest, Jordan—

with the good reverend bringing up the rear—straight. Reverend Poppa Nogood would be my most difficult challenge. The Negro presided over one of largest churches in the city and used it as a playground to play bedroom footsie with the little harlots in his congregation.

Turning their lives around would be crucial, and help in my mother's recovery. It made sense. Stress and worry had delivered her to death's doorstep in the first place. What good would it do if I sacrificed my life to give her a kidney and her family continued to act like well-accomplished heathens? I was trying to come up with a solid game plan, but the lack of heat was making it impossible to think. I was freezing my nuts off as I uncomfortably sat in the passenger's seat of the tiny Ford.

My cell phone vibrated. My brows clenched together out of disgust. Rico read me like I was a John Grisham novel.

"Baby mama?" he asked with a smirk on his face.

"Yep—my little child support-threatening Genghis Khan with stilettos," I said as I rubbed my knee. The joint venting its displeasure was painfully demanding an explanation as to why I had stuffed my big, six-six ass in a tuna can on wheels.

"No disrespect, brah, but your baby mama is meaner than an anabolic, steroid-addicted broad on her menstrual."

I started laughing so hard that I almost coughed up a lung. "Yeah, you're about right, partner. Malisa has been tripping lately, and threatening to dime me out to the child support bloodhounds every time I step outside of her little box. I think she's cheating on me, too."

"I said that the broad was evil—but I don't think— seriously, you think she'll cheat on you while carrying your seed?"

I really wanted to go there and tell him about my suspicions of her so-called cousin, Kirk. Kirk was a drug-dealing moron who was over my house every time that I looked up. My girl had lived a pretty checkered life before we met on that tragic night where shoving a ten-spot inside the heifer's underpants at a bar called Simply Naked had turned into a cash shakedown with daily threats of child support. Her family and friends were always shrouded in secrecy. I didn't know much about them, so I had reason to question if she and Kirk were really related. Something wasn't right. I couldn't worry about it, though.

"Man, I wouldn't put it past her." My cell vibrated again. This time, a smile spread across my face that was wider than the Detroit River.

Rico was quick with the comment. "Can't be the baby mama!"

I just kept smiling.

He snatched the phone from my hands and read the caller ID.

"Maria?" He looked at me as if to say with a Ricky Ricardo accent: *Lucy, you got some 'splainin' to do.* "Nigga, you look like you're the only one creepin'."

I snatched my phone back. "Ain't like that at all."

"Tell me what it's like, cuz."

"Oh, that's right. Well, you don't know about the stab wound."

"What stab wound?"

"Damn! We haven't chopped it up in a while. I thought I told you about me curb-stomping three Mexicans—one who had a switchblade."

"Switchblade, knife wound, three Mexicans—what the hell is going on, man?"

"Just had a few things on my mind. You know how we do it. I just forgot to tell you." I cradled my cold, throbbing knee with both hands. "I was at a pub in Southwest Detroit."

"What the hell were you doing out there?"

"Can I finish?"

"You got the flo'."

Literally and figuratively, we froze as the headlights of an approaching car shined through the back glass of the Focus, brilliantly illuminating the small car's interior. I was rather uncomfortable in sitting with my back to the entrance of the one-way street. I felt vulnerable. I was a little leery with putting my safety in somebody else's hands. The nerves in my stomach tightened as the approaching vehicle slowly moved in our direction. We both let out a nervous sigh of relief as an elderly black lady passed by driving a vintage Toyota Camry.

"I sat at a booth and this little gorgeous Spanish tamale walked over to take my drink order. She was flirting with a brotha, so I started laying on the charm."

Rico impatiently ran a hand down his face. "I ain't trying to collect Social Security before you finish your story. Just in case you don't remember, we will have some stank-ass drive-by shooters rolling through in a few. Get on with it."

"Anyway, Mr. Impatient, as the drinks started flowing, my little Spanish Harlem continued about her game. Our flirting didn't go unnoticed. Three Mexican gang members sitting at the bar started mean-muggin' me."

"You know how they can be about their women."

"Right. They sat there drinking and taking it all in until they couldn't take our show anymore. They approached. We ended up outside scrappin'. One of them pulled a gun, and another one pulled a knife., When it was all over, they were all knocked the fuck out, and I suffered a knife wound to the leg."

"Wisdom—the girl, how did you get her phone number?"

"Here's the thing: she slipped it into my pants pocket before we went outside."

"You know you crazy, right?"

Rico received a text message. Gone was the humor from a second ago; it was replaced with a serious mug belonging to a zone where violence voided rational thought.

"It's about to go down, homie." Rico informed.

Butterflies danced around in my stomach as I saw the headlights of their vehicle slowly turn the corner. I wasn't a punk, but I wasn't stupid. Being alive right then meant everything to me. My mother was my world. I had to make it out alive. I was going to die so that she would live. A silent prayer for our trap to work went up into the night sky.

I twisted my body in the seat to see the drive-by shooters creeping down the street and driving an older Suburban. The passenger windows slowly descended as the GMC drew closer to our bumper. I recognized the barrels of the weapons that protruded from both windows. AK-47s were about to make short work of Mama Lemon's house when the street lit up like Times Square on Christmas Eve. The red and blue lights of police cars—both marked and unmarked—zoomed from every direction and blocked in the Suburban as police jumped out with their weapons pointed at the SUV.

When the police had all the young cowards in custody—only then were we informed to step out of our vehicle. I still couldn't understand why Rico chose to sit in the little Ford in front of the house. The reasoning he gave didn't make any sense. I guess he wanted to be front and center if shit went sour.

After the cops cuffed and stuffed all the thugs in police cruisers, Lace was purposely left out. He was still wearing handcuffs when I walked up on him.

"Bitch!" he growled. "I'm gonna fuck your shit up, nigga!"

I wanted to grab his ass and give him what his mama and daddy had failed to, but tonight belonged to Rico. I saw him talking to a few officers. A tall, light-skinned officer dressed in regular clothes nodded to the uniform standing behind Lace. It was on. The officer removed the handcuffs as Rico started to move in Lace's direction. The red and blue lights bouncing off the windowpanes of surrounding houses drove a few neighbors out into the cold climate to investigate.

"Now, youngster," Rico said with a very comical but twisted expression on his face. "Let's see if you're really a gangster."

Lace understood the message. The pit bulls were unleashed and about to establish a pecking order. Lace rubbed both wrists.

"I owe you anyway. You still got the gun you and your boy jacked me for?" Lace asked.

They circled each other.

"I'm telling you now like I told you then—kindergartners shouldn't play with dangerous weapons," Rico joked.

I was seeing it, but still not believing it. The police were standing around watching. I even thought I saw money exchange hands. My boy must've had some strong pull inside the police department to organize a detail like this one. I felt sorry for the youngin. Highnoon had definitely put the squeeze on his boy, Molechin, and now Mr. Golden Gloves was about to go all Floyd "Money" Mayweather on Lace's ass. Rico was chomping at the bit to see how bad he could hurt this punk. It had to be the fantasy of every professional boxer to get into a haymaker-throwing brawl with a nonprofessional.

Where some of the sidewalks were covered by packed-in snow, the street belonged to slush and black ice. None of that mattered to Rico, as my boy dodged a couple of Lace's head-hunting jabs and laughed. Rico toyed with the schmuck before unleashing a brilliant three-punch combination—two to the body and one delivered upstairs, which put Lace on his ass.

To hell with the smelling salts, I thought. The police could've tried to revive the lame by passing raw sewage under the drive-by-shooting worm's nose. He wouldn't be getting up anytime soon. The Negro was out for the count.

"I guess that's done, huh, champ?" I said, trying to hold a straight face.

"Get up!" Rico yelled at Lace's unconscious body. "Remember that the next time you try to harm somebody's family!"

As the police dragged away what was left of the young hoodlum, I got ready to go. The fun and games were over. I had to set my mind on a course of action that would bring about desired results.

"Wisdom, I don't know what's going on with you, but if you ever need me, just call." My best friend let me know he was in my corner.

I gave him dap and limped back toward the mail van. Tomorrow I would be dropping by the hospital to see Momma. I had seven days—one week to straighten out the lives of my family members.

WISDOM

SUNDAY...

spent all day Sunday at my mother's bedside. The next seven days were going to be hell, and I wanted to give Momma all of me for at least one day. Because after today, there was no telling if I would see her again in life.

Of course, it saddened me whenever I looked at her. Tubes were everywhere. She looked like a sick octopus. And to add more stress and worry on my gray hairs, I couldn't reach my sister. She was supposed to meet me down here, but Tempest never showed or answered her cell. I figured it was strange. At one moment, she loved our sibling connection, and the next, she totally ignored my calls. I didn't wanna put too much stock in it. My sister was a grown woman. If she needed me, she knew how to get in touch.

Besides, the first person on my list to turn righteous again was my father. The good reverend. I didn't exactly know how I was gonna pull this miracle off. But what I witnessed the day before was enough to get the creative juices flowing. It was nothing but God who had softened

Highnoon's stone-cold, rock-hard tablet of a heart and allowed me this opportunity. So I knew everything was possible, and I didn't have a single, solitary moment to waste.

"Wiz." Momma spoke for the first time since I'd been in the room. "You okay, boy?" Momma's voice was low and weak. Her hair was matted to her head and her face was swollen beyond belief. She didn't look like the beautiful girl who had given me birth.

I gently rubbed her hair. "That's why I love you. You're always worried about the next person."

She offered an exhausted smile. "Wiz, I'm tired. I'm ready to go home." This wasn't good. Even I knew that when older, Baptist folks who'd been ill for quite some time started mentioning "tired" in the same breath as "going home," they were ready to give up the fight.

"Momma, just hold on. Everything's gonna be alright." I waited for my words to sink in. "You remember when you used to tell me about how when you didn't feel like you could hold on any longer?'

She nodded her head.

"How God would be right there to walk for you when your legs were giving out?"

She smiled up at me. "Okay, honey. I'll try and hold on, but it's hard."

"I know, but please...you have to trust me on this."

"Boy, you know something I don't?"

"I know you'll be alright." I rubbed her face gently.

"Where did you get so much faith from?" she asked as if she didn't know.

I was trying hard to keep my tears at bay. "You, ma'am. I learned about faith from you." I hugged her tenderly, but she couldn't fully reciprocate my embrace. The tubes acted as restraints.

"I love you, Wiz." A single tear cascaded down her fluid-filled cheek.

"I love you back, Momma Jones."

I looked at her for one long eternity, and tried hard to capture her in my mind as though I were taking a mental Polaroid.

"Look, Momma, I have a little business to take care of. I'll make sure I come back and see you. Deal?"

"This old lady'll still be here when you get back." That made me feel better, knowing that my mother was going to try to hang in there. Her new kidney would depend solely on her will to live. I kissed her jaw and went off to save souls.

I was driving around on a Sunday night and listening to a slow, relaxing groove by The Art of Noise, a synth-pop group that received their start in '83 out of the UK. I wasn't a huge fan of the group, but a fan of one cut in particular, "Moments in Love." I always played the slow and inspiring joint in the eleventh hour of a crisis. The tone of the tune started out soft and easy and slowly worked its way up into a haunting crescendo belonging to the story of trial, tribulation, but eventually, break-through—or at least that was my sappy perception of the song.

As I carefully drove down the slippery streets left behind by a mild snowstorm, I was trying desperately to wrap my mind around what could possibly be the last seven days of my life. It was one thing to know that everyone would face down death one day, but the teeth belonged to a different beast in actually knowing the time and day. Every task that I didn't accomplish inside the span of seven days would be left undone. I thought about how my death would affect those left behind, and how my life could've turned out if I hadn't taken my hardheaded ass to the basketball court that day—on the eve of the NBA draft, for Christ's sake. I was a friggin' number one draft pick. I would have been able to buy my family everything they dreamed of. My ol' girl would've been straight. I could've merely shown my Visa Black Card and handled my business like any other self-respecting millionaire snob with loot. Negroes would've been coughing up kidneys at retail price. Instead, I chose to participate in a game with a cat who I knew was hating on me with every beat of his cold, black heart—a fool who hadn't hesitated at the moment of my vulnerability.

Doing to Pogo a few days ago what he'd put on me years back was merely a fraction of payback, a mild form of punishment compared to the years I had fantasized about buying some airtime on a local cable channel and featuring myself torturing him for the duration of the show until the punk was dead. But for now, returning the favor by introducing his face to the cold, hard ground after he fell six feet from the air had to suffice. It wasn't Christ-like, but I would go to my grave knowing that the joker would remember me every morning he looked in the mirror and cried while trying to brush broken stumps that used to be healthy teeth.

An old, white Ford Bronco—made famous by O.J.—was sitting at a red light on northbound Telegraph and Six Mile. I was on the southbound side of the main street, getting ready to jump on the Jeffries Freeway when I spotted the SUV. I knew it was him when I laid eyes on the vehicle. The roads were slick and black ice was present under a couple of inches of fresh snow. I had to be careful when making the Michigan left around the center medium. I pulled behind.

Bingo!

Confirmation came when I read his customized plates: *No Mercy*. He must've made me because once the light turned green, homeboy was peeling out—the back of his truck fishtailing as rubber searched for traction underneath the white stuff. Traction was nothing to the front-wheel pull of my mail van. I didn't think it should've been his deal, either—being that his SUV had rolled off the assembly line with four-wheel drive. But black ice was still ice. The Bronco merely spun wheels until it caught asphalt and shot off down the street. I was right on his ass, shadowing his every move. It was late, so there weren't too many on the street, but I was worried about the police in Redford. They liked to set up speed traps in real dark areas. Forty-five was the posted speed limit, but we were a couple of nickels over it.

I had this mofo red-handed. He'd been stalking my every move. Showing up all over the place—a total mystery. I didn't know who the white man wearing the Ray Bans with the buzz cut and driving the white Bronco was. The fool had shown up at my job once, then again by a Coney Island restaurant, lurking, stalking, and staying close to the shadows. But this time I'd gotten the drop on him and the fool was running like a scalded dog. He slipped and slid out of one lane and into another, swerved around a Pontiac, and barely missed clipping an old, silver Impala with heavily tinted windows., He kept his foot on the gas as the SUV swayed from side to side, looking at times like he was going to flip it. The Impala lost control and I barely avoided hitting it. My rearview wasn't short on showing the action. The Impala careened toward the snow-covered island medium and hopped the curb, then slammed headlong into a huge tree trunk. I could only pray that the occupants were okay.

I gained a little ground on the chump when he must've hit some black ice, jumped the curb, and plowed right into the wrought iron gates of a cemetery. The coward didn't waste any time getting out of the wreck and bailing through the huge opening. Buzz Cut was not getting away from me. I slid my van on the sidewalk. With adrenaline pouring through my body, my mind anticipated getting to the bottom as to why the *Top Gun* reject had taken such a shine to me. He'd had a couple-seconds head start and was laboring to get through undisturbed, knee-deep snow that covered the headstones and grass area. The narrow road that separated and cut the place into sections was clear. Once he made it there, it was going to be *Bye-bye,Buzz Cut.* I ran and jumped, trying to make up the distance, and landed with the snow just below my knees.

Caliba's remains rested in a place like this. I had made several attempts to go visit her gravesite, but never carried through. I felt guilty, as though I'd killed her with my own two hands. I had to pull my focus back to the pursuit. The chase was in front of me. The snow acted as human glue paper, slowed my pursuit, and delayed me from beating the reasons out of him for why he'd been following me.

Once he finally broke free of the deep snow pockets, he was off to the races. He ran up a pathway and between two large crypts. The snow wasn't so deep in that area. I wasn't too far behind. When I got to the large crypts, the cat was nowhere to be found. Sirens wailing in the distance stopped my search. Footprints had ended at the door of the stone chamber on the right. He was inside hiding, but I couldn't do anything about it. Not with the Redford Police closing in. The company van being at the scene wouldn't have gone over too well. Besides, I needed that van to get me through the next seven days. As I hot-footed it back, I was afraid that Buzz Cut would remain a mystery.

If I didn't discover his identity within the next week—anything not done…would have to stay that way.

WISDOM

(SEVEN-DAY COUNTDOWN)
MONDAY, DAY ONE…

"Amen, Reverend!" a fat guy sitting in the back of the church bellowed on the last pew.

The pudgy brother needed to be ashamed of himself. The too-tight suit he was wearing—or wearing him—fit him like spandex.

"Say that, Pastor!" shouted an elderly lady wearing one of those church hats the size of a small Buick. The old bitty sat right in front of me, and even I was having trouble tracking my father's movements because of the hat. With her being so old and fragile, that heavy hat had to be wreaking havoc on her flimsy, thin neck.

My knee was killing me. Trying to chase down the white dude last night had brought the kind of pain that made me want to put a gun up to my temple and pull the trigger. I didn't have time for figuring out my mystery stalker wearing Ray Bans. My father's church was hosting an evening revival—kicking off the next five days of scripture, praising, singing and of course, the offering. Pastor had to get paid, right?

I was sitting in the middle of the church. No mask. No disguise. Just my plain, stressed-out mug. The reverend had quite a turnout. He hadn't noticed me yet, but I guessed that was largely in part to him not being able to keep his eyes off Sister Walker. I knew her name because the home-wrecking broad had gotten up earlier and read the announcements. I wondered how many people in the church had noticed them openly flirting with each other. I didn't know, but Sister Lawson looked like she was about to blow a gasket. I knew Sister Lawson. I had caught her and my father at the Red Roof Inn right before the family brawl. And word around the campfire was that her settlement check from the city had helped finance my poor, lost soul of a father that sweet Cadillac Escalade ESV truck parked neatly in the spot reserved for the pastor.

What could I say? I wasn't there to judge; I came to save. That's why I was sitting out in the congregation. Plus, I hadn't heard my father preach in a while.

Despite Pastor Jones' shortcomings, the man could preach. His words were pure poetry, served with a hefty side of *Have Mercy*, and neatly wrapped up in a double side of *Good God!*

"Jesus Christ served as an unblemished sacrifice." the good reverend preached. "Ain't that something? God's unselfish nature." He stopped and looked at his congregation for the effect. "Yet, some of you can't shed that selfishness to tithe."

"Tell 'em, Pastor." One of the deacons pumped his fist.

"Saints, you act like the money that you're holding on

to is yours. When in fact, it's God's money. If it wasn't for God, a lot of you wouldn't have money. You'd be just like those weary, sign-toting souls asking for a handout at the stoplight or the freeway exit." Poppa was a leader, born and bred. True to form, he went into the pockets of his beautiful black robe with yellow trimming and removed a white envelope. "Pastors are not exempt from giving God what's His." He held his tithe envelope in full view. A deafening hush fell over the guilty members.

I lay back, trying to wrap my mind around the fact that this man was begging people for their hard-earned money so that he could finance his own little trick operation. I was totally aware of the whole ten-percent thing, but that was when a church was running properly and didn't have a heathen at its helm. Tithing took a lot of prayer and discipline—people giving money to a church in hopes of being blessed. God forgive me, but the people didn't really have it to give in the first place, There were folks whose homes were a closed door away from foreclosure, repossession, and eviction. It took a lot of faith to give to a church whose leader was as crooked as the letter *S*.

"The scripture for giving comes from Malachi 3:10," the pastor said.

My mind was on other things. Like how I was going to turn his wretched soul back on the right track. I'd come here hoping that I could meet with him to talk some sense into him.

He finished by saying, "Brothers and sisters, you're robbing God by holding onto what's His." One of the deacons lugged out the tithe box on cue.

"They're not robbing God!" a heavy, muffled voice yelled from the back door of the main aisle.

I didn't know about anybody else, but my blood ran cold at the sight of two mugs with ski masks, both brandishing automatic rifles.

"This is not a robbery," the littlest one warned. A third one, at gunpoint, marched in the greeters and a few others who where lollygagging around in the vestibule. "This is an attempt to collect a debt. Sit down and shut up, and you won't be harmed." He waved the rifle across the congregation. "I will warn you once, people. Put your cell phones away. If I catch anybody trying to text, call or film this shit for YouTube, I will not hesitate to put yo' ass on the news. Any heroes will be laid out in a box at the altar—closed casket."

With the exception of a few saying, "Oh my God," and a couple of them whispering, "Jesus, help us," the church grew as quiet as a graveyard on a deserted island..

"Brothers." My dad finally got enough nerve to speak. "Exactly what debt could you be collecting in a church?"

"You." They snatched weapon slides back. "Mutha-fucka," the fat one said as he wobbled toward the pulpit, his weapon following behind him. "You didn't heed the warning, Pastor." He beckoned with the muzzle of his weapon. "Come down here, you hypocritical heathen."

I felt more helpless than a man with no arms or legs

trying to put out a small fire. My mind worked with the thunder of nature, coldly calculated their strengths, and probed for any weaknesses. Sure, I was a big guy, but that would only make me a bigger target. Not to mention that I didn't want to put any of the members in harm's way by attempting something foolish. I would have to ride this out and pray like mad that the boys in blue would be somewhere nearby and not at the doughnut depot.

"Brother," my father said. The weapon was at his back as he marched down the aisles. "I'm sure we can work this out. God will forgive— "

"Shut up!" the mountain with legs barked. "Just keep walking. Save the fire and brimstone speech for these brainwashed people in here. You have a debt to pay."

The punks were disciplined. They'd done this type of work before—maybe a bank or two. I couldn't possibly understand what they wanted from my father. This couldn't have been a robbery. These clowns were only interested in my old man. Their movements were crisp, army trained.

The fat creep marched my dad down the main aisle. I was sitting in a pew right off of that aisle. I gritted my teeth as they walked by, the old man finally catching my eyes. My heart was savagely thumping against my chest. I felt perspiration on my palms.

The masked creep was in striking distance, but my father's eyes begged me not to do anything stupid. My struggle for personal restraint was harder than government cheese.

This can't be happening again, I thought to myself. Same robbery…different scenario. First, Yazoo's dad, Frank. We had stood around helplessly while the man took his final breaths before descending into the murky depths. Just like that, Zoo had been robbed of his dad. Now this. I couldn't sit there. I had never told my dad, but he meant everything to me.

God, I silently pleaded. It couldn't be ending like this. My father's evil deeds were catching up. Would he be killed before I had a chance to straighten him out? Before he had a chance to turn the corner? *Lord, please give me the chance.*

I saw only three men. Common sense told me that these guys probably rolled deep. This was a big church and they were well armed, which meant more had to be holding things down outside. I hoped nobody tried to grow some balls and oppose these cats. There was no telling what they might do to my old man. I didn't know what the hell he'd done, but the ol' goat had sure gone and gotten his plums in a twister.

Breathless and helpless, we watched them march our leader out to a fate only known by God.

"Anybody who sticks their head out these doors will get a hole in their collection plate," the smallest of the three warned us as he thrust his weapon forward, and enforced the threat.

They shoved Pop out the doors, along with our hearts and prayers.

REVEREND POPPA JONES

The thugs stopped being polite after they exited the church. There were more of them than I thought. The three who'd made the initial contact followed me out, while the other three trained their weapons on the doors of the sanctuary with stern orders to shoot first and ask questions never. There were a total of six. It was a blessing that all my members had been on one accord today. I was afraid if there had been anybody dragging in late today—or at this moment—they would've been considered dead on arrival.

I was equally surprised to see Wisdom in church. It had been a while since I'd last seen him. And if I hadn't pleaded with him by using eye contact, he would've ended up on the floor with huge holes blown throughout his body.

Without warning, the fat one shoved me down to the asphalt. He pointed the weapon directly at my forehead. The others started stomping at Fats' command.

I was kicked and stomped for a good three minutes before Fats yelled at them to stop. The other two backed away as Fats stepped up, holding a cell phone. He shoved it up to my ear with wicked laughter.

"Somebody needs to holla at you, Preacher," Fats said. His laugh was still wicked..

My body felt like it had been thrown from the balcony of a seven-story apartment, then run over by an eighteen-wheeler on the streets below.

I looked at Fats like he was insane. I went to move, but the terrifying pain streaking across my chest caused me to stop in my tracks. Ribs could've been broken. Grabbing my ribcage, I tried to slow down my breathing. "Hello."

"You must've thought I was joking," my past said. I could hear her brimming with satisfaction. "You just not gonna do me like the rest. I told you that I want you to suffer. Ain't you heard? Hell has no fury like a pregnant woman scorned!"

I spat out a puddle of blood and knew darn well that God was fed up with my mess. This was my Egypt. His wrath. The thief in the midnight hour. My back was up against the wall. I had hit rock bottom.

All of my sins were coming to bear. I knew one day I would have to answer for my wayward conduct. Misleading God's sheep, squeezing their pocketbooks for my own personal gain. It was strange what came back to memory once God started knocking at my door. I could remember a sermon from an old, down-home preacher. He warned about treating God's church as a personal piggy bank. The old man preached that if a man kept reaching in the bank, eventually, he would draw out debt.

I owed God. Every ounce of me owed him. He gave me His Son. I gave Him my grief. There was nothing like the debt of a religious leader whose hands were caught in the cookie jar of God's tithing box. The goon was right about me owing debt—even though he was talking about mortal debt. The jerk didn't know it, but he was delivering a message straight from God.

"May God forgive you for interrupting His service and disrespecting His house with those weapons of destruction." I spoke into the phone, and spat up a nasty glob of saliva-saturated blood.

Afterward, I didn't know whose gun butt struck first. The phone flew from my hand and so did blood from my nose. The jackals were on me like a fat man on a four-piece chicken dinner with a biscuit.

I tried to ball up to escape some of the punishment. I couldn't because the pain from fists and flying gun butts drowned out rational thinking. I thought I was dead after a couple of minutes. My body went numb. I couldn't feel anything. I didn't try to fight back. In a roundabout way, I accepted this attack, embracing it as God's remedy for the bad ways in which I lived. I took my medicine as a man. The more my attackers put the boots to me, the more I felt God trying to stamp out the lustful demon nestled in my flesh. My eyes. Touch. My heart. The way I'd blackballed Deacon Slydale. Satan's misdeeds were draining from every hole in my body.

I allowed myself the budding opportunity to remove

my mind from my body, thinking if I lived, how was I going to tell my wife the real reasons behind the assault? Breaking the news to her about a brand-new baby in her condition wasn't gonna be easy. But I was determined to get my life together, and not because my attackers chose to wear steel-toe boots instead of sneakers. It was time for a change.

The voice from my past was claiming to have the baby any day now. This time I'd really messed over the wrong woman. She was a woman who'd proven to be more wicked than any harlot enjoying her trick on a pew inside a church. A woman who had absolutely nothing to lose. The mother of my soon-to-be baby was one miracle away from being my daughter-in-law.

WISDOM

I waited a few moments before I approached the door. All the while, I expected to hear gunfire, and then feel the hot nastiness from lead penetration. My heart was running a marathon. I got as low as my six-six frame would allow, looking back at the deacons to see if any had the plums to back me up. They were quivering and shaking in the corners.

Slowly, I pumped myself up to take a peep through the small window in the door.

The coast was clear!

I didn't see a soul. My imagination was working me over big time. I kept imagining my old man being fitted for cement shoes, then trying them out on the bottom of the Detroit River.

Once out in the vestibule, I walked to the main door and prayed that they hadn't abducted my father. I pleaded with God that they left enough of him lying in the parking lot to recover.

Surprise and shock registered across my face as I glimpsed over my shoulder to see an empty floor that should've been packed with concerned and angry members, ready to fight from here to eternity at freeing their spiritual leader. Instead, all I saw was a ghost town of a vestibule. I expected to see tumbleweeds and funnel clouds of dust blowing across the carpets as if I were standing in some desolate street in the West.

Opening the door, I exercised extreme caution. I slithered out and peered over some snow-covered brush. My instincts took over. I dialed some numbers into my MetroPCS. The next thing I knew, there was a lot filled with flashing red and blue police lights, an ambulance, and a few in plain clothes. Large snowflakes started to fall. The parking lot looked more like the scene right after a failed presidential assassination.

They'd roughed up the ol' man pretty bad, and left him lying flat on his back in an unconscious state. The entire parking lot had been shoveled. The rock salt had melted the ice left behind, which spotted the lot with pools of dirty water.

The emergency technicians revived him. They should've taken him to the hospital while he was out. The stubborn, pig-headed fool refused any further medical treatment, ignoring the warning of internal damages.

"I ain't going anywhere." Poppa groggily barked at one of the two technicians.

A short black man, with a granddaddy of a receding hairline and unsightly razor bumps on his chin and neck, looked at me. "Young man, would you talk some sense into him?"

"Pastor," the white tech said calmly. "Please reconsider." He looked at me with genuine concern, as if he thought I could make Pops obey. Poppa was sitting on the back bumper of the emergency truck. They'd torn his clothes off him. His suit jacket had been ripped off and the buttons from his shirt were scattered across the lot. His shirttail was out and his beady chest hair was exposed. "Pastor, you have a few bumps, a couple of nasty abrasions, a split bottom lip—not to mention a few questionable broken ribs."

"And because you're talking so slowly," the black tech butted in as he fit Poppa's left arm with a blood pressure cup. "I want to add a possible concussion." He pumped the thing and waited for the results. "One-forty over ninety-five. Your pressure's up".

"Hey, Hercules," I said, standing over Poppa. "If you're not going with them, you're not going back in the church"—I pointed—"to preach."

"Since when did you start telling me how to run my church?"

I folded my arms defiantly. "Since the trauma to your head has rendered you incapable of making sound decisions for yourself." Nobody but authorized personnel were out in the lot. The members hadn't been allowed to come out yet. Detectives were inside interviewing every last soul.

I knew none of the members could describe the attackers beyond the fact that they wore ski masks and brandished hardware that couldn't be purchased from Home Depot.

A tall, neatly dressed black man with an immaculately cropped Afro approached us, pad in hand. Detective Strong had taken a statement from me when he'd arrived on the scene. Until Poppa was decent in the head, I acted as his mouthpiece.

"You ready to talk to me now?" Detective Strong asked Poppa in a smooth baritone voice. His vocals suggested that he should've been on tour instead of slushing through the snow chasing criminals. The brother was also stylish on top of it all. A black cashmere topcoat hung from his big, broad shoulders, giving off the illusion of sheets clamped to a clothing line, blowing around in a summer breeze.

Poppa stared back wide-eyed. "All I can tell you is that the poor lost souls wore ski masks and carried AK-47 assault rifles." Poppa was still sitting on the back bumper being attended to. One tech fumbled with an instrument I'd never seen before, while the other tech bandaged Poppa's head.

"I spoke with a few members of the church." Detective Strong flipped the pages of his notepad. "They all said that the perps weren't after money." He flipped again. "In fact, one of the men yelled that out upon entry." Detectives Strong's neatly trimmed eyebrows knitted together in a questioning fashion. "Pastor, have you been receiving any threats, any disgruntled members—anybody that would want to do you bodily harm?"

The look my father gave me before he answered chilled my bones. "Not to my knowledge," he calmly said. He was lying. The bum knew something. My theory suggested that he'd stuck his King James into the wrong woman's pulpit.

Trying to convince this fool to turn over a new leaf was gonna be harder than persuading a pimp to give up his whores and take a job as a greeter at Walmart.

Detective Strong glanced around the parking lot at his officers feverishly working, and tried to find an ounce of something to shed some light on a situation that clearly puzzled him. He blew cold smoke from his mouth as he removed a card from the inside pocket of his coat. "I know that the trauma to your head might make it a little hard on your memory. " He handed Pops the card. "If you think of anything that might help this case, please call me—regardless of the—"

"I won't hesitate to call." Poppa rudely cut Strong off. Something was getting his goat. Detective Strong had somehow struck a nerve. The detective studied Poppa like he was some big-shot archeologist trying to decode the mysteries of ancient Egyptian hieroglyphs. Then he let his facial muscles relax.

"Gentlemen, have a good day." Strong walked away with his coattails blowing around in the wind like some action hero evaporating into a windy sunset.

Poppa snapped at the techs. "Are you all through?"

"Pastor," the black tech spoke, "I'm going to ask one more…"

Poppa shot the tech an unholy look. "Brother, God gave the doctors their skills. But occasionally, He heals without them." He looked at the other one. "You saints have a blessed day." With those chosen words spoken, Reverend Poppa Jones went staggering off in the direction of his office. I started to get that feeling in the pit of my gut. This thing ran deeper than the good reverend was letting on. I could see I'd bitten off more than I could chew. All I could hope for was that the reverend wouldn't take all seven days to be put back among the righteous.

Poppa Jones slowly staggered into his office. To avoid being questioned by members before time, Poppa used the back door to gain entry—me in tow, my hand on his shoulder to guide and sturdy his stride.

No matter how Pops tried to front, the ol' man was deeply shaken. I would be, too. Those punks went through all of that trouble to send a message. But what kind of message?

"Sister Green," Poppa spoke in a Daffy Duck kind of tone into the intercom on his desk.

"Pastor?"

"Get Minister Smith on the phone."

Minutes later, the soft, lovely voice spoke clearly through the intercom, "Pastor, the minister is on line one."

I sat in one of the seats in front of the pastor's rich mahogany desk and took in the splendid beauty of his glorious study. I hadn't been there in a while. The old man had made many modifications. He'd sure come a long way from those dingy, gloomy-looking, cramped quarters he had started in.

Pops instructed one of his associate ministers to go to the sanctuary and calm everything. Afterward, he was to lead the congregation in prayer and give an early benediction. I could only imagine the chaos among the members. There would be loads of jokes, gossip, and rumors circulating behind Poppa being forced from the pulpit and stomped in the parking lot. I could hear those old bitties firing up the phone lines already.

"Oh my God!" Sister Green shrieked. She stood in the doorway with her hands up to her mouth, shivering. "Pastor, are you alright?"

I craned my neck to see the beautiful face behind that sexy voice.

"Yes, Sister Green," Pops said and slightly smiled. "I'm fine."

Fine was what Sister Green was. The sister was a straight-up dime piece. Her behind looked like two melons bouncing around in a pillowcase.

"I was in my office. I didn't know anything had happened until Sister Long called me on my cell, and let me know," Sister Green said as her eyes roamed over me in search of recognition.

Poppa went into his mint jar and popped one.

"Sister Green," Poppa said and waved his hand in my direction. "This is my son, Wisdom Jones."

I stood and took her slender, vanilla hand in mine. "How do you do? It's a pleasure to meet you."

"The pleasure is all mine, Wisdom." The sister craned her neck and took all of me in. I would've felt violated had she not been so damn fine. "Pastor, why didn't you tell me you had a basketball player for a son?" Her flirtatious smile seemed to place my dad back in that sour mood I'd witnessed minutes ago.

"That's because I felt no need to," he scolded.

Quickly, Sister Green's pleasant smile melted into a look of pure confusion. The grown woman suddenly wore the look of a goofy adolescent.

"Sister, can you leave me and my son alone?" Without a reply, she retreated for the door with her tail between her legs. She was getting ready to step over the threshold when Dad said, "Hold all my calls."

I waited until she closed the door. "That's about all the rudeness I'm going to stand," I said. I sat back down. "Besides treating Momma like garbage and leaving her to die, what has crawled up your blowhole? Oh, and who in the hell were those creeps in the ski masks?"

"Don't know." His words were short and pointed.

I shook my head in disgust.

I could tell that he was tired of living a trifling life of hurt, lying and deceit. The look was a picture of emotions painted on sleeves, which summed up how I felt. I felt like an angel of mercy on borrowed time, trying to do a good deed before I earned my halo, wings and a very relaxing vacation, padded by eternal rewards in Heaven.

"Son, I'm sorry about your momma..," he apologized. I could hear his voice breaking. "I didn't mean to leave her at that restaurant. It hurts me to know that I'm the one responsible for her heart attack. I'm sorry, son. I'm so sorry."

It wasn't until he moved his hand from his face that I witnessed tears. I couldn't believe it. This Negro was showing some signs of humanity. Up 'til this moment, Pops had been a hard, cold, cruel man with the slogan "Weakness can get you killed" stamped on his forehead. But I saw nothing that resembled his former arrogant attitude now. All I saw was a tired, old battleship looking for some special place to dock and drop an anchor of burdens. The huge, brown grocery bags underneath his bloodshot eyes portrayed a man who'd been tormented between heaven and hell. A shamed spiritual warrior who'd come up short on that much-anticipated rite of passage.

I leaned down to massage my throbbing knee. The romp through the snowy mountains of the cemetery had increased the pain. Once the adrenaline stopped pumping, my joint was on fire. At least in a few days, I wouldn't have that problem. Speaking of underlying facts, I wouldn't have any problems once Highnoon satisfied his blood-thirsty taste for revenge.

"Wisdom," Poppa started out and dabbed at his eyes with tissues. "What do you want me to say? That I'm a religious leader who doesn't believe in his own product? Is that what you want to hear?"

I continued consoling my knee, *religiously* unmoved.

"I didn't want all of this responsibility. It was God who saw fit to leave this burden on me." He whined as I if were a sucker for bullshit. He blew his nose and looked me dead in my eyes. "Don't sit there looking down your nose at me, Wisdom Jones. You don't know how it feels to be a preacher who leads those to water, but doesn't drink himself."

"Oh," I said. "Spare me the pity party. Does it look like I'm living the life I always wanted? But that doesn't give me a platform to dive off into a pool of sin because I've been burdened down with truckloads." I rose up. "Now does it?"

"I've tried to satisfy—"

"Who...yourself?"

"My family the best way possible. What can I say? I've failed. I couldn't do both. One would suffer. Man cannot serve two masters."

"Aw, save me the sermon, Reverend. Your family had your back. But your whores caused you to stray."

"Respect the Lord's house."

I yelled, "You respect it! Besides, the word *whore* is mentioned in the Bible."

"Son, God knows that I have my sinful desires—my breaking points. And as a pastor, I know better than others about breaking God's covenant, but that only makes Satan come at me just that harder. Son, I'm only human."

"Pops, that's weak. You know as well as I do about how women bring out the weaknesses of men. Ain't a man on this miserable planet who hasn't been tempted one time or another—ask Sampson."

"It ain't that easy."

"Why haven't you checked on Momma?"

"Because I couldn't bear to look at her after what I've done."

"Man, you embarrassed her. Then you drove off and left her at that"—I almost cussed—"restaurant."

He looked down at his desk, guilt written from hairline to chin.

"You didn't even have the decency to call me and inquire about her. *And what did you do?* You moved out the house and shacked up with some bimbo." I was trying to keep my anger in check, but it was damn near impossible in my infuriated state. "Yeah, I know. I know everything. Pop, you're foul. I smell you from here."

"Son?"

"What?" I was looking him dead in his eyes.

"The baby ain't yours." He blurted out what sounded like a confession.

"What baby?"

The old goat choked up for a minute, looked down on his desk, and clasped his hands.

The bum coughed. "Malisa's."

A deep, unholy silence foiled the ol' man's startling revelation. The stupid, apologetic look on his face set off a four-alarm fire inside my spirit. It felt like heat from a fire's blaze, but I couldn't see the actual flames.

I pinched the bridge of my nose. "Whose baby is it, Preacher...if it's not mine?" I calmly asked, although I already knew the betraying answer. I just wanted to hear it from his treacherous lips.

His eyes dropped from mine as if the answer rested on his desk. "Mine."

The first tear that escaped my eye activated a floodgate of emotions, stomach butterflies, and tormented memories.

Without word or warning, I was out of the chair. I slid across the desk, headfirst, and knocked his trifling ass backward without remembering when or how. I grabbed a handful of his tie.

His eyes were wide with fear. He clutched at my hands and attempted to free himself.

"Son." He breathlessly pleaded with me. "Don't do this. She came on to me. She said that she would start rumors in the church if I didn't comply."

"Bullshit." I snarled. Because of the army of tears sliding down my face, I couldn't see him. Everything was blurry. I held onto his tie as if I were a fishing pole and he were a desperate fish, fighting for life, trying hard to escape my line. "If that was so, why couldn't you come to me?" I tightened my grip. I heard the struggle going on in his lungs for air, but I couldn't loosen my hold on the bastard.

"Didn't…know how." He tried to inhale. I was like a snake—constricting. As he exhaled, I tightened my grip. He clawed at my hands. "She…she was naked…naked at the time. Couldn't…walk away."

"Ya'll been laughing in my face, forcing me to think the baby was mine."

I was set on squeezing all the lies out of him like juice from an orange. The Negro didn't deserve to be walking among the living. He had violated me in a major way.

Garbage! I had to remove it from the dump. It wasn't mine to do, but I felt an undying urge to kill. I desperately wanted to rid myself of the haunting pain that had tormented my family for years, the demon that had ripped my family apart and planted seeds of corruption. Each of my family members was struggling with a demonic branch that had broken off from Poppa's main tree of wickedness. That branch manifested, impacted our lives, and doomed us before we had a chance to start.

"This must not be your day, Preacher." I was squeezing so hard that my teeth were hurting from angrily grinding them together. "You already had one ass-whooping. Now I'm about to finish the job them ski-masked punks started." I squeezed until something popped. Not the sound of bones crunching and breaking, but the rational pop of a civilized thought, an epiphany. I had no right to strangle God's anointed. Absolutely no right to think wicked thoughts on God's property—even if the ol' man was wrong. God was judge, jury and executioner. When it was time, He'd deal with Poppa's wretched soul.

"You ain't worth it," I said. I nearly felt like Celie in *The Color Purple*. I relaxed my grip and let his worthless carcass fall to the floor.

"Thank...thank you," he said. Through my tears, I saw him taking deep breaths, holding his throat, and gasping for air.

"No," I said as I looked down at the mess I still loved as a father. "Don't thank me. Best make peace with your evil deeds, Preacher."

I left him on the floor. It looked like he was in a praying position, but I didn't know. It was no longer my concern.

I strutted out the door and felt ten pounds lighter. The secret was out. I didn't have a baby. And after I saw Malisa, I wasn't going to have a woman either. For the moment, I was happier than roaches in a bakery.

Sister Green's desk was vacant. I figured the sexy sister went to get firsthand gossip from Sister Long, or she'd been scared off by all the furniture moving around in Poppa's office.

I didn't give a damn. Either way, Poppa had gotten the message. What sane-minded man wouldn't? Especially after facing death twice in one day. If this didn't put him back on the straight and narrow, I didn't know what would. Then it hit me like a concentrated kick in the nuts. My happiness was short-lived. I was due to be murdered in six days. So either way it went, I would be rid of Malisa's trifling, scandalous, lying behind. The thought came to me like a stab in the gut. I connected the ski-masked punks with Malisa. Her handiwork was written all over it. She was just that ballsy to arrange something like that. I'd even go so far as to say that her faithful gopher, Junita, had a hand at supplying the ghetto A-Team. After all, for months, the broad had tried to control me by the threat of child support.

Amusedly, I shivered at the fact that I'd been going behind my old man. The bare thought of visualizing him and my soon-to-be ex in a midnight, sexual romp nauseated my stomach and churned my bowels to the point of release. I only wished that I could stick around to see Malisa pull that child support crap on the good reverend. I felt for the baby the most. My little brother or sister had a rude awakening on the horizon. A harlot for a mother, and a Bible-slanging, backsliding Judas for a father.

Momma was going to be the most thrilled. She would live, but with a broken heart.

Outside, and back in the mail van, the heat was as lukewarm as usual. I was going to miss this van. I'd told my supervisor that I was going to run some errands for my mother. It wasn't too far from the truth. He understood. Stanley Focus said that I had his prayers, and he had even given me the week off.

Looking through the window, I glanced up at the sky.

Lord, one down, two to go. But something in my gut warned me that Poppa wasn't gonna go into the light of righteousness that easy.

The schmuck!

WISDOM

TUESDAY, DAY TWO...

y ol' man was up to his old tricks. I was sitting down the street from Sister Lawson's house. I'd sat there the whole night after following him from the church. This was not the way I should've been spending my last six days on earth. I hadn't had a chance to properly introduce Malisa to the curb. Take the steam right out of her muscle-bound ego. For what I had planned, she might just have that baby right where she stood.

Sister Lawson lived in a nice area, but it was still the hood. So I didn't look too out of place sitting in the mail van.

It was nine o'clock in the morning and my eyes were burning by the wildfire of sleep deprivation. I picked up my cell and dialed the hospital. I got a little scared when a lady answered the phone. Nurse Betty told me that my mother had gone for some tests. She informed me that Momma would be back on the floor in a few hours. She said that Momma was stable.

I hung up, yawned, and stretched my tall frame. The cramps in my legs were screaming bloody murder, with my knee yelling at them all about having seniority.

An elderly black man came out of his house carrying a shovel and staring at me. Since last night, an inch or two of snow had accumulated. His look of suspicion heightened with every scoop of snow.

I didn't want him calling the cops. I had to act fast, so I rolled down the window.

"Excuse me, sir," I said in a voice reduced of bass. I didn't want to scare him.

"Yes," he said cautiously.

I held a dollar store police badge up, prayed it served the purpose, and hoped that he kept his distance. The lenses insides of his wire-rimmed glasses were industrial strength, and as thick as aquarium glass. I figured as long as he remained a few feet away, I could pull it off.

"I'm Detective Nelson," I lied. "Have you witnessed anything unusual?"

The old man squinted but stayed put. "No, Detective. Can't believe I have."

I went into my showbiz routine. "I'm on a stakeout. We have probable cause to believe that someone on this street is engaging in drug importing and exporting. So if you have any information, please let me know."

"Well," he said, "I ain't seen nothin' around here like that, but if'n I do, I'll let ya know." He smiled a toothless grin. "Anything to help the law." He obliged me with the tip of his ball cap.

I nodded while rolling my window up, and felt sorry for the old dude. Today had to be the coldest day of the winter, and this old guy was out in it shoveling snow.

' the old toothless man said as he held up a
nowed that old toothless grin. "This prob-
oblem."

,Jesus!" I praised, and slid from behind the
o the blistering cold wind. God is an on-
d heard Pops preach that in the pulpit, but
his mess, I hadn't really believed until then.
, sir." I shook his mitted hand. "I'll make
ome kind of award for being such a good
d lying to the old fella, but I couldn't do
behind bars. I took the can and ran around
. I looked down the street as if I believed
ng to sit there until I fixed my problems.
gas, I was forced to listen to the old-timer

ed you to be a lawman." He scratched his
chin. "Figured that out last night while I
that Ving Rhames fella frolic around on
e new *Kojak*."
s on Dad and where the hell he was going.
o be rude, but I wasn't listening.
d you," he whispered as if not to offend
e Ving Rhames' version better than I do
He cracked a foolish smile, and winked
e he had said something worthy of saving
like Ving Rhames was going to ride in on
used in the movie *Rosewood*, guns blazing
from Highnoon.
gas cap on in a hasty motion. Gave the

A sigh of relief escaped my lungs.

Like a refreshing breath of air, Maria's angelic face made
her way into my frontal lobe. I was about to call her when
my cell rang. To my surprise, it *was* Maria. I smiled as I
picked up.

"Hey, Papi," she greeted.

"Hey, Mommie."

"Ya busy?"

I looked down at Sister Lawson's house. Nothing.
"Nope, what's up?"

"Just wanted to know what you were doing today."

My other line clicked. The name displayed on the caller
ID made me want to throw up.

"Maria, hold on."

"Okay."

I clicked over.

"Where the hell have you been, muthafucka?" Malisa
yelled into the phone.

"Excuse me?"

"You heard what the hell I said. I told you what I was
gonna do if you dissed me again, didn't I?"

I patted my mouth, yawning. "Turn my social security
number over to the child support folks." I blurted out a
lazy, uninterested response.

"You think I won't?" she threatened louder.

"If you think the baby's mine, go 'head." I countered,
and threw my first card on the table.

"You yellow bastard."

"To qualify being a bastard, one must not know the

father's whereabouts," I said sarcastically. "My pops is running around here"—I glanced down at Sister Lawson's house—"somewhere around here."

"When I get through performing down in front of that Friend of the Court judge, you gonna need three jobs to pay ya child support, bastard." She hung up.

I was laughing so hard that I forgot the phone automatically transferred me back to line one.

"That must've been some call from Chris Rock," Maria joked, laughing, too.

"Maria, I'm sorry. That was a lunatic masquerading as my baby's momma."

She chuckled a little.

"What were you saying?"

"I was wondering what you were doing today."

"What ya got in mind?"

"Today is my day off. Would you like to go out?"

My pops stepped outside wearing a trench coat. He started his truck and began cleaning the snow from his windows with a small scraper. In minutes, he was done, lumbering back into the house. The cold smoke escaping the exhaust told me that he had left his truck on to warm.

"Wisdom?" Maria said. "You there?"

"Maria, I have something to tell you," I said in a serious tone.

"You wanna come by my apartment?"

"I ain't gonna have to battle with Paco and his crew, am I?"

She giggled. "No, s
days ago. So you shou

"Good." I reached i
and some paper. "Go

I had just finished
preacher stepped to t
goodbye.

"You pervert," I said
phone.

"Say what?"

"Maria, I'll call yo

"I'll cook you din
She hung up.

I watched as my
inched out of the d
direction. I let my
started the van. It st
from the curb, the s

"Damn," I cursed.
act of defiance. Bea
bring it back to life
to have it idling all
was rebelling until

"How could I h
angry drum solo on
out and I was sitti

The knock on th
tion from my lap

"Detective
gas can and
ably fix yo' p

"Thank yo
wheel out in
time God. I h
because of all

"Thank yo
sure you get
citizen." I hat
anything from
to the gas tar
Pops were go

Pouring the
babble.

"Kinda figu
gray, whiskery
was watching
television as t

My mind w
Wasn't trying

"Twix me a
anybody. "I lil
that original."
his right eye li
my neck. Sure.
the horse he'd
and saving me

I screwed th

old-timer back the can, thanked him once again, and was out. I didn't know how far two gallons would take me, or even if the fuel injection would be kind enough to accept my generous offering. Fuel injection vehicles could be wishy-washy after running out of gas. They sometimes needed adjustment from a professional auto mechanic. I turned the key, hoping that wasn't the case, and sent emergency prayers up. The engine growled a couple of times before turning over. I left Old Man Toothless, who was grinning like a jack-o'-lantern, on the curb.

My old man was nowhere to be found. After I filled up at the service station, I continued my search, starting with the obvious. The church parking lot was empty. I couldn't believe that just yesterday, it had been the scene of a vicious attack. I asked myself what the world was coming to when criminals disregarded God's house of holiness and instead used it as a venue for staging kidnappings and carrying out ruthless acts of aggression.

The questions would remain unanswered. My angry, ringing cell terminated my thoughts. I had too much on my mind to be trifling with a woman who was dead to me. Truth be told, I was kinda glad that Pops had hit Malisa with his mojo. That made it that much easier to walk away. I wasn't feeling her like that anymore. I felt sorry for putting my hands on my dad, but he had broken all the rules and crossed the lines. And as I glanced at my cell going off, I figured what's good for the rooster was also good for the hen. Before it was all said and done, Malisa would be put in her place, too.

My ghetto MetroPCS jumped off. I recognized my brother-in-law's digits right away. This had to be bad news. My brother-in-law and I almost never bumped our gums on a mobile. There was a deep tightening in the pit of my gut. As I answered, I braced myself while trying not to think negative thoughts. I didn't want to give the devil any juice to work with.

"Brother-in-law, what it do?"

"Wisdom, have you heard from your sister?" Darrius asked with fear ringing off every word.

"Naw, D. I ain't heard from her since the hospital, after Momma's heart attack." The snow had started to descend from the sky in a fury. Visibility was cut to shreds. I reduced my speed and tried my best to slow down the panic surging through my body. "You haven't talked to her?"

"You know I've been in Chi-Town on a business trip since last Thursday. We haven't been on the best of terms. We had a big argument Thursday night. After a fight, she sometimes gets in one of her moods and doesn't want to be bothered. So I give her space—you know how stubborn your sister can be. After she calms down, Tempest usually calls me. I haven't talked to her since Thursday night. And I have to admit that I'm getting kind of worried."

My sister had been missing since Thursday night. Did he mean to tell me that it'd taken the soft punk three days to get worried? I can see why Tempest was creeping on this SpongeBob of a man. I wanted to give him the crash course on how to man-up and wear a pair.

"Darrius, have you tried to call the police and file a missing person's report?"

"No. I didn't think it was serious. Just thought that she was somewhere blowing off steam."

Didn't think it was serious, my ass. My brother-in-law had an incredible head for business, but his nose for common sense was plugged up—a complete moron.

"Listen, where are you? We need to go to the police station," I said. I failed badly in trying to hide my growing anger for stupid shit.

"My plane just landed. I got my car at the Park-N-Lock, which is not too far from the terminal. Wisdom, meet me at the shop. I'll be there in an hour."

"Darrius, go to the police station and report my sister missing. I'll get at you first thing."

"All right. I'm on my way, just as soon as I pick up the car."

I hung up on his stupid ass and dialed my sister—her cell went straight to voicemail. I was horrified at the possibilities. Detroit wasn't exactly the safest of cities for a woman to be running around in by herself. A decade had seen Motown torn down by a stingy economy, job loss, poor housing market, crime and drugs. A woman like Tempest would be a lick for any deviant with a gun, a mind for plunder and a will bent on destruction.

My job had just gotten harder.

TEMPEST

eechie pulled up his pants while admiring his brown, lean, muscular physique in a dresser mirror. He was feeling himself—swag on overdose. He was a man who had planted the flag of conquests inside the earth of his territory that spanned for miles. Geechie was a hands-on guy who micro-managed his turf with an anal eye for every detail. Nothing went down without his permission. His vicious-ness was legendary. Violators were made an example of in public, and by using extreme methods of violence: drive-bys, beat downs, and one time dousing a man with gasoline and setting him on fire. The victim hadn't been allowed to get within ten feet before Geechie's goons cut him down in a hail of gunfire.

He flashed a smile and forced his top lip up to reveal a perfect row of super white teeth. Geechie took pride in his million-dollar, commercial-friendly grill. He simply loved himself. Cruelty and narcissism usually made great bed partners in the production of evil men like him, tyrannical rulers who maimed, tortured and murdered their way to their thrones. They ruled their worlds with absolute power, and stacked plenty of money along the way. To Geechie, it wasn't about money anymore. He was swimming in the stuff. Challenges for a guy like him were few and far between. He was the king-snake who nobody wanted to cross. The police on the payroll, a few politicians in his pocket—Geechie was one of the undisputed heavyweight drug czars inside the city limits.

Cats like him possessed an insatiable need in sharpening that edge. His only problem was an ungrateful snake, slithering around inside his organization with hands in Geechie's pockets. It was a small problem—yet one he had to deal with. But Geechie always found creative challenges to indulge his sadistic fantasies of total domination. Like seeking out married women and sexually driving them to the brink of divorce, Geechie was the type who disrespected the institution of marriage every chance he got. Especially if she was one of those women who thought that her shit didn't stink. He fancied himself as a broncobuster who took those women wild with strength, independence, and strong will, and rode them until they were weak, defeated and begging for his attention. His mission was always to find that one and feed the broad a steady diet of thug love, sit back and watch her square-ass husband chase behind her— all while leaving a salty trail of tears, like a pussy-whipped sucka.

Geechie laughed as he looked at the image in the mirror of a woman who was motionlessly lying on her back, butt naked and on top of an earth-tone comforter of the king-sized bed behind him. She had been one of those women. Strong. Beautiful. Confident. One of those bedroom-ruling, left-right-up-down bitches who felt that she was superior to a man because of her education, thriving businesses, and her circle of sophisticated, male-bashing heifers.

Tempest wasn't so beautiful now. She lay on the bed, a broken and pathetic image of a once-powerful diva. Snot and tears connected on both sides of her face, just underneath her nose. Tempest's body quivered. Her eyes blankly stared up into the ceiling like her soul had been trapped there.

Geechie turned away from the mirror and passed his hand back and forth in front of his nose. "Damn, ma. You stank. That odor between your legs is vicious." He threw on a regular shirt and grabbed the Glock from the dresser top. "You smell like you ain't had a bath in four days. Good thing I wore a rubber. Yo' pussy smell like you got an infection. Nasty bitch." Geechie laughed at his cruelty.

There was no movement from Tempest. The only signs of life were tears.

He pointed his weapon at her. "See, I can end your shit right here today. But that wouldn't be any fun, now would it? All I wanted was for you to run a couple errands in a few prisons—basic shit, no heavy lifting. You tried to get cute. And there is always a penalty for cuteness."

With his free hand, Geechie grabbed Tempest's left ankle, and with muscle, he yanked her off the bed. He didn't even give a damn about the back of her head smacking the carpet. A portion of his anger being projected at her was in response to his dog, Creature. Somebody was gonna pay for murdering his prized pit bull.

Through all the harsh treatment, Tempest still didn't utter a sound. It was like she had temporarily detached herself from her body. As he dragged her in the direction of the closet, Geechie continued. "I told you that I was going to fuck you a few more times before I put a bullet in your head." He opened the door of the closet and pulled her in. "Damn, ma! Yo' ass smell like cum and shit. That's what happens when you don't obey your master." The walk-in closet was decent sized with a single rack of clothes and a few boxes of sneakers. It went dark after Geechie closed the door. "I did make a promise to you, ma. Before I do away with you, I'm gonna bounce down to your hair shop and pay yo' lame-ass husband a visit—stomp him into sucka meat." He licked his tongue out like he was getting off on her misery. Geechie patted the door with his right hand. "Don't get too lonely in there. I'll be back. You remember that line from Schwarzenegger? I'll be back, my princess. I love you!"

Geechie tucked his gun and walked out of the bedroom.

MY WORD IS BOND

Geechie was running short on patience these days. Matter-of-fact, the young cat was running short on everything. Starting with the gut-wrenching loss of his prized pit bull, Creature. Somebody had more than murdered his best friend. The vet said the dog had ingested a very concentrated form of acid. A steak had been the peace offering. The dog didn't see it coming. Death in the humiliating form of a T-bone.

The mutt was just one of the ingredients in Geechie's troubling recipe of rotten luck. Someone had been knocking off his dope spots right and left. His pockets were reeling and taking a tremendous pounding. And now with no mule, Geechie couldn't even compete with the rest of the hustlers who were smuggling dope into the penitentiary upstate. Tempest was the only girl he knew with a clean record who could get his drugs into the prison and she had opposed him. He had no choice but to make her suffer.

Geechie had somewhat of an inkling as to who was responsible for the sudden drop in his bank account, but time forbade him to move on it. He had to be sure. The same fool who he took as suspect was one of the hustling niggas who was responsible for keeping the rest of his empire afloat.

Something had to be done. He couldn't keep taking losses and expect to stay on top, and sustain the respect of peers. Pretty soon, one of the younger, hungrier rollers would grow some apples and try to come for the title. That wasn't gonna happen. Geechie would make sure of it.

The first stop on his bus schedule to redemption— Fine Lady's Hair Salon, Tempest's bread and butter. Niggas had been hitting up his pockets, so he felt compelled to make this tramp feel his pain by breaking her off a good chunk of payback. After all, he'd warned her ass about what would happen if she didn't play ball. So with all that out of the way, Geechie bopped his way through the salon door, pulling up his sagging britches and heading straight for the office.

He smiled at the pretty ladies who were leaving, their hair done all up in the boastful, dazzling, slick styles Detroit was famous for all over the country. They returned his smile. A few even admired his hip-hop flavor.

Geechie had timed it perfectly.

The end of the day brought emptiness to the place. Not many witnesses. He didn't care though. He was Geechie. The name invoked fear alone. Anybody left in the joint after he finished would automatically know to keep it tight-lipped. He was sure of it. By taking their identification, he would warn if anybody talked, there would be no more hair to do, or hands to do it with.

"Can I help you, sir?" Tempest's husband asked and rose from behind the desk. Darrius looked to be troubled by the face now staring at him, like he realized something he didn't. He'd seen the young man before, but he was having trouble placing the face.

Geechie said nothing. It was as if he was getting off on the confusion going on behind the well-dressed man's eyes. After all, Geechie had gotten off plenty of times in every hole in Darrius' wife's body, introducing her to a real nigga. If her husband had been a real man, Geechie wouldn't have been in possession of the lame's wife.

"Sir, could I—"

Before he could finish, Geechie smacked the dog crap out of Darrius, almost knocking the brother out of his expensive Gucci loafers. Darrius was bent at the waist and holding the left side of his face, panting like he was about to pass out. The loud, fleshly noise drew a few nosey bodies from the parlor, but they quickly retreated at the sight of the young kingpin. For they, too, recognized the serpent in the hen house. Call it *hood instinct*. The recognition Geechie received mirrored that of the respect given by the mighty elephants and big cats in Africa's Serengeti to the highly venomous black mamba.

Darrius wasn't from that part of town. So he didn't recognize death standing before him wearing Timberland boots.

"What's your problem?" Darrius asked in pain, standing

fully erect—his hand still favoring the left side of his face.

Geechie smiled wickedly. "Yo' whorish wife."

Wife wasn't out of his mouth good before he clocked Darrius in the left temple with a serious haymaker. Darrius' body hit the carpet like a throw rug. He was out like a light. Geechie could've stopped and walked away after the pulverizing punch, but he was all about punishment and making a statement.

With straight malice in his heart, Geechie collared Darrius, pulling his unconscious body to its feet like a WWE wrestler.

"I bet you didn't know ya wife take it up the ass, did ya?" Geechie planted his left foot and threw Darrius' body into the copier.

Crash!

Boom!

Pow!

Darrius hit the floor first—the copier fell on top of him.

Geechie grinned, continuing to taunt, and pulled up his baggy jeans. "Such a cute ass. And man, what a mouth. The things her mouth did to me—sweet biscuits and gravy." Geechie kicked the machine from Darrius. He stood there admiring his handiwork, rubbing a hand across his smooth, freshly done cornrows. "But I don't expect yo' bitch ass to appreciate such a fine freak of work."

Darrius groaned and moaned something that put an everlasting smile on Geechie's smug grill. He put a cupped hand over one ear.

"Hunh...what cha say, nicca?" Geechie pulled Darrius to his feet again, noticing a few stylists watching his performance and smiled as if he were posing for the paparazzi. "Yeah, ya'll bitches watch this. See, if Tempest would've acted like I told her to, I wouldn't have had to do this. "

Geechie unleashed a helluva uppercut. He put so much force on the blow. He hopped on one leg, put everything he had behind it, and held up his jeans during the torture. The blood that gushed from Darrius' mouth sprayed the walls. Somehow, Darrius withstood the blow, surprisingly, even tickling Geechie's funny bone.

"What the hell's holding you up, fool?" Geechie laughed as Darrius reeled back and forth between the two realms of consciousness as if his Gucci loafers were rockers. His face looked like ground beef: cuts, lumps and blood.

A well-placed Timberland boot to the privates put Darrius on his back clutching his plumbing.

"You don't even deserve a broad like that, nicca!" he shouted, and spat on Darrius as he rolled around the floor in excruciating pain. "Can't even protect her." He picked up a picture from the desk. It was a moment in Paris from the couple's happier days. "Do you know what this trick did after she came home from this trip?" He took Darrius' moaning as a green light to continue. "The lil' skank rode my Johnson in the backseat of my Yukon."

"Nooooooo," Darrius yelled weakly—his hand outstretched in hurt and pain, blood pooling from the corners of his mouth. "I love my wife—"

"You know, I could almost tell that when I was fuckin' her." The windowpane shattering and screams from some of the hairstylists did little to mask the sound that Darrius' ribs made as they snapped, crackled and popped to the power behind Geechie's size-twelve Timberland boot.

I was on my way to the hair shop to see Darrius. I'd talked to him a little while ago and he told me he'd gone to the police department and made the missing person's report. Tempest still hadn't called. Hadn't heard from her since our tearful reuniting. I felt that coldness in my gut. Something wasn't right.

I couldn't let it bother me right now. I had to force my head back into the game. Once she surfaced, Tempest would be my next sheep to herd back into God's live-stock of righteous creatures. But for now, I had to concentrate on the old man. He'd given me the slip, but my time was ticking. God had given me this chance to straighten my family out. At times, it seemed too heavy of a burden to carry. I was going to need the hand of another cowboy to help steer the herd. I made it up in my mind to put off the search, for right now. I had to go and check on the whereabouts of my sister.

I drove, and thought that it was time to bring Rico's

He took the glazed-over look in my eyes as a *yes!*

"Listen, we got things to do before all that takes place." I turned the radio down. "I need to know if I can trust you to keep your emotions in check. We screw this up and my momma is a goner."

Rico put a fist to his heart. "I'm down and dirty with you 'til the end. How do you know Highnoon's playing with a righteous deck of cards?"

"I took care of that. I just need you to follow my lead and be prepared to back my play. My people need to be brought closer together. While I got breath in my lungs, I'm about the Man's business."

"Sounds like a plot for a movie. It's crazy but I want what you want. Even if it means the bullet I eat with your name on it. I'm down and dirty."

Highnoon and Rico shared tumultuous history. Neither man liked the other. I wouldn't go so far as to say *liked!* They hated each other with an unbridled abhorrence. Rico was a couple of years under Highnoon and me. The two used to compete for everything: money, women, anything with value. Neither man backed down. The line had been crossed one day when Highnoon tried to punk Rico in front of some girls. We were little Negroes, but reputations meant everything in the hood. So Rico and Highnoon squared off. Rico hung in there for a little while. After the dust had settled, Rico was almost un-conscious, leaving Highnoon to gloat about how he was a full load when it came to swinging joints. And that's why Rico's a former Golden Gloves champion today. It's amazing how one ass-whooping could drive a man right to the end of the road and pick him up where destiny began. That's why I wouldn't be caught in a war without Rico. He had my back as well as my front.

Here it was, so many years later, and I could still sense the bitterness in Rico's voice. I got the feeling that he would *twist* Highnoon if given the opportunity. That's why I had to keep a close eye on his unstable ass. I couldn't risk him putting a bullet in Highnoon before the deal went through. My boy didn't care about Highnoon's treacherous reputation.

"Yo' ol' man could be anywhere by now. Where the hell you supposed to start?"

"Don't know." The fleet of police cruisers in the parking lot of my sister's shop sent chills up my spine.

"What the hell?" Rico said.

We pulled across the street from the scene and parked in a huge lot. An ambulance was present. We started across the busy intersection, deep in our own thoughts. I swallowed hard. I mean, this crap couldn't be happening again. I'd just gone through this chaos with my pops. *God, what are You trying to do?*

I approached the police cars, with foul play flashing in my mind. I hadn't heard from my sister. I was scared as hell that the stretcher the EMT techs were bringing out held her remains.

"Who are you, sir?" a boyish-faced, white cop asked. He jumped in front of me with one hand on his gun, the other extended toward my chest.

"My sister owns this—" The sight of Darrius' bandaged head, bruised lips and black eyes stole all my words. I didn't know if he was alive or dead. He wasn't moving. My first thought was how Popeye had done Monique—Jordan's girlfriend. Popeye's work was more vicious than this. Extremely graphic. Someone else was responsible here. I went to talk to Darrius, but the brother looked to be unconscious. My heart was in my throat and beating with the dreadful possibility that this was directly connected to my missing sister.

"Where's my sister?" I asked the policeman.

The white cop looked at me like he was ashamed to say. The cold air had his face red. "We don't know yet."

"Okay," I said to the officer. "We'll try something a little easier, like who the hell did this?" I pointed to my brother-in-law's badly beaten face.

The cop hunched his shoulders. "I'm afraid that we don't know that, either. The victim doesn't know and none of the stylists seems to be talking."

"You mean to tell me that somebody could come here and cause all that damage"—I pointed in the shop— "without nobody seeing anything?"

Rico pointed to a few of the stylists. "What about them?"

"Like I said, in case you weren't listening, they said they didn't see anything," the cop said.

The fear in their eyes was evident. Someone had scared them senseless.

"Rico, the girls are pretty frightened," I said. I looked

at the EMT techs loading Darrius' body in the truck. The brother was out like a light. Until he regained consciousness, he wasn't gonna be any help—that was if he woke up with a sane mind.

Sure, the police were taking statements. Trying to dig up leads. But even I knew that that was as far as it was going. This mess was getting more complicated by the minute. I had to find my sister.

"Listen," Officer Red Face said. He had his chest stuck out in that arrogant policeman manner. "When we get something, we'll be in touch."

"Bastard! What do you think?" Rico asked as we made our way back across the blaring horns and oncoming headlights of rush hour traffic.

I wasn't really surprised to see one of my sister's hairstylists standing next to my van, smoking a cigarette with her arms wrapped around her body to conserve heat. I didn't know Tamika all that well, but she wasn't standing out in the cold without a jacket and freezing her ass off for no reason. Both disgust and horror lived on her face like she would never forget what she'd witnessed. And though the sistah styled hair for a living, hers was jacked. She was a dark chocolate-skinned woman with terrible acne and teeth that looked worse than her hairdo.

"Now I ain't supposed to tell you that Geechie beat the shit out of your brother-in-law." She took a deep pull on the cigarette before flicking it to the wet ground and heeling out the butt. Tamika started walking in the other direction. "Like I said, I'm not supposed to tell you that Geechie has your sister, either."

I said nothing. I was stewing in my own caldron of insanity. I was so heated I was seeing red. I was so scared. Scared for Tempest. God only knew what was running through her mind. I could feel it in the pit of my soul. We lived in a society where all kinds of lunatics stalked the sleeping world. Professionals of the big-game hunting of human beings.

Jeffrey Dahmer, John Wayne Gacy, Ted Bundy—all psychos with a powerful hankering for control and domination. Geechie was just as bad. The man had a fiendish reputation of taking whatever the hell pleased him. I shivered with a rage only known by God.

"Geechie!" I yelled, losing control of myself. Rico was the type of guy who didn't scare easily. But this time I saw a little fear as he stared into my bloodshot, bugged-out eyes. It wasn't the usual fear that one might have for one's life, but the fear that one exemplifies for a friend who's walking the borderline of insanity.

I opened the door and slid my big body behind the wheel. "Geechie's dead. Nobody puts their hands on my family and lives."

"What's the call, big boy?" Rico asked in a low, sinister tone that mirrored my high intensity. "I'm down either way. It won't hurt to check that nigga out. Being that's the only thing we got to go on."

"I know you have the contacts to find any and everything out, my friend. Can you find out where the Negro rests his head?"

"Consider it done." Rico whipped out his cell and made a call. I figured I better call and cancel my visit to see Maria.

"Hello."

"Hello." I spoke in a worried tone that betrayed the norm.

"Wisdom?"

"Yeah...it's me."

"What's the matter, Papi?" The concern in her voice was growing by the moment.

I was becoming accustomed to that concern, almost dependent.

"My sister..."

"What's wrong?"

"My sister's been kidnapped," I said, trying my best to chase away denial. There was silence on the other end so loud that I almost missed something that sounded like glass splattering over the floor.

"Wisdom, I'm sorry. Is there anything I can do?"

"Don't cut your feet."

"Huh?"

"The glass—don't cut your feet."

"You no worry about that. If you need me, just call."

"Okay. Please stay by the phone."

"I will." Maria seemed like the type of woman that didn't have to be told that. I felt foolish after I said it.

"I'll call you later."

"Wisdom, be careful, please."

I clicked off.

"Got it," Rico exclaimed, ending his call. He held up a piece of paper. "Layer Street. That fool's got a major supply house on Layer Street in Dearborn Heights. That nigga must be itchin' to get busted, out there in the land of honkies?"

"No. That's pretty smart, especially if he keeps the traffic down. Plus, he doesn't have to worry about nobody breaking in...except us."

"Whatever. Let's do the damn thing."

Dearborn Heights was our destination.

I stopped at a red light. The black Cadillac truck sitting at the stop on the opposite side of the intersection drew my attention. My ol' man had some broad with him. She was giggling all up in his face.

"This fool," I said. Right then and there I had a choice to make. Either I could drop everything and follow him, or pursue my sister. The yellow cab on Rico's side gave me an idea. "Rico, jump in that cab and follow my ol' man."

"I don't think that's a good idea. What if you and Geechie get into it? You gonna need me." He patted the weapon through his clothes.

"Trust me. I got this. Quick, before the light changes, hop out and grab the cab. Call me back with his location."

While his face held resistance, Rico jumped out and hailed the cab. The gray, scraggly-bearded white man was startled at first, but when Rico waved a huge wad of bills at the window, it was on. The light turned green and the driver made a U-turn in hot pursuit. I watched through my driver's side mirror as the cabby's taillights disappeared in the darkness.

I used the directions Rico had written down to get to Layer Street. It was a little bungalow home sitting in a real quiet neighborhood.

Discretion had gone out the door with rational thinking when my sister was snatched. With baseball bat in hand, I walked up to the glass block basement window facing the backyard. The lights were out and nobody seemed to be home. I got in position like I was about to rip a pitcher for a home run. One hit shattered the damn thing.

There was no time to admire my *breaking and entering* skills. I didn't know if anybody heard the glass submitting to my baseball bat. For all I knew, the police could've been on their way as I stood. I gave one more look around before slithering like a snake on my belly through the window, headfirst—which was stupid, because I'd be defenseless if the fool had a dog. I fell down on my hands and allowed the rest of my body the proper passage, glass fragments crunching under my hands. Back on my feet, I looked at the measurements of the window, thanking God that I hadn't put on any extra weight.

To my surprise, there was no dog—which threw me. Dope dealers' egos were huge. Most of them prided themselves as ruthless. It was that ruthless nature that dictated to them the breed of dog, the pit bull being the most popular breed of choice. They were aggressive and violent, a mirror image of the owner. Plus, the dog provided excellent home security for those paranoid types.

I fumbled through the darkness of the basement and worried about a silent alarm or startling one of Geechie's house niggas from sleep. Houses that carried large quantities of drugs didn't have alarm systems. One act of nature could trigger it and bring nosey police from here to doomsday. And a major player didn't want anything to do with the law. Especially out here in Klansville Dearborn. So I relaxed while searching for the stairs, praying that Rico's cabby kept up with the Reverend's SUV in the snow. I was worried to death about my sister, though.

My mind was fumbling over thoughts while my feet stumbled up the stairs. Times like these made me wish I smoked. Smokers always carried a lighter or two. A good flame was all I needed to navigate my way up the eerie black staircase. Slowly, I propelled myself up to ground level. The stairs cracked and creaked under my Timberland boots.

At the head of the staircase, I could see dull light coming from the kitchen. The doggy obituary that was stuck to the refrigerator door by a banana magnet freaked me out. A color picture of a powerful-looking, light brown pit was featured as the guest of honor. It even displayed the birth and death date. Just like a human obituary.

Oh, this nigga had gone too far. My guess was that this

schmuck had lost his dog and was still in mourning. The Negro even had the dog's bowls filled with food and water. Like the offering would tempt the dog to forsake his heavenly cloud and come back to his owner. This fool was a couple of sandwiches short of a picnic. The name on the obituary was all I needed to work my theory about gangsters and their dogs. Who in the hell would name a dog *Creature?*

I was inwardly laughing until I heard something that sounded like bumping and thumping coming from the back rooms of the house. My mind cursed my hands for dropping the baseball bat after I'd smashed in the window. I was weaponless. There were no knives lying around in the kitchen. Nothing but a stupid can opener.

I was a big body, agile, real stealthy, and moved around on the basketball courts with all the gracefulness of a ballerina. So I tip-toed deeper into the house on plush carpeting. The sounds became louder and more distinguishable—like muffled panting. I figured I'd stumbled on one of Geechie's goons having a sex session. That was until I peered into a windowless room opposite the bathroom.

What I saw caused a rage to circulate through my system. This was beyond explaining. Beyond any reasonable comprehension. My stomach went queasy and my heart pumped with the same intensity of a lion in predatory mode. Anger flared my nostrils like the hood of a dangerous cobra ready to strike.

Without giving much consideration to the pistol laying

on the nightstand, I rushed right in and pulled the fat, sloppy-looking, grown-ass man off the underdeveloped teenage girl.

"We wasn't doing nothing"—was all he could say as I immediately went to it by delivering two quick punches to his abdomen and slammed his ass against the wall. The sucka crumbled at the toe of my boots and gasped for air.

The little girl's eyes were wide with fear. Her mouth was duct-taped and wrists were bound to the bars of the fake brass headboard by handcuffs. She twisted, yanked and pulled in her long legs, drawing them into a defensive posture, like she was about to kangaroo-kick the hell out of me.

"You're going to be all right." I tried to reassure her. Down at the foot of the twin bed, I grabbed a nasty-looking sheet and covered her body. I thanked God that Pigboy hadn't gotten off her bra and panties. I shuddered at the thought of how it could've turned out for the youngster if I hadn't come here in search of my sister.

"Who the hell are you?" Pigboy asked from the floor in a daze, still on all fours and trying to catch his breath. He was wearing leopard print bikini underwear. Disgusting. His big belly hung overlapping his privates— thank God. His chest hung lower than any woman's breasts I'd ever seen.

This could've been my damn daughter. It angered me all over again. I raised my foot and stepped on the fingers of his right hand like I was stomping roaches.

"Fuck!" he cried out in pain.

"The key for the handcuffs." I demanded.

He pointed to the nightstand. I took them and released the girl's wrists. Next, I grabbed the nine-millimeter pistol and stuck it in my waist.

"Who you?" he asked again.

"Her daddy," I responded. I wore the granddaddy of all evil looks. The girl's eyes looked surprised as her hands removed the strip of tape from her mouth.

"Her daddy?" Pigboy snorted. He missed the wink I gave the girl to play along. "Do you know whose house this is, cowboy?"

I smacked him across the head with one of my frying pan-sized hands. "Don't give a blue hell. This is my daughter. You raping her; you might as well be raping me."

The sight of the digital camera sitting on the tripod incensed me. That's when I removed the pistol, raised it up, and brought it down across Pigboy's head. He let out a howl, then collapsed while holding the gash with both hands as if the pressure would stop the blood flow. Negative. The blood welled up through the cracks of his fingers.

"Oh my God!" Pigboy squealed. It never ceased to amaze me that folks never called upon the Lord until they were faced with the reaper of their wrongdoings.

I held the pistol on Pork Chop, looking in the girl's direction. "Pumpkin, get dressed and take yo' ass home. I'll deal with you when I get there."

The girl never broke stride in picking up her clothes, spitting on Pigboy, and running from the door. She stood on the other side of the threshold with tears in her eyes. She mouthed, "Thank you."

I nodded. She was gone. I heard the front door slam behind her.

"So, Pigboy, I see you and your boss like bullying women."

"What you talkin' 'bout?"

"You were trying to rape my daughter, like Geechie kidnapped my wife." I lied.

He looked up with his head bleeding like a stuck pig. "Don't know nothin' 'bout that," he said, a look of pain on his face, still holding a bit of homeboy attitude.

I squatted on my hunches and violently grabbed a handful of his mini-afro....

"Damn!" he yelled and made the ugliest of ugly faces.

The barrel of the Glock slid smoothly underneath his chin.

"Now," I sinisterly said while watching him. "Tempest— you know a brown-skinned momma with long hair... seen her?"

I pulled his hair tighter to reinforce the right response.

"She was out to his house in Southfield. Geechie took her—" I grinded the barrel into his skin—"I promise you. I don't know if she's still there."

"What do you mean, you don't know?"

"I heard that he had taken her to Chicago."

"Chicago?"

"I know he left for a few days. Don't know if he took her. That's what I heard, but you know how rumors are. He should be back in a couple days—please don't kill me." Pigboy pleaded. "I'm telling you all I know."

"I don't like scum-sucking pedophiles. Like 'em as much as I like hemorrhoids. God's giving you another chance to change your ways—being that you tell me where the house is. If you don't"—I pointed the weapon at where I thought his penis would be—"I'll make it so you can't get your disgusting groove on ever again."

I didn't have to wait too long for cooperation. The ugly Negro started singing like a canary.

I took the digital camera.

"Listen, Pigboy, keep your mouth shut. You alert Geechie of my presence and not only do I come back to carve up a pig, I'll turn this"—I held the camera up—"over to the police. I'm watching you. Any more little girls...I come gunnin', understand?"

He nodded his head *yes*.

"Do you know what it feels like to live on borrowed time?" I asked.

He was just nodding his head *yes* to everything. And I knew that. He was still on his knees when I raised the gun in the air. With cat-like speed, I bashed him over the head with the weapon again, real hard! He hit the floor, unconscious.

I lied. First opportunity I came across, I had plans to

turn the film in, starring Mr. Underage Lover, to my boy, Sergeant. Hunt, who headed the Narcotics Division. He would take it from there.

Geechie wasn't gonna be thrilled about losing a soldier from his crappy organization.

Stepping from the house, I tucked the pistol into my waist. I had plans to ditch it first chance I got. I didn't like guns. My temper was too bad. Looking up at the darkened skyline, I wondered what was going through my sister's head. If that snake touched her—God help him.

Behind the wheel, for the first time in a long time, I thought about Jordan and Yazoo. I wondered about their whereabouts. I wondered if my time would run out before I got a crack at them. Doing all of this running around had tired me beyond belief. It was as if I could actually hear the clock ticking.

Nothing was easy. This was my test. I accepted it. I wasn't sure if this would turn out messy. I just hoped that it didn't have to be no unnecessary bloodshed. But faith was built by blood. The world was exonerated by the blood of the Lamb. David wasn't allowed to build God's temple because his hands were stained by too much blood. I just hoped nobody had to die, but if it had to be, then that's what it was gonna be—bloody!

WISDOM

Tuesday night had become one gigantic *hit* and *miss*. I found where Geechie's main house was located. This cat had digs in Southfield, Michigan. Which surprised me, 'cause Southfield was one black homeowner away from being the new Detroit. The majority of the white folks had retreated, leaving ancestral homes in search of an exclusive community. The bulk of the drug-dealing morons avoided Southfield to live in high society. So when I found out that this dude lived there, I was joyfully relieved. Breaking and entering out there would be a piece of cake. My skin blended in with the brand-new Nubian settlers.

The *miss* came in the form of Rico's cabby not being able to keep up with the four-wheeling reverend. Rico had reported to me that Poppa Jones had been driving like a madman, blowing through traffic lights. I couldn't wrap my mind around this blatant disregard for human life. My guess was that Pops couldn't wait to get that floozy home. The promise of sex might've caused the ol' dude to toss the rules and regulations out the window.

My pops was many low down things, but not a bad driver. Undoubtedly, Rico's assignment had drawn a blank. The setback would cost time, no doubt. Precious ticks off the clock that I didn't have. Now with four days left, I had to kick this soul-saving rescue endeavor up a couple of notches. Not only did I have to go back to the drawing board at finding the preacher, I had to find Jordan and free Tempest. My biggest challenge would be my older brother. Saying that he was the oldest didn't sound right. For years, people looked at me in such a manner. One would guess that all my brother's immature ways typecast him as my younger sibling.

My head was whirling with worry. Didn't get much sleep last night. My soul was tormented. Yet, on the top of my pile of worries, I still had to serve big, bad Malisa a large plate of righteousness.

"Papi," Maria said, smiling. She entered the bedroom carrying a beautiful tray. "I made you eggs, toast and bacon. Can't forget your juice. I know you going through something, but you need to eat."

I sat up in her bed, the covers sliding down my muscular pecs, allowing her to properly sit the tray over my thighs. The girl even brought me the morning paper to read.

"I thank you for understanding my living situation. I don't have a girlfriend anymore and I'm glad you understand. I hope I won't inconvenience you by staying with you until I can get everything situated," I said, and forced myself to take a bite of toast.

"Let me do this." Maria spread a napkin across my chest and removed the toast from my hand to butter it.

"Don't worry about it. I don't need much sleeping space."

Maria hit me with that ice cream sundae-flavored smile that she'd seduced me with at the bar.

"But you need your space, Papi. Look at you. This bed is king and you still no fit." She had on a simple housecoat and big, fuzzy bunny slippers. Her hair was pulled back into a ponytail. It didn't matter what the lady wore. She had class. And class made Sears look like Bloomingdale's.

I tried to laugh a little. This woman was what I'd been looking for all my adult life. This situation only solidified the fact that God had to have a serious sense of humor. I'd finally found somebody decent, but I was due to be executed in a matter of days. Even I had to have an internal, hearty chuckle at that.

I was going back and forth inside my mind at disclosing to Maria the reason why this breakfast didn't matter. And for that matter, from here on out, food wouldn't be needed. Food was meant to sustain life. Mine was almost up. It was only right that I told her the deal. Despite the short length of time Maria and I had known each other, the girl was now looking at me with wedding bells in her eyes.

My angel tried to feed me another piece of toast.

"Maria," I said. I refused her, and finished what was in my mouth. "I have something to tell you." She fed off the seriousness in my eyes.

"About your sister?"

"No. I made a deal with the devil."

"What do you mean, 'deal with the devil'?"

"I got in a bad way with a really bad man for all the right reasons."

The silence in the air was bananas with tension. I removed the tray from my lap and set it on the floor, scooting closer to Maria on the edge of the bed.

"My momma needs a kidney." My eyes dropped from the weight of sadness. "She'll die if she doesn't get one."

Her eyes took on hurt like she was genuinely sharing my pain. She didn't know it, but the look on her face made me brush the napkin off my chest, reach out and pull her into me.

"I'm sorry for you," she said. "I didn't know you were going through all this." Maria squeezed tighter, burying her face deeply into my chest. I smelled her hair. Baby oil. Smelled good. She made me feel good. A moment of peace in the middle of my stormy trip to the grave.

I figured I'd drop the rest of the bomb.

"I made a deal with a cat named Highnoon. To make a long story short, he's the perfect donor for my mother. The only thing is that this fool wants my life to save my mother's."

"You mean like a slave."

"No. I mean like *dead*. My cousin killed his brother centuries ago and because he couldn't get at my cousin, I've become the sacrificial lamb to pay my cousin's tab."

She pulled away from me with tears in her eyes. "What are you going to do?"

I took a long pause. I could almost see her wearing a black dress.

"Maria, I have no choice."

"The police?"

"By the time they get up from the doughnut counter, I'd be dead."

"How long?"

"Couple of days. He gave me seven days to put my house in order. Get my family back on course with God."

"I finally met a *chico* who's not gay or a gangster, and he's gonna be"—she gulped—"killed in a couple of days."

"I'm sorry for bringing you into this."

Tears slowly rolled down her cheeks.

"I'm here for you, Papi." She took my hand and put it to her heart. "This Highnoon, maybe there's another way around him."

"You sound like my best friend, Rico."

"He's right, you know. You just got to have faith."

"Maria, I'm going out of my mind."

"Have you heard anything on your sister?"

"No." I lied. "The police haven't contacted me." I shared tons with her, but I wasn't gonna share how I broke my way into one of Geechie's joints, smacked up his worker, and beat information from his brain. The girl already told me in so many words that she didn't like gangsters. So if my actions didn't qualify as gangster, I didn't know what else did?

For the next hour, Maria listened attentively while I painfully described the curse on my family that my ol' man was responsible for. The preacher couldn't keep his wiggle worm in his pants, and because of it, my family suffered. How it impacted each kid in very different ways. Jordan's curse with crack; Tempest's curse was the same as my ol' man's, but Yazoo wasn't my dad's, so the curse didn't apply. He'd been scorned. Blamed God for the tragic death of his ol' man. How I had four days to shepherd my family back on the path. Somehow influence Jordan to stop smoking, Tempest—first I had to find her—to close her legs to the public, and turn Yazoo from his God and family-loathing ways.

During the course of my couch-trip, I short-circuited, malfunctioned, and unloaded all my burdens on poor Maria. I'd felt it coming for some time. A breakdown. The whole nine. Tears and all. My knees were bending from the tremendous weight on my shoulders. Somehow, I was made to carry the cross for my entire family. Wasn't comparing myself to Jesus Christ, but it felt like I was marching to the cross. How Satan meant the crucifixion for evil, but God saved the world by giving His Son—Romans 8:28-29. Highnoon was my cross; my sacrifice would save my mother and the hearts of my family members. I was strong before, but now that my hour was upon me, I was losing it. Couldn't take it. Didn't want it. Wanted to get rid of it.

"Father, please remove this burden from me!" I cried and fell into Maria's lap. "I can't do this. I just can't do this."

I cried while Maria held my head in her arms, rocking me as if I was a newborn. I was hoping she wasn't looking at me like I was some sniveling punk.

"Wisdom, you're gonna be just fine. You're a special chico. God has plans for you. I believe that. Just stay strong. You say that you have four days. Don't waste them by sitting here. I have faith in you. I know you can do this." She kissed my forehead and dried my tears. Maria was strong, yet docile—docile yet supportive, supportive yet loving. If this went like she said, I was looking forward to marrying her and having a sack full of collard greens and taco-eating babies.

A wild thought began to percolate through my mind. A good, strong man was only half until made whole by the other portion of woman. God was all the strength man needed, but still He blessed the roots of man with the solid fertilization of femininity. It was a little premature, but I wanted my roots fertilized by Maria. I still hadn't gone there about how my preacher-father knocked up my trifling ex. I figured I'd save that little gem for another bed and breakfast confession.

Restored, strengthened and energized, I stood, washed, then dressed to get back on Dad's trail while waiting to make that move on Geechie's crib in Southfield.

I took one long look at my Aztec princess. She was beautiful. Inside and out. I wanted her on my team. This woman was in my corner. She wouldn't mistake my tears for a weakness. Her gift was strengthening her man. I could feel that. I gave her a forehead kiss and was out.

I was back out on the prowl. My first call was to the church. I quickly found out that the good reverend had cleared his weekly calendar. A little flirting went a long way. Sister Green informed me that Pops had told her that a vacation was long overdue. A part of me couldn't blame the ol' man, after being dragged out at gunpoint and dusted off in the parking lot. How could he explain something like that to the congregation? The gossip and the rumors swirling around the church had to be bananas. And judging by the way Poppa Jones had been blowing through traffic lights last night, my hunch was that he was probably on his way out of town then.

My knee was hurting and my clothes were dirty. I had been wearing the same gear ever since I'd found out that Poppa had laid holy hands on Malisa. I feared what would happen if I went back to my old digs. It was stupid. All my clothes were there. I hadn't heard from Malisa since Monday morning. The stakeout. For all I knew, the crazy broad could've pulled a *Waiting to Exhale* move on the few stitches of clothing I had left.

Pops was gone.

Boom!

Leaving me holding myself, wishing for better days. I wanted to go back to Maria's and crawl beneath her bed. I wanted to believe her, but sections of my heart told me that I was in way over my head. Who was I anyway, a *savior?* Didn't think so. Far from. The woody I'd gotten from just sleeping under Maria's comforter last night defined my fleshly imperfections. And what was I thinking about? Staying with another woman? Well, it wasn't like I had other places to choose from. Rico was staying with his mother. Their house was seriously overcrowded. Couldn't bunk there. I guess I could've stayed in my mother's condo, but I didn't want to go all the way out to Farmington Hills.

Aww, hell. When it all came down to it, I was full of it. The truth was that I didn't want to be alone.

The streets were clear today. Looked like the city boys had gotten up off their wallets and salted the roadways. Didn't much feel like chasing souls today, so I went to see Momma.

"Hey, ol' lady," I said as I walked into her room.

"Wis, how you?" she responded and offered a phony smile. She was hurting. I could see it in her eyes.

"You must be doing pretty good. They've taken some of the machines away, huh?" I frisked my hand over her hair. She looked tired. I could tell that she was giving up the fight. Affording the Reaper the opportunity to swing his scythe. Momma's body looked like she was being possessed by the Stay Puft Marshmallow Man. She was so swollen. I felt kind of bad. If it wasn't for my stupid idea of trying to straighten out people who didn't want to be straight, Momma could've been on her way back to the land of excellent health.

"I still got this old smelly IV in my arm. They still

come by here to clean my blood with that awful machine."

I sat in the chair next to her bed.

"Where's Tempest?" Butterflies flew through my stomach at the mentioning of my sister. "She ain't been by in a couple of days."

I lowered my eyes to the floor.

"I talked to her yesterday." I lied. What was I supposed to do? The truth probably would've killed her right in front of me. I couldn't have that. If she died, the deal with Highnoon was still standing. The chump would do me regardless.

"Wiz, where's my daughter?"

"I think she went with Darrius on one of his out-of-town business meetings to Chicago. You know how she like to shop and things."

"She didn't tell me nothing about that."

"I know. This was something last minute." I pulled my eyes from the floor. I had to try and sell this like a used car salesman attempting to unload a jalopy. Momma was wise. The lady could sniff out deceit from miles away. I had to be convincing. Conniving. "She's gonna drain her bank account dry if she doesn't slow down her spending."

"Boy, what you talking about?"

"Darrius went on business, but Tempest went to shop at the high-priced stores on Michigan Avenue."

"Lawd, have mercy." She slapped her hands together. "Here I am laying up in this hospital and that chile paintin' the town."

A nice looking nurse walked in, said hello, and changed Momma's depleted IV bag. After she jotted something down on Momma's bed charts, the chocolate lady gave me an encouraging smile and then left.

"She selfish, ain't she?" I continued my deceitful character assassination.

"Ain't even called me."

"Selfish, boy. Selfish." I would rather Momma be mad at Tempest instead of knowing the real deal. Figured once I got Tempest back, they could clear the air. I was determined to get my sister back, even if that was the last thing I did. I would reunite my mother and sister. The others would have to learn or burn. Live in eternal grace or fry holding a flame of disgrace.

My momma coughed and it sounded like death. "Son, if I don't make it out of this hospital— "

"Momma, don't go sounding crazy."

"Look at me, Wiz. I'm not getting any better. I'm tired, boy." She coughed again. "You saw that father of yours?"

"Naw, ain't tryin' either."

"Don't be that way. I didn't raise you like that. He's still your father. No matter what went on between us. Make sure that little rugrat of yours knows who the grand-daddy is after I'm gone."

"Stop it."

"Listen. If I die before your father comes to his senses, go by that yella heifer's house and tell him to come pay his respects."

"What yellow heifer?" I asked.

"Sister Walker."

"How?"

"Had him followed." I let her talk. "One day, he left the house and one of them private eyes was right on his tail."

Feeling a brand-new surge of hope, I asked, "Momma, where does this lady stay?"

"Out there in Sterling Heights. Get my purse. I got the address."

Call it fate, or faith. Hell, it could've been pure luck. Whatever it was, I'd take it. The long shot. The big gamble. I removed her purse from the closet.

"Here, boy," she said as she went into her purse. She handed me a piece of paper.

I held the paper up. "Momma, why?"

"Love, boy." She gazed up at the ceiling. "Just dumb love."

"Momma—"

"Get out of here. Go find your father." Her eyes spoke volumes. She turned onto her side, facing the window. Guess that was my cue.

I took it and ran. I had a mission to complete. Whatever I started, I had to finish. Force of habit.

Tick, tock—the clock reminded me. Highnoon's ugly face was drawing nearer.

This was the first time I paid attention to all the billboards off the Lodge Freeway. Everything from casinos telling folks that it was okay for them to come and gamble their life savings away, to advertisements featuring some of Detroit's finest professional athletes. The Detroit Pistons had Tayshaun Prince's narrowed, light-skinned, freckled face gazing down from a gigantic billboard and reminding me of what my life could've been like, had I not torn up my knee. I was one of those jocks who didn't continue his education. Lost all desire to graduate on that fateful day. I guess I could say that my desire to carve out an above-average living for myself in society had shattered also—right along with my ACL. Hence, I was unprepared for a brutal reality. I'd be rich if I had a penny for every down-and-out athlete who never factored in injury. Not stopping for one second to think about how one career-injuring setback could bring about a lower class of life, never-ending unemployment lines, humiliating wages, task-master-type supervisors and degrading homelessness.

I drove with my mind fumbling and stumbling down memory lane. I remembered the night I let a few moments of betraying passion come between me and my ex, Caliba—the one I should've been married to with a sack full of kids by now. The woman who should've been my everything. I hadn't been responsible enough to handle a woman like her. My infidelities. The life of a Michigan State basketball superstar. Groupies flocking—catering to my every desire. People kissing my ass just to get a piece. I'd gained everything only to lose it all. Caliba had turned to drugs to cope with discovering my indiscretions. Her subsequent cocaine addiction. The destruction of a life. Caliba, a gifted student studying law. Her free-fall from a scholarly throne and landing into a hellish pit of depression and crack houses. Until she was no more fit to clean raw sewage. The drug over-dose. A piece of me had been buried with her on that cold, rainy day in January.

I didn't wanna sound like Fred Sanford, but I looked up at the cloudy skies and whispered, "Caliba, I'm coming to join you, honey. So save me a seat at the table."

I was lost in the past until my present found the hell out of me. I answered my cell.

"Where the hell have you been, nigga?" Malisa asked in a nasty tone. Star-six-seven had disabled it and left me virtually in fear of answering. For every gadget made, there was always a way to circumvent it.

"You have a very nasty mouth."

"I know that shit. I'm due any minute, and yo' ass out there lollygagging somewhere."

"You got your cousin, Kirk, there."

"Nigga, that's it! Kiss yo' check goodbye. Friends of the Court will be seeing me real soon. And don't worry about coming back here because yo' junk gonna be on the street…" The phone sounded like it dropped. I thought the girl was just throwing a tantrum when I heard a scream.

"Shit, my water broke!" she yelled in the background.

"What do I do?" I could clearly define Kirk's terrified voice. Malisa was breathing hard and heavy. She sounded like she was locked in a battle at gaining control, and struggling to implement the techniques she'd learned from those Lamaze classes.

"Hello," I said.

It sounded like there was a scuffle for the phone before my cell went dead.

That had to be one of the weirdest moments of my life, I thought, swinging a left onto Rico's street. I swallowed hard. My little brother or sister was on the way into the world. I felt sorry for the youngster. The situation was still a strange one. No matter how I twisted it, it was some crazy, deranged crap.

I forced that mess from my mind, blowing the horn in front of Rico's crib. My boy rumbled out in a leather bomber, faded jeans and Timberlands.

"What's the word, fool?" Rico greeted, then stepped in munching on a chicken wing.

"You got it, killer."

"Yo' ol' man was like ghost last night. That old cracker cab driver couldn't keep up. I even offered to throw a yard his way to step on it. Couldn't keep up. The roads were too slick."

"That's all right." I pulled off. "Think I got a new lead."

"How?"

"Don't ask."

"How's Maria?"

"She's cool."

"Looking forward to making her acquaintance."

"Bet you are."

"You hear from the police?"

"Ain't looking for them pigs to do nothin'."

"What you find out at Geechie's spot?" He sucked on a chicken bone.

"I broke the basement window out, went inside, right?"

"With you so far," Rico said.

"I went up the stairs and into the kitchen. This fool's dog had died and this idiot had a funeral with all the trimmings. Complete with obituary. Dog's picture on the front and all."

Rico rolled down the window and chucked the bones. "Oh...snap."

"So I start hearing sounds coming from the back room. I look inside. Why one of Geechie's fat-ass goons got an underage little girl up in that piece, duct-taped, cuffed and stripped damn-near butt naked, trying to get his freak on."

"One thing I can't stand is a Chester. In the joint, niggas like that got they manhood took."

"I tried to beat his head in."

"You should have."

"This punk up in there dressed in leopard print bikini underwear."

Rico almost coughed up a liver, laughing.

"Punk," he said, still cracking up.

"After I let the girl leave, I wrecked that fool. Plus, I threatened him by promising to take the digital camera he was filming with to the police."

"I know you gonna serve that pervert, right?"

"Yep." With that said, I pulled the van right into the parking lot of the precinct. Rico was holding a heater. He stayed in the van while I went looking for Officer Samuel Hunt. Samuel and I had started as gangsters, both working from two different places of society. I ran the streets while Officer Hunt ran the dealers who ran the streets. Through many different shakedowns, we'd forged an unbreakable bond. Still holding fast today. Eventually, he cleaned up his career.

If I said it, then it was gold. So when I handed Hunt the camera, he ran it straight to the lab. Officer Hunt was very familiar with the cat who was trying to star in his own personal porno. Had popped him a few times. Calvin Jefferson. The sissy had a rap sheet a mile long. Petty thefts, but mostly sexual assaults. The APB went out right then and there.

Hunt and I kicked 'hood history for a few ticks, dapped each other, and then I was out.

"What Officer Hunt have to say?" Rico asked.

"The clown's name is Calvin Jefferson and he's a baby rapist."

"Sick. What they gonna do?"

I checked both ways before pulling out the driveway. "Hunt said within the next four hours, Mr. Jefferson's gonna be gettin' chased around the cell by Big Dick Bubba."

We shared laughter.

"What's on the agenda now?" Rico asked.

"That clown told me that Geechie's got my sister."

"Let's roll on him."

"No. He said he'll be back in a day or two."

"How can you trust he ain't lying?"

"The puddle of piss I left homie lying in told me the fool was telling the truth."

"What now?"

"Well, now we gonna go and find a home-wrecking broad in Sterling Heights. But first I need to make a stop." I pulled into the lot of a local hardware store.

Poppa wasn't gonna give me the slip this time. His truck was right where I'd expected it to be: in the driveway of that home-wrecking Jezebel.

Out here in high society, I couldn't pull my detective routine. I had to be stealthy. Cunningly original.

"Okay," I said to Rico. "This is the plan. We can't sit out here and wait him out. Sooner or later, one of these white folks gonna get suspicious and drop a dime. So, homeboy, this is what I'm gonna need you to do. You're gonna drive around the block until I hit you on your cell and let you know that the coast is clear."

Rico looked confused as we pulled behind the good reverend's ride.

"So what cha saying?" he asked.

"I'll call you if I have any problems. If I do, come in fast."

"What you got planned for the ol' dude?"

I held the ski mask up that I'd purchased at the hardware store. "I tried to talk some sense into the ol' dude, but now it's time to scare the living crap out of him."

"You a fool," Rico said. "Be careful."

"Yes, ma'am." I joked, getting out of the car.

Immediately after that, Rico slid into the driver's seat. It was one in the morning and peaceful out here in White City. Not another soul was stirring. I crept through the inky darkness like an angel of mercy, captivated by the brilliant display of thousands of stars. I stopped to admire the twinkling going on in the heavens. It was the kind of scene that was hindered by man-made lighting back in the city.

"Wiz." Rico strained to whisper. "Quit gawking and be 'bout yo' bidness."

I snapped out of it. Soon I'd probably be among those twinkling stars.

Rico pulled off as I went to work with the screwdriver. Putting a flimsy towel up to Pops' back taillight, I thrust the screwdriver through the plastic and applied pressure. The towel acted as soundproof and muffled the cracking into plastic splinters from the shattered tail lamp. This act shorted out the alarm. Quickly, I went to work at jimmying the lock of the back cargo door. I'd still had *it* after all these years. My carjacking skills were a little rusty, but it was just like riding a bike—after driving for so many years. The lock sounded like sweet music to my ears when it opened. I scooped up what little plastic I could and folded my big body into the truck's cargo area. I thanked God that Pops had removed the third seat for some reason. I just hoped when he came out in the morning, the ol' dude wouldn't come around to the back. The jig would be up.

REVEREND POPPA JONES

ister Rita Walker lay on my bare chest lightly snoring. I lay there in the dark recess of her master suite and took inventory of my crippled life.

Questions buzzed around my mind like vultures circling something dying in the desert. Like why I couldn't shake Sister Walker? What kind of perverted hold did she have over me? And why had I allowed her to talk me into coming over here? One word summed up my life: sinful. I'd walked out on my wife, and left her to battle kidney and heart problems alone. Shortly after that, I moved in with Paula. What was going down under her roof had been enough for God to bring His vengeance to my front door. But I was alive for a reason. He was giving me another chance.

The ribs on my left side were still a little sore from the stomping. I positioned the sister's head so that she wouldn't aggravate that area. One would think that after I was tore up by those animals last Sunday, I would've straightened up. But here I was in all my backsliding glory.

Who was I kidding? It sure wasn't God.

My mother had a saying: "A hard head brings a softer behind." I still had a rock bottom strapped on back there. I'd turned my back on everyone and everything. I thanked God that my mother was dead. I know that that's some kind of profound statement, but I was serious. It was she who put the Bible in my crib. She saw the anointing on my life. She sent me to serve under the pastor of her church. She believed in me. Had she been living today, the stress of my backsliding would've surely delivered her to the grave.

I had Sister Green clear my schedule for a week. It had been a long time since I'd gone on a vacation. It was long overdue. I was getting away from the church and all those gossiping hens. I needed to try and plot my next move. Probably go to an island. Take Sister Lawson. Sister Lawson had the money. Sister Walker just had the loving. And since good loving didn't spend, Sister Lawson won the trip hands down.

I wasn't really worried about the state of the church. Even though my new baby's momma had sent those thugs up in the house of God, I would blame the mishap on Deacon Slydale. Once I returned from the islands, I planned on calling an emergency church meeting. My flock loved me, so they would believe anything I said. After I got finished, Slydale was going to come off like he was the head of the Mafia. But that still wasn't going to fix the fact that I had sexually jacked my son's girl-friend. I left him with another brother-sister, instead of a son-daughter.

I didn't blame Wisdom for coming after me in my office. For my betrayal, I deserved death. I was sure Malisa had more surprises for me. The heifer had eighteen years to torture my bank account. Wisdom might've been pissed that day, but something in his eyes suggested that he was happy that I'd taken his place on the chopping block. Maybe that would be my punishment? Maybe the child would drive me to an early grave?

My wife and kids were the last things on my mind before I joined Sister Walker in dreamland.

Jumping up from a hair-curling dream, I opened my eyes to stare down the barrel of a full-fledged nightmare.

Even though it was pitch black inside of the bedroom, I could see the silhouette of a man's face. The nickel-plated pistol in his right hand seemed to defy the rules of darkness. The thing shone like half-dollars falling from heaven.

I was certain that he put a finger to his lips when he said:

"Shhhh. Move and I'll fill you full of the Holy Ghost." He spoke in a quiet but creepy voice. Eerie demeanor. Sinister. "Preacher man, if you scratch your ass the wrong way, you're dead."

Shadowman produced another glistening, nickel-plated special. He held me in check with one as his silhouette walked around to a sleeping Sister Walker, nudging the fleshly lump with the barrel.

"Poppa," Sister Walker said. "Stop playing. You know

you can't handle round three." She opened her eyes and screamed like a tortured soul.

"Rita, you look like you've seen a ghost," the stranger comically stated.

"Do you know him?" I asked Rita. I kept my eyes peeled on the shadow.

"1 Samuel 3:13. For I have told him that I will judge his house forever for the iniquity which he knoweth."

That was it. I knew exactly who this man was. I didn't have to see the face to know who the voice belonged to. It was the stranger from the coffee shop. The scary-looking guy who called himself Red Rum. He'd quoted that scripture before he left Starbucks.

"Do you know who I am?" he asked me.

"Brother Red Rum." I answered, trying to hide the fear in my voice. My breath caught in my throat. "Of course. The whole King David and Bathsheba story—now I understand. I'm King David who took the only thing that you had."

"I'm afraid that you didn't do a very good job of talking me off the ledge, huh, Preacher? You are in serious trouble. I'm judge, jury and executioner. You will be judged by me, you false prophet."

"I thought you were—" Rita was cut off.

"Dead. I am dead to you, dear. I staged the whole animal-eaten thing. I've been watching ya'll for quite some time." He walked back to my side. "Get your clothes on, Pastor. We're going for a ride."

"I need some light," I said.

"Back up," he commanded.

I moved away from the lamp on the nightstand at my side of the bed. He switched it on. The light flooded the room, and shone light on our dreadful situation. There he stood, dressed in black cargo pants, a thick hoodie, and steel-toes boots, both guns trained on my chest, a far cry from the fancy duds he was wearing at Starbucks.

He reached into his hoodie and removed a business card. He flicked it at me.

I slowly picked it up from the floor. It was mine. I had given it to him at the coffee place.

"I guess"—he waved one of the guns in his wife's direction—"me and honey over there won't be needing marriage counseling."

"What do you plan on doing to me?" Sister Walker frantically asked.

"Until death do us part, honey," he chillingly stated.

Rita started crying uncontrollably.

"*The Shining*, Jack Nicholson—the whole Red Rum name was slick," I said as I pulled on my slacks. "It took me some time to remember where I'd heard the name from. Stephen King's *The Shining*." I was trying desperately to buy some time, for what—I really had no idea. Merely hoping for a miracle.

"Wellington, please don't," Rita pleaded through tears.

"Shut up, whore!" He yelled for the first time and broke his creepy calmness. "I put you up in this big house. Bought you nice cars and what do you do? Give all my money to a false prophet." His creepy laughter was enough to raise the hairs on my back.

I found myself being dragged out of that church all over again. But unlike the pit bulls that scrambled my brain in the parking lot that day, this man was ten times spookier. Everything from his voice, his laughter, to his movement screamed out *maniac*.

I slid into my dress shirt. "Red Rum is *murder* spelled backward."

"I thought you'd appreciate it."

I wasn't moving as fast as he wanted. My lack of enthusiasm merited a barrel at my temple.

"Please...Wellington." Sister Walker cried, tears rolling down her face as she hid her naked body behind the comforter. "Don't hurt him."

His deranged laughter split the silence. "How could you betray me with this false prophet? What did he do, lay hands on you? Did he promise you that after his wife dies, you'll be her replacement?"

My body was shaking uncontrollably as I stood and slid into my pants.

"Yeah, I know about your wife. It's my job to find out things about scumbags like you. If I was her, I'd die, too."

His statement cut me to the bone.

Poor Wilma.

I'd given her nothing but grief. My wife was a good woman. It stunned just that much harder to hear the truth from a total stranger.

This is it, I thought. This could be my last ride. Something was telling me that prayer would be useless. God had disconnected my private line. Time to face the music.

At this very moment, Wisdom's words had come back to haunt me. After my son had left my office, he told me to make peace with my evil deeds. Lying up in another man's house with his wife wasn't exactly making peace. But at any rate, I buttoned my shirt. I was almost finished dressing when the Negro grabbed me behind the neck and violently slung me over a loveseat, headfirst. As I flew through the air, I thankfully cleared the loveseat, but God intended for me to meet something much harder. The wall was unforgiving. I slid down it, a broken wreck. Dazed a bit, I could see this Negro walking toward me, guns out front. It was the first time I'd noticed that he walked with a slight limp. Rita was in the background screaming like a white woman in a horror movie.

"To me," he said, "backsliding preachers are the lowest forms of life. Ten times lower than a child molester." He leaned down and put one of the barrels to my temple. "I got plans for you, Preacher. Shooting is too good for you. Plus, I like to take pride in my work"—he motioned with the gun—"on your feet."

"Noooo!" Rita screamed. She was out of the bed and on her feet. She charged her naked body at Wellington. "You son of a bitch!"

Wellington was smooth. I could tell he was schooled in martial arts. With one gun shoved into my back, he smoothly caught Rita on the left temple with the other weapon. She dropped without a sound. Her naked body lay sprawled across the carpet. I couldn't tell if she was alive or dead. My heart went out to her. But I had my own problems.

He chilled me with more ghoulish laughter. Wellington gazed upon the naked body of his silent wife.

"It's hard to find a faithful woman today." He harshly shoved the pistols into the small of my back. "Move it."

On our way out of the house, I listened to this madman rant and rave about the folks at his job.

"I worked for the CIA until they discharged me. Medical reasons," he said as he marched me out at gunpoint. "Damn, that truck is yours?"

I said nothing. I was afraid to know what he was thinking.

"Tell me, Preacher. How many of your members do you drive past every day on the streets begging for change? Just so you can make your payments."

"Don't judge me." I got up enough nerve to say something in response.

"Judge you?" he uttered. "You got it all wrong, Preacher. I'm the one who's going to send you to be judged." He pushed me up to the truck. "Keys?"

Wellington looked back in the direction of the house as if he expected his wife to come pouring out.

"Forgot something. Don't you move." He backpedaled, keeping his pistols trained on my chest. When he made it to the doorway, he placed one of his weapons underneath his shirt, leaned in and grabbed some rope. I wanted to break and run, but the Negro was no doubt a trained marksman. It would take little effort for him to turn me into Swiss cheese. Not to mention, if I did get away, all the commotion I would bring upon my ministry. All the scandals that would arise. I was having visions of news reporters shoving cameras in the faces of my members. Snooping around, trying to dig up more dirt. Chasing my family for stories. Then there would be people coming out of the woodworks to crucify me. Slydale and his gang—scorned, frustrated and looking for revenge. That would be nothing compared to what my newest baby momma would say. After she sold her story to TMZ, I would be King Pimp of the pulpit.

He opened the back door.

"Get in."

I did as I was told. I'd rather be dead instead of seeing my church crumble. I probably would hang myself afterward anyway.

Quickly, he bound my hands and feet.

"Remember at Starbucks when I told you that I needed to be talked out of killing the man who was fucking my wife?"

I said nothing. I figured it was a rhetorical question.

"I'm gonna kill you, Preacher." He admitted the truth. "Now we have us a little ride."

WISDOM

My dad's nuts were in the grinder again—I couldn't believe it. He'd been dragged from the church a few days ago. Now he was being kidnapped from another man's house by what seemed to be Sister Walker's husband. I'd only heard half the conversation. God seemed to be beating me to the punch at resurrecting my father's virtuous spirit. It took superhuman restraint for me not to leap from my hiding spot and helped my wayward dad.

This was it. My father had messed with the wrong woman. This dude sounded like a certifiable psycho. First that church thing, now this. Both situations involved guns. Made me feel kinda glad that I'd kept the Glock I'd taken from Pigboy. Felt my waist to see if it was still there. Keeping the gun had gone against all my principles. *Better safe than sorry*, I always said.

God must've heard my prayers. Instead of stuffing the pitiful preacher into the cargo area where I was stashed, and discovering me, the psycho shoved my father into the back passenger door.

From what I could gather, this nut job used to work for

the CIA. Usually, I would question anybody else, but this whack-job's voice confirmed it. He was real calm, cool. Didn't say more than necessary. A phony would've been the opposite: loud, arrogant and boisterous. This cat was for real. Being that Sister Walker didn't follow screaming at the top of her lungs, I shuddered to think of what had become of her.

Damn, I had no way of alerting Rico. Couldn't call him on his cell. I would give away my position. When I'd jumped in the back of this truck, I hadn't planned on this going down. I was just gonna use the mask to try and scare my father straight. Too bad this crackpot had beaten me to it.

"How about a little music, Preacher?" the nut-job asked in a voice as if he and my dad were very good running buddies.

My dad said nothing. From where I was posted up, I could feel the seat my father was lying on shaking worse than a hooker standing on a cold street corner. As if to send my dad a stern message, the lunatic played "Stairway to Heaven" by the O'Jays.

The radio popped on and the lyrics started.

I guess my dad got the message. He started shaking worse than the spin cycle of a washing machine. We backed out of the driveway with the psycho whistling along with the beginning of the song.

Pulling off, I had the strangest feeling. I felt somehow that Rico was following. I hoped homeboy hung loose for all of our sakes. The cat driving my ol' man's precious gas-guzzler was seriously unstable. And if it came down to it, the ex-CIA agent could be deadly—lethal.

I was relieved the psycho chose to taunt my ol' man with music. It drowned out the hip-hop ringtones I'd programmed into my cell. The ringtone I'd given Rico was one of DMX's songs. "Where the Hood At" would've given me away. I held the phone down so that the nutcase wouldn't detect the screen lights. I wanted to pick up. But I couldn't. I just prayed Rico was on his game tonight.

I could feel the truck turn right. My body shifted. The sudden increase in speed could've meant that we were probably on the freeway.

DMX's song rang out again. Five minutes later, "Cater 2 U" from Destiny's Child's *Destiny Fulfilled* CD rang out. Maria left me a message when I didn't answer. I had a moment to relish in the happiness that she'd brought into my chaotic world, that was until Malisa's cell number appeared on my caller ID. I hadn't given her a ring tone. But if I had, it would've been the tone from Michael Jackson's "Thriller."

What could she want anyway? Her water had burst the last time I'd talked to her. I hadn't wished her any complications, but I hoped the labor pains had been extremely hard and harsh. That's when I was hit with a startling revelation. We were driving in an expensive truck with a broken taillight. This late at night, the police would surely be attracted to it like sharks drawn to the scent of fresh blood in the water.

Drive-by shootings, the cops were nowhere to be found. Robberies, the pigs were nowhere around. Muggings and dealing with old ladies—cops were always slow in responding. But for defective equipment, the cops would be all over it like hungry police at an all-you-can-eat doughnut buffet. It would not be good if we were stopped. The police were bumbling idiots, and left to their own devices, they would surely find a way to get my father killed.

"How does it feel to know you're gonna die, preacher?" The creep's laughter had evilness to it, a fiendish pitch only known to banshees and ghouls. My blood ran cold.

"Hey, Preacher, can you remember that chief of police who came up missing?"

"Lord, please!" Pops yelled out in torment.

"Chief Craig Monroe was his name. Police are macho and hard when in uniform, but when you got one dangling on a meat hook, pulling out fingernails, toenails and pubic hairs, it's amazing how they break down crying. The chief wasn't no different from all the others."

Pops cried louder. For even he knew when a killer started confessing murders to someone, it usually meant curtains for the victim.

"Don't cry now, Preacher. You weren't crying when you were banging my wife, now were you?"

I was pretty shocked. Didn't know my ol' man could

hit the high notes. This ruthless bastard was toying with him, getting off by torturing my dad. Pops would be ashamed if any of his members could hear.

"Please don't kill me. I'll go away. You won't ever see me again."

"You're right about one thing, Preacher. I won't see you again, and nobody else will, either, for that matter."

Dad yelled that much harder.

"You see, Preacher, my wife's got a problem with not being able to keep her legs closed. The chief was just like you. Manipulative. Slick-talker. Both of you so-called leaders seduced her with the King James." He chuckled like he was about to reveal more of himself. "I caught the chief and my wife coming out of the motel together. Smiling and laughing like they didn't have a care in the world. Knowing my investigative background, my wife should've known better. Caught the chief coming out of his house when I took him. I learned a lot, working for the CIA. Alternative ways of killing a man. Some more painful than you can imagine."

I could barely hear the CIA maniac over my father shouting The Lord's Prayer at the top of his voice.

"That's not going to help you, Preacher. God knows you're an adulterous piece of crap, for Christ's sake. But anyway, the chief didn't go quietly. Put up a tough fight. But I've been trained in the area of combat. I'd toyed with him for a minute until I got bored. That's when I broke his leg and arm."

The truck started slowing down. We were probably exiting the freeway. The clock on my cell told me we'd taken a twenty-minute ride. But where to?

My question was answered moments later when the smooth, hard pavement turned into a dirt road. I could hear the sounds of rocks crumbling and striking underneath. I was tossed about like debris in a windstorm.

"...for thine is the kingdom, the power, and the glory, for ever and ever. Amen" Poppa Jones finished "The Lord's Prayer."

The psycho drove the truck, laughing at my father.

"Cut that mess out. You'll be face-to-face with Him in a minute, Preacher."

REVEREND POPPA JONES

There was something sinister about the lunatic. I had realized it the first time I'd met him at the coffeehouse. I couldn't believe I'd sat at Starbucks and given crisis counseling to somebody who sat across the table, passing himself off as disgruntled, and two seconds away from bagging his wife's lover. It was creepy, the way this man had held his composure while sizing me up, knowing all along that I was the self-serving snake responsible for stealing his wife's honey.

This was the first time I'd noticed that I wasn't wearing a coat. The ropes cut into the flesh of my wrists, and there was a chilly nip on my arms.

I wiggled around on the seat and tried to relieve the pain in my wrists. Nothing matched the pain in my heart. Pretty soon my wife would be a widow. The thought killed me. I couldn't say that my children would be fatherless. They'd been without me practically throughout childhood. I wasn't there to see Wisdom's first basketball game, or Tempest's graduation. Wasn't there to see Jordan take his first baby steps. Who was I kiddin'? I wasn't even there when the boy was born.

The very thought of all my trifling ways sickened me. Sickened me to the point of vomiting on my leather seats.

My whole body was tight. My chest pounded like a war of nerves had begun to take over. I broke out in hot and cold sweats. My mouth tasted bitter from bile, and my palms were moist from fear and the anticipation of death. In what wild ways would I be tortured? This Negro was demented. Those CIA agents could be ruthless, especially ones who'd flown over the cuckoo's nest.

Out of nowhere, tears leaked from both eyes. My sight went blurry and I was transported deep into the pit of my soul. All the sorrows I'd committed. Lives I'd destroyed. Most of all: my broken covenant with God.

Somewhere in the depths of my dirty soul, I saw the faces. They were just standing around blankly staring ahead. Their eyes were focused on something. Curiosity drove me to jostle my way through the crowd. I wiped away my tears only to see somebody all laid out in a casket. As I pushed farther, I found out that *I* was the guest of honor. I had the full undertaker's facial. Instead of the lively, vibrant look, my face looked flat and hard. Hands folded, resting on my chest. I stared out at the crowd to see Sister Walker, Sister Lawson, the young woman I skydived from her window, her aunt I had sex with, Slydale and his crew, and everybody else I did wrong.

"We're almost here," Wellington announced like we were on our way to the beach.

"Wellington, you don't want to do this."

"Why not?" he asked. "If I don't do this, then you'll think it's okay to continue acting wicked."

We hit a huge pothole, jarring the truck. I bounced around so hard that the ropes tightened. I felt they were going to sever the hands from my arms. Wellington stopped the truck seconds later. My stomach knotted and I felt my bowels slipping.

"We're here, Preacher," Wellington sang out. "It's time to pay the piper."

"Wellington, please— "

"Shut up!" he growled. "Stop saying my name like you know me."

"The Lord said to forgive a man, like you would want Him to forgive—"

"Preacher, if you're trying to reach me, I've just cut your arm off."

He whistled while opening the door. I struggled against the ropes, praying they would loosen so I could free my hands. I could hear the wacko whistling as he walked around the front of the truck to the other side.

He opened the back door.

"Come up outta here." He pulled me harshly by my neck. I screamed, dropping headfirst to the icy ground. I hit so hard my teeth grinded together. My head exploded in pain. Five different shades of blue blinked behind my eyes like disco lights. The rest of my body fell over to the cruel earth.

"That looked like it hurt, Preacher," Wellington said.

Wellington was a pretty handsome guy, but the hideous look on his long face said that he was beyond reasoning.

The Negro reached down and pulled me to my feet. I stood too fast and felt lightheaded. *Phew, it was cold out.*

But I was shivering more from the look on his face than from the bitter, cold climate. The winter night was beautiful. The moon hung full in the sky like it had been painted. We stood in an open clearance surrounded by a spooky forest. In the distance I could see nothing but inky darkness peeping from between the trees.

Wellington pulled both guns from his waistband, pointing.

"Move it to the back of the truck."

I hopped, trying to keep from falling flat on my face. My head being informally introduced to the cold, hard ground had opened up a nasty gash on my forehead. The fall had done more than rattled some teeth. I felt a coolness oozing down my face. I couldn't feel or see it, but I knew it was blood.

"Stop," he ordered. We were a couple of feet from the back of the truck. "Turn around."

My feet were bound together like a captured slave. I struggled to turn. Whatever strength I harvested, the sight of the freshly dug grave drained it. A shovel was stuck in the middle of a massive mound of loose dirt.

My mouth opened. Nothing but cold smoke escaped.

"Turn around. Face me, Preacher."

I didn't want to. I'd rather not see it coming. In so

many ways, I was a coward. I hid behind the King James. Standing in the pulpit preaching one thing, but showing God another.

I reluctantly obeyed.

"This is what it's all about. See how scared you are? I'll bet my house that if I gave you a second chance to live, you'd change your ways. Right, Preacher?"

I saw where this was going. This was about me begging, groveling for mercy. Handing him my manhood wrapped up with a nice, pretty red ribbon on top. Sleeping with another man's wife served as the ultimate humiliation. Some men committed suicide behind learning about their wives' unfaithfulness. Couldn't handle it. Whatever damage I'd caused this man I wasn't going to re-charge his manhood by sacrificing mine.

"Pride, huh?" Wellington asked, cold smoke bouncing off every word. "Ain't it the greatest ruler in the downfall of modern civilization?"

I said nothing. Just kept reciting Psalm 27 inside my head. David's victory over his foes. Expressing the confidence that he had in the Lord. I'd made peace with this punishment. I wasn't fit to shepherd my flock. My stomach fluttered with anxious butterflies. Wished he would stop toying and get it over with.

"Hey, look, if you want to have foolish pride, be my guest. I was kinda hoping that you would've said the correct answer to save your miserable hide. But—what the hell—on your knees, Preacher."

I fell upon the cold, cruel, unforgiving earth. My knees smashed into the frozen clay. He kept me honest with the pistols. Again he tucked one into his waistband. Then with sheer savagery, the bastard tore my shirt off my body. He didn't stop there; Wellington removed my shoes and threw them into the darkness. We could hear a thump far in the distance, and then something scurrying for cover.

"Don't want none of your kids following behind you." He looked upon my bare chest as if getting a charge out of the power he possessed. "You don't deserve to die with a shirt on."

"I guess I should die like a dog, huh? Not even a decent burial. No headstone. Depriving my family of closure."

"Yes. Dogs deserve to die like dogs. Sleep like them. Don't come at me with that sideways mumbo-jumbo," he screamed, foaming from the mouth like a crazed dog. His cool demeanor was slowly unraveling like the bandages of a thousand-year-old mummy. I tried to stay as calm as possible. His mania seemed to be feeding on my fear.

"Just so you know"—he pointed in the direction where the shoes traveled—"your company is out there." He smiled at the confusion going on behind my eyes. "No. Not my wife…if that's what you're thinking. But over there is where the chief's maggot-infested carcass is buried."

"I thought I was mentally screwed up. But you're sick." He flashed the grin of the insane. "Nobody knows it but you and me"—for the moment something caught his attention—"but pretty soon, just me."

It was pretty dark out, but I could still see the back end of the truck move faintly.

"If you believe in the religion you sell to your congregation, now is the time for prayer." Wellington pulled the other pistol out, pointing one at my chest and the other at my head.

Death was locked and loaded. I looked up at the sky, wondering if God was going to go through with this well-deserved termination, blinding the skies to the atrocities going on underneath. The maniac would be the last person I saw in this world. It was at that moment that I wished I had another chance. All the right I could do. My wife and kids. All the lost souls in the church. I would go straight. Do right by my flock. I couldn't promise that I wasn't going to fall short. Nobody could promise that.

I was locked in heated prayer when the back end of my truck dramatically rocked from side to side. Up and down like something was trying to break out.

God?

"What in the name of heaven?" I asked, my mouth hanging open.

"What are you trying to pull, Preacher?"

I hunched my shoulders as if to say, "Not me."

Wellington Walker slowly walked over to the truck. He stared back at me.

"Stay put." He grabbed the door handle. That's when I noticed the broken taillight. I didn't know what to make of it. When I left Sister Lawson's the other night, everything was fine. My mind concluded that some baggy pants thug had been trying to jack the truck—around the same time I was being marched out of Rita's house at gunpoint. The startled youngster probably jumped into the back and stowed away. My heart went out to him. Once found, Wellington was sure to kill him. It looked like there were going to be three bodies buried out here instead of two.

A chilled gust of wind wailed, blew up through the trees, rattled the frozen, naked branches, and made a clanking sound. Wellington cocked one pistol behind his ear. "Come out slowly and I might let you live. If you don't, I put lead into your marrow."

There was no answer, only the wind whistling through the trees. A light snow started falling. Huge flakes floated down like feathers from a dove. I could see Wellington mouthing a silent count, his laboring breath inflating and deflating his chest.

Then it happened!

Wellington snatched open the door as if it were the door leading to a room filled with Pharaoh's riches. The huge black boot he harshly received to the mouth was rich with surprise.

A shocked expression ripped across Wellington's face on his way to the ground, the pistols sliding across the frozen terrain.

"Motherfuc— "Wellington tried to yell but the bloody teeth he was spitting out cut short his profanities.

A figure dressed in black slid from the truck. Standing fully erect, this stranger was enormous. Gigantic. Huge. Six-eight or bigger. A ski mask concealed his identity. I didn't want to call it a man. God was a god of mystery. This thing could've been *anything*. Was it here to save? Or was it here to destroy?

At that moment, Wellington was probably asking himself that same million-dollar question. His eyes widened with fear. The guns were probably his only chance against the colossal intruder. He scrambled after them for dear life. Wellington had almost reached one when the figure dived on him, punching *him* in the back of the head.

I couldn't believe what I was seeing. I expected Rod Serling from *The Twilight Zone* to step from between the trees, smoking a cigarette while trying to explain the unexplainable. Death had been postponed for the moment while Wellington "The Grim Reaper" Walker battled with the newcomer. I didn't know what this was about. Maybe one of Wellington's CIA buddies had been commissioned to take him out. Maybe. But I was dead either way. Whether God or a CIA operative commissioned this, I had done too much dirt. Far too much to keep on living.

Determination won out with Wellington retrieving one of the weapons. He was on the bottom, the stranger on top, struggling for control of the gun. Wellington was trying desperately to point the barrel at the stranger's head, but the bulldog grip that he had on Wellington's pistol hand prevented further advancement, and flying brain matter. The strain from the struggle caused the weapon to discharge, lighting up the night, shattering my back window.

I watched the two entangled bodies jockeying for possession. I prayed they'd shoot each other, cancel each other out. Another shot whistled past my head. I was through watching. I tossed myself into the hole Wellington had dug for me. Felt like I broke a hip bone when I landed.

I was out of harm's way. But if this thing didn't go down like I prayed, I'd positioned myself in my final resting place.

WISDOM

"Let go!" the lunatic demanded as we continued to tussle over the weapon on the cold, hard, jagged tundra. We rolled around like two kids in the backyard wrestling for possession of a Power Ranger action figure. My Timberland boot had done its job. The lunatic's mouth foamed with bloody saliva. The straining caused his mouth to flop open like no muscles were attached. I laughed at the bloody, jagged stomps that used to be healthy teeth.

This ex-CIA retard was cock-diesel. He wasn't a tall man, but he was very muscular. Robust. And for an older guy, this cat was in shape. He wasn't huffing and puffing like me. My right arm trembled as I held the hand clutching the pistol. I banged the pistol hand against the freezing ground, forcing another premature blast. The night lit up once more. One more bang against the ground and the pistol flew from his hand. I didn't know why he hadn't thought of it before, but the spook brought his right knee up into my groin.

I let go, clutching my painful privates. The hefty attention I was paying myself cost me. When the pain finally subsided, I looked up to see the psychotic stare in his eyes over the barrel.

"Now I don't know who you are, masked man, or where you came from, but I do know where you're going. You just made my job harder. Now I have another grave to dig." He took careful aim. I closed my eyes, thinking about how Highnoon would react from being cheated when I heard a metallic clank. It didn't sound like a gunshot, but I opened my eyes slowly, searching my chest to see if I'd been hit. The stupid, faraway gaze in the madman's eyes confused me. That was until he fell— face first—to the frozen ground. Standing inches behind the spot in which the ex-CIA agent had timbered…

"Saving you is beginning to be a full-time gig," Rico said, a shovel draped across his shoulder like he was standing inside the batter's box awaiting the perfect pitch. Rico offered his hand and pulled me from the ground.

"Punk," I said to the lunatic's unconscious body. I whispered something to Rico while nodding at the hole Pops had dived into.

Rico stepped back into the shadows. I had a plan and didn't wanna confuse the ol' man. I made sure that the lunatic was out before I went to fetch the pistols, still feeling the pain in my balls. The pain pulsating in my knee was thumping faster than the thud of my heart.

I'd been one eyelash away from being buried out here with everybody else. Had to thank God for His intervention. Without Him, I would've been another trophy on the wall for the ex-CIA idiot. I laid the other weapons on the ground and removed the one I'd taken from Pigboy out of my waistband.

"Preacher," I called out. I tried to make my voice sound gruff and intimidating. There was no response, which led me to frightfully believe that one of our stray shots had taken him. My heart palpitations were heavy. Short steps took me over to the hole. My pops was lying on his back, his eyes closed.

"Preacher, open your eyes." His eyes popped open as if my words carried miraculous powers. I offered my free hand, pulling him out.

"Who are you?" he wanted to know.

He was shivering like I couldn't believe. The lunatic had snatched his shirt and shoes. Stripped him almost butt naked.

He glanced at the gun in my hand. "Are you going to kill me?"

"To answer your first question: I'm the voice of Him calling in the winds. I'm the rounding up of His stray sheep. Change your ways, Preacher. The Man upstairs wants you to change your ways. I've been sent to deliver this message." I showed him the pistol. "If you step out of line next time, I won't be here to help you. I'll be the one sent to destroy you."

"Okay, I will," Pops spoke, relieved. "Praise God. Glory be to His name." He looked at the human lump on the ground. "What are you going to do with him?"

"Not your concern, Preacher. He'll get what's coming to him. Killing the chief of police should earn him hell in a cell." I untied his hands and feet. "You're free to go."

The ol' man hurried to the driver's door. I grabbed the lunatic's right leg, dragging him to the front of the truck.

"Remember"—I looked to the stars—"He's watching."

He jumped in and brought the engine to life. The ol' man pulled off, leaving me to the task of recycling the rope. I hogtied the psycho and dragged him in the direction of the flashing headlights. The CIA creep groaned a little. I was real careful when I slugged him across the head with the pistol, sending him back to La La Land.

Sliding open the cargo door, I muscled the lunatic's body into the van.

"You better be glad that your boy was on his game. I got nervous, not waiting for you to call me. So I circled and came back around, lucky for you"—he nodded his head at Mister Super Spook—"hate to think if I would've went along with *your* version of the plan. Who the hell is that anyway?"

I was one tired and battered soul.

"The husband of the woman my ol' man was creeping with." I stumbled into the passenger door, breathing like I'd just run a marathon. After I checked the strength of the ropes, I said, "Let's jet."

The CIA cat was out like a light. I kept the pistol on the creep for precautionary measures. I'd watched a segment on the Discovery Channel about how CIA agents were trained to be slick escape artists. If the schmuck even blinked wrong, I was ready to bust a cap in his ass.

It took us a minute to find our way out of the woodland maze. I made sure that my mental note-taking of the location was on point. I would leave no stone unturned when handing the directions, that creep in the back, along with his pistols over to the police. It would be their job to dig up the frozen police chief.

Rico and I discussed the entire ordeal on our way back to the city, stopping to laugh at some of the humorous details: My ol' man shivering his butt off, how I let an older, less physically imposing man get the drop on me. Poppa Jones' intense begging for his life. And how Rico had crept up behind the man and leveled him with the shovel. I forgot I'd even had one in the van.

"I sure hope yo' ol' man's through playing pimp-daddy," Rico said. The dumb smile on his face made me laugh. It wasn't the laughter belonging to a jovial soul, but the tortured, sick bellowing of a demented human being.

"Hey, what's—" the CIA creep groggily said before I cracked him over the head again.

Slowly rolling, I kicked the lunatic out of the cargo door at the precinct with a note affixed to his back—his two guns with him. The two police officers coming out of the station tried to run out and catch a glimpse of the van's plates. No dice. The headlights were out and Rico had his foot to the floor.

Tick-Tock, the clock was ticking.

Thursday morning was here. And I still had three more of my folks to scare straight. My eyes burned from lack of sleep. I could barely think straight. See straight. But if I expected to achieve my task, I had to be quick. Geechie was up next. I was going to rescue my sister, and find a way to bury Geechie's drug-dealing behind... forever.

WISDOM

THURSDAY, DAY FOUR...

I couldn't go another step without a fresh change of clothes. I was dreading my final trip back to my old house. Now was the best time if any. Malisa was still at the hospital. The cow had given birth to an eight-pound baby boy.

My little brother.

The back-stabbing hussy still didn't have a clue that I was wise to her little game. I hoped like heck that Poppa would delay letting her know that the bones were out of the closet. I figured as long as she was left ignorant, the more time I would have in springing a trap on that rat. I laughed at the media attention that a humiliating paternity scandal could bring to my dad's doorstep. The frightened look in my ol' dude's eyes last night told me he'd turned the corner. As in getting out of Satan's bed and going back to full-time duties for the Lord.

Rico was still hanging strong. After delivering the reverend's stalker to the police, we went back to Rico's to chill and do a little drinking. The rum and Coke had gone against my better judgment, but my nerves were riding high in my throat. Death was on my heels and I needed something to give it the slip. Something potent.

I couldn't sleep because every time I closed my eyes, Highnoon's ugly face kept reminding me that I had a couple more days to handle my business. So I stayed up drinking and playing spades with Rico and his sister at Mama Lemon's spot. I hadn't been back to the house since Rico had monkey-stomped Lace for trying to bring the fight to his mama's front door. I couldn't believe Mama Lemon's house had three bedrooms and twelve people living under one roof. The overcrowding wasn't a problem for me. The more the merrier.

We were now in the van and headed for Malisa's. It was time for me to confront my demons.

"I ain't gonna have to put one in that nigga, Kurt, am I?" Rico questioned, showcasing that evil grin.

"Is there one day where you don't have bullet-riddled bodies on the brain?" I asked.

"No," Rico said as he looked out his window at life in the ghetto. "Living in the ghetto, you can't get caught slipping. Gotta stay sharp. If you soft, you lost. Too many of my friends are in the dirt because they went soft. It's real out here. I refuse to go out like that. So if that means thinking about popping a few fools every day to keep that edge, then that's how I gotta think."

While listening to Rico's five-and-dime mumbo-jumbo, I noticed my cell ringing. The number was blocked as usual.

"You got him," I said as I answered. I tried to throw

off any potentially irritating callers. The voice I heard sounded like a gift from God.

"I need to meet you," the male caller said. But if I knew my brother, Yazoo, it was more like demanding than asking.

"Name the time and the place."

"Three o'clock. The parking lot of the White Castle—Warren Avenue."

"Be there," I said, not even waiting for a response. I ended the call.

"Yo, who dat?" Rico asked.

"You'll see sooner than later. But right now I need you to help me get my crap out of Malisa's crib."

"That should be one trip, huh?" Rico joked, smiling.

I laughed. It was a pretty sad laugh, though. I didn't have that many clothes. I'd been working for the majority of my adult life and I still didn't have two nickels to rub together.

"That's real funny coming from a house so crowded, five of ya'll got to step outside to make room for somebody to turn the television," I blazed back.

We snapped good-naturedly back and forth while traveling the rest of the way to Malisa's.

"Dude, looks like somebody done cleaned ya'll the hell out," Rico stated. The echo of his voice seemed to bounce off the walls of the empty rooms.

The entire crib was completely emptied. Gutted like

a fish! Almost like nobody had ever lived there. I frantically ran from room to room looking for any signs of life.

Nothing!

It was only after I slowed my heart rate that I found a note attached to my mangled NCAA trophy for Most Valuable Player. If I'd paid attention when we entered, the thing would've stuck out like a sore thumb.

I stepped up to the mantle in the living room with curious eyeballs.

"What's that?" I waved Rico silent while I read the letter aloud:

Ha, ha, ha, nigga. I guess by now you lookin' around scratching yo' head and nuts, wondering where the hell everything is. In case you don't know, the baby ain't yours. Yo' crusty father told me that he told you. Shit happens. Get over it. If you would've been handlin' yo' bidness, I wouldn't have had sex with the preacher for money. At first it started out that way, but somewhere in all the dollar signs, I started developing feelings for the old man. Plus he was swinging a mean joint. I'm kinda happy the baby's father is yo' father. At least he won't inherit yo' loser ways. Let's face it, superstar, you're a loser now and you'll always be a one. Couldn't make it to the NBA. Hell, you're barely holding on to minimum wage. I know I ain't working. Tell you the truth, but I need me a real man, Boo-Boo. Not some little boy….

I read on, despite my sudden urge to kill her stupid ass.

Yup, I was responsible for sending the crew in the church and dragging the preacher out. That were Kirk's crew. While I was havin' yo' baby—oops—yo' father's baby, I also sent Kirk

*and the boys to clean house. Don't bother lookin' fo' yo' shit
'cause I burned it. And don't bother looking for us because
we're moving out West. My new Boo, me and the baby—
yup, Kirk is not my cousin, stupid. He is my man. Oh yeah,
he told me to tell you that he loves the wonderful job you did
in not taking care of business. The only thing I left you is this
broke-ass trophy. It's broke just like you.*

"Man, don't let that rat boil yo' blood." Rico tried to
lighten the sting from the letter. "Good riddance, tramp.
Raggedy Roach. Wisdom, you can't let that little bug-a-
boo blow yo' head, man. You done come too far. Your
mama needs you. As much as I hate this contract you got
with this Lownoon busta— "

"Highnoon," I corrected.

"—High, low, hoe, that punk nigga—you know who
I'm referring to. As much as I don't understand this, I'm
supportive. We've put in too much work to turn back.
Give that stank broad a rest."

Rico was right. The little pep talk brought me back to
reality.

"God don't like ugly. Karma's a monster. That stank
broad'll get hers."

"You're right, man. Let's get back to putting my family
back on track." I extended a fist in the air. "One down,
three to go."

Rico met my fist with his. "Three days to go. We can
do this. Who's next?"

"We have to find my sister, and I think I know just who
can help us."

"That's cool," Rico said as he walked toward the door. "But where we gonna start looking for Jordan?"

That was a good question. The mere thought of what we had encountered on the last *Jordan* run was enough to make my bowels run loose. Not to mention almost being shot by those two ugly, crack-slangin' baby ghouls we'd bumped into in the cemetery.

"Don't know. Something will come up."

"It just better," Rico said.

The afternoon traffic was surprisingly light for this time of day. We were sittin' in the parking lot of White Castle. Rico was getting his grub on. I watched while my boy gobbled down one burger after another until the sack was finished. Rico sipped some Coke and burped.

"You wanna let me in on the mystery? Who we meeting, black? What's with all the secret squirrel jive?'

"Easy, partner." I pulled out my cell." Patience, pal."

"Whatever." Rico didn't like to wait on anything. His motto was simple: *Give it to me now, I'll wait when I'm dead.* The boy had the attention span of a toddler. Waiting made him real fidgety. To pass time, I called Momma. It was no surprise that my ol' man answered Momma's phone. He told me that he was wrong for his treachery. Said that he was down there begging Momma's forgiveness. Said it wasn't a good time to break the news about the baby.

I respected that. I told him to kiss Momma, and then I wished him blessings.

A black Range Rover roared into the parking lot, loud-ass rap music banging from the expensive SUV. The tinted windows left the driver invisible to outside eyes. The speed demon almost had an accident with another car, speeding, trying to beat a burgundy Cadillac Seville to be served first at the drive-thru window.

Rico picked up one of the little burger boxes and examined it. "White Castle must be cookin' with crack." He chuckled, watching as the Caddy laid on his horn in disapproval. "Niggas trying to kill each other to get at these gut grenades."

I was getting a little irritated. This fool had left me waiting. I knew it was his method of operation, but this was pushin' it.

The Rover pulled into the spot next to us, banging a DMX tune. I was already peeved about having to wait past the agreed upon time. Now this idiot chose to eat his burgers and have a party next to me.

"This fool keep bumpin' his box trying to floss," Rico said. He looked over me at the black truck. "He gonna be minus some music." He pulled up his coat and exposed the handle of a nine-millimeter Glock.

"Wait." I peered deeper into the tinted window. I got out the van and knocked on the Rover's tinted window.

Looking back, I saw Rico exiting the van, pistol in hand for all to see.

"Rico," I said, "put that thing up."

"Yeah, Rico, put *that* up," Yazoo echoed with his window down, the music now a low rumble.

Rico's face mirrored the surprise on mine.

"Look at Mr. Big Time," Rico exclaimed with great relish, tucking the pistol back underneath his coat. Today was colder than penguin booty. The grounds were wet and salt pellets crunched underneath our Timberlands. Michigan's winters were notorious for being unpredictable. And so was this punk stepping from his expensive truck wearing a flamboyant fur. He caught my admiring eyes.

"Sable." He rubbed the coat as if it were his best friend. "Nothing but the best for the kid."

Rico slapped him five. "I know that's right."

I was unmoved. I didn't give a damn about material things. "You said two. I was here at two." I scolded him.

Yazoo shook his head and smiled. "Same old Wisdom. Your car or mine?" Yazoo was arrogant. I couldn't miss it. Didn't feel like hearing him brag about his wealth.

So I said, "Mine."

Yazoo turned up his nose like the mail van was a germ-infested cesspool.

"Whatever. Let's do it." Yazoo looked toward Rico. "Take my truck for a spin.

"You ain't gotta tell me twice," Rico said, already scooting behind the Rover's wheel.

I had to admit: I was a little envious—despite the warning by God of being envious of people obtaining material possessions through the pursuit of evil works. I looked on as Rico peeled out of the parking lot. For the moment, I'd lost my best friend to star-struck syndrome. That's why Rico was thinking about turning pro. He said that boxing would be his ticket out of the ghetto. He could then buy his mother a huge house. Not to mention a Range Rover for himself. Right about now, Rico was in four-wheel heaven. The music that had aggravated him earlier, he now kicked like an NFL punter.

"Sell out," I spoke in the direction Rico had peeled out.

We jumped in the van. It was obvious Yazoo didn't give a damn if he insulted me. The dude sat tentatively on my seat. Kept raising his thighs to see if anything was stuck to his two-hundred- dollar jeans. The schmuck sat straight up, so that his precious sable wouldn't touch the reclining leather of the seat.

"You too good to sit in my van, huh?" I asked with a little attitude.

He looked around my van like it was beneath him. He rubbed a finger across the leather of the recliner part of the seat. Saw a little dirt on his finger. "See this dirt. My coat cost too much money to be stained by this crap."

"Why you tryin' to disrespect me, Yazoo?"

He smiled. "No disrespect. I pay good money for my stuff. I'm just careful where I sit, that's all."

I shook my head at the phoniness. When just yesterday, this bum was on the shoulder of the freeway, kicking the tire of his stalled-out hooptie in bitter frustration. Now he was Big Money Grip.

"What you want with me?' I asked.

"That stupid girl went and got herself in trouble," he said.

"What stupid girl?"

"Yo' sister. She went back on her deal of carrying drugs into the prison for Geechie. He went out to her fancy crib in Bloomfield Hills on Friday morning and kidnapped her stupid ass."

I was trying to check my anger. I couldn't. But I had to. The memory of me choking him out at the family meeting was urging me to repeat.

"Did you know about him playing the bongos on Darrius' head at the shop a little while ago?"

"Bongos?"

"He went by the shop and tore it up with your brother-in-law."

"He broke it off on Darrius?" Yazoo smiled.

"Glad to see that you are amused," I said with attitude. "If you knew Tempest was in trouble, why the hell you ain't do nothin'?"

"Because it's a money thing, baby. You wouldn't understand."

"Make me, Yazoo."

"I work for Geechie."

I shot him a look laced with hot molten daggers.

"Well, Geechie's reign is just about over. The nigga is losing money, respect and connects."

"That ain't tellin' me why you just sat on your ass and allowed this to happen."

He smirked. "Still missing the big picture, little brother. Hey, genius, if I would've gone in trying to play hero, Geechie would've made the connection. And I'd be locked in a closet like he's doing your sister."

"Naw, brah, I do understand. You don't give a damn about your sister. Anything that can't help fatten your pockets, it ain't no use to you."

He waved me off like I was an annoying fly at a family barbeque.

"Like I said, I got plans for the nigga. Nothing's gonna stand in my way. If you wanna go get her, I'll tell you where."

Now it was my turn to look at this fool like he was the newest germ in town.

He handed me a small piece of paper. "That's the address." Yazoo looked up to see Rico whipping into the parking lot. I found it strange that there was no music. Yazoo made ready to go. "Geechie won't be there after eleven. That will be the best time to break in."

"How do you look at yourself in the mirror?" I asked.

The arrogant son of a bitch popped the imaginary collar of his coat. "I'm paid, baby. I ain't got a problem with looking at myself." He screwed up his face and gazed around my van. "The question is...how do you look at yo'self? Come work for me and I'll take you out of minimum wage village and fatten yo' pockets, baby."

"No thanks, *baby!* I'll manage. I'd rather wait on God."

He laughed until he almost choked. "You need to get off that God business." He removed a phat bankroll of bills from his pocket. "This is my god, baby. Now and forever. I'll keep my god and keep the pockets phat. You keep God and stay broke." With that, Yazoo stepped from the van. I watched Rico slap him five. I opened the door but didn't get out.

"Hey, kingpin, do you know where Jordan is?"

"Naw, I don't keep up with the crackheads." Yazoo dapped Rico.

"Zoo," Rico said, "I was trying to impress some broad in a Benz and blew one of your kicker boxes. Why don't you get an estimate and—"

"Don't even worry 'bout it, playa. I got it. Money ain't nothin' but a thang." Yazoo dapped Rico again, jumped into his truck, rolled down his tinted window, and blew an arrogant kiss at me. "Wiz, when you get yo' mind right, get at me. I'll make yo' paper tight."

He rolled the window up. The Range Rover pulled off. The punk didn't ask about Momma, nor did I feel a need to give him any details. He'd made it clear that money was king. Nothing or nobody else mattered. It was at that point I made Yazoo the last person on my list to turn. He would definitely be the hardest. I really didn't think the efforts would be worth it. He was dead to his present family. His new family was greener, had more numbers and big pictures of immortal ex-presidents. His pockets were now home to a few past White House heavy-hitters like Washington, Grant and Jackson.

"Yo. You smell that weed scent on Zoo, man?" Rico asked, slipping back into the passenger seat.

"Yep. The same one you're now wearing."

Rico smiled foolishly. His eyes were glossy and emulated the shape of a smiling Asian.

"He—I...you know what happened—"

"You can't even get the lie out. Save it. I know you smoke a little weed from time to time." I put the truck in drive. "I ain't mad at cha."

"Zoo done changed, man," Rico explained, His voice was void of the anxiousness it held earlier.

"I know. Before he was an irritating, broke little creep, but now that he has money, he's more irritating than ever. Maybe the weed's to blame for his *Pinky and the Brain* philosophy of taking over the world."

"Say what?" Rico said.

"That fool's planning to whack out his boss, Geechie." I drove slowly out of the parking lot.

"Snap. So that's how Zoo's getting his riches," Rico said. "Well, that nigga better wait in line. When I catch Geechie's punk ass, I got plans to put some hot ones in him."

Thoughts swam madly around inside my head like a swimmer in a hundred-meter freestyle competition. "You know that rat of a brother stood by and let his boss snatch Tempest from her crib."

Rico's eyes regained natural composure.

"The rat even gave me the address where Tempest is being held."

"Is it the same as the one fat boy gave you?"

"Yep. But that ain't the point. This fool didn't even do anything. Geechie could be brutalizing my sister. Yazoo said that Geechie is locking my sister in closets. He said that she'll be at that address later on. Until then, I have to live with the fact that my sister is probably being tortured right now. I'm helpless 'til tonight. Don't know what I'd do if something happens to her." I was desperately fighting to hold back the river of tears. "We can't even involve the police either. Geechie has police on the payroll. He gets wind of the tip and Tempest could be dead."

Rico reached over, patting my shoulder. "Tempest'll be alright. You'll see. We're gonna find her. That's my promise to you. She's my sister, too. On my soul, Geechie's gonna pay. Word is bond."

"I've got to find a way to get Geechie and Highnoon pissed at each other. In the warehouse that night, I kinda pulled Highnoon's coattail to Geechie's plan to take over the city."

"What plan?"

"I lied and told Highnoon that Geechie was gonna try him."

"Oh, I get it," Rico said and snapped his fingers. "Pit 'em against each other. Hopefully get 'em so riled up that they'll be at each other's throats."

"Yep."

"How?"

"Don't know yet. I gotta get Geechie off my sister's back. Because once we save Tempest, what's gonna stop that punk from getting at her again? Especially after"—I swallowed hard—"I lay it down for my mother."

Rico's face dropped. I could tell that my boy wanted to say something about my standing contract with Satan. But out of respect for my decision, he remained silent.

"You see how everything worked out for my ol' man? Once they dig up the body belonging to the ex-chief of police, that CIA whacko will be put away for life."

"We'll think of something," Rico said, looking in the direction we were now traveling. "Where we going?"

"Cemetery."

"Looking for Jordan?"

"Geechie will be gone after eleven. We might as well try and run down Jordan first."

"Let's do it," Rico agreed, smacking his thighs, and pumping himself up.

I drove along the streets of an area totally devoid of cops and the law. A part of the city where walking to the store could get my face on one of those postcards that come through the mail with profiles of missing people on the front, an urban environment where crackheads roamed the streets like mindless zombies in search of the euphoric state rendered by that elusive, first-time high. Jackers loomed behind every bush. Dope pushers and prostitutes shared the corners. And if the kidnappers missed a person, the hot lead from the drive-by shooting found 'em.

"This place makes me appreciate where I live," Rico admitted.

We were cruising through enemy territory, searching, hoping to catch Jordan on a corner buying some crack. The winds howled and whipped, rocking the van as if it were a child's swing in a storm. It was unbelievable how the cold temperatures didn't stop or slow down the crime elements on these streets. It was business as usual.

"Yeah, I know what you mean," I said, disgustedly staring at a prostitute. The nasty heifer had her skirt hiked and was pissing on the curb. I could even see the cold smoke fogging off the stream.

"No home training," Rico said.

"Naw. It's the choices she made. You never know. The mother probably taught her values like yours and mine, but somewhere along the way, she made a bad choice."

"Like selling booty?" Rico offered, chuckling.

"Something like that."

We made a left on a residential street named Graves. The name was befitting. Almost every house had been torn down. And the ones that were standing looked like they were next on the demolition list.

"The zombies are thick on this block," Rico said. He removed his pistol, held it down and out of sight, popped out the magazine, and inspected the rounds.

"Must be a crack spot somewhere around here." My heart was deeply troubled. I looked at the slow moving Black Americans. People who could have been doctors, lawyers—heading Fortune 500 Companies. Instead, I saw zombies whose brains had been fried like chicken by chemicals. Souls had been sold to the dealers with the lowest prices, their thought processes replaced by the primitive instincts of a junkie-hunter-gatherer.

What the hell? I yelled inside my mind as I watched one of the zombies a block up break from a crowd of smokers on the left-hand side of the street. He was moving more like Usain Bolt.

Rico was still leaning down, checking his weapon when I floored the van. The thing launched forward, throwing Rico's head against the dash.

Thump!

Rico looked up just in time to see Jordan do a Tyson Gay up the street.

"Damn," I said and strapped on my seat belt. "We've just been made."

"That boy can run," Rico said.

My brother must've come to his senses, finally figuring that he couldn't out run the van. The boy disappeared between two houses. I jammed down hard on the brakes. The van screeched to a halt and careened to a stop.

"Stay with the van," I yelled to Rico, who was already out and running in Jordan's direction. I slipped in some water, lost my footing and fell hard on the ground. I jumped up from the puddle with my left pants leg soaked.

Between the houses, running full steam, I saw Jordan speeding up the alley. He had a sizeable lead, and was adding to it.

Stride for stride, I matched his, closing the distance.

"Stop, Jordan!" I commanded loudly. I didn't know a crackhead could possess that much wind speed. Jordan never broke stride. Never once looked back. His legs kept pumping and arms flailing.

The schmuck bent another corner. I followed, but not seeing the drunk on the ground, sleeping in his own vomit…

Crash! Boom! Bang!

I fell over the drunk, slamming into the side of a big dumpster. My momentum almost put me through the side of it.

"Oh my God!" I yelled. I lay on my back, grabbing my surgically repaired knee, rocking back and forth—in extreme pain.

"Hey, buddy," the old drunk said, "you just ruined the best sleep ever." His hair was unkempt. His long, black overcoat was stained by vomit and seriously needed an iron. The old bum removed a wrinkled paper bag from his coat and shoved it up to his five o'clock shadowed-face. "Can't even get decent sleep anymore." He had his nerve to cut his eyes at me. The homeless dude flipped me the bird and then staggered away, drinking from the bag.

My pain was intense, an eight on the pain scale. I was so focused on my throbbing knee that I didn't notice the blood oozing down my head. Just like that my past had come back to haunt me like an eighteenth century ghost scorned by the diabolical way it was murdered.

As I tried to rock my pain away, time vaulted me back to a place where running up the court, breaking opponents down with a lightning-fast crossover was a happy way of life. Record-breaking nights, big-breasted, big booty groupies, but most of all, the house on the lake—all within my grasp slipped through my fingers like sand through an hourglass at the snap I'd heard on the concrete basketball court that fateful day.

I rocked for my shattered dreams. No longer caring where I was. Not concerned for my safety.

I rocked.

Not even caring that my injured knee was probably sending out distress signals of vulnerability to the criminal element.

I rocked.

Not interested that the predators had probably sensed the blood in the water and were closing in for the kill.

Time slipped me. I didn't know how long I'd been in the alley holding my knee. Daylight was slowly succumbing to approaching darkness. Rico had to be flakin' out.

I picked myself up off the ground and painfully limped back through the snow the way I had come. Not even flinching when a pit bull charged the fence of its enclosure, barking, teeth showing, slobbering. There was nothing the mutt could do to me that Highnoon didn't have planned.

Hot pain shot through my knee as I miscalculated putting too much pressure on it. A cold gale whipped through the alley, penetrating my thin layer of clothing.

Malisa had torched my wardrobe. The broad had left me with just the rags on my back. I didn't have much, but now, I had even less. A black, leather bomber, jeans, Timberlands and some funky drawers. The puddle I'd fallen in earlier had soaked the only pair of socks in my life right now.

I limped through sub-zero darkness humiliated, broken in spirit, defeated and shivering. Chilled to the bone. I refused to submit to defeat. The dog could still be heard in the distance. Barking like he could still smell my heinous thoughts of finding Malisa and choking her out. Knowing that I had a couple days left on earth switched my mind back to business.

Jordan was gone. I'd slipped up. Stupid. Thinking he wouldn't recognize my van. How lame of me. Who wouldn't recognize the company's logo of a stick figure in a running position with a mail sack draped over his shoulders? A lummox. An embryo could've planned better. The blown chance would force Jordan underground. He'd never resurface after my latest episode of incompetence.

I lumbered between the two houses I'd jetted through earlier. A look of relief flushed across Rico's face. He ran out to help, grabbed my left arm and draped it over his shoulder in an attempt to take weight off my knee.

"What the hell happened to you, man? I've been hittin' you on the cellie," Rico said.

I stopped, quickly patted my coat and pants pockets.

"My cell! I lost it! My only damn means of communication!"

"Don't you think your knee's more important?" Rico tried to reason.

"You don't understand. I have no money or time to get a new one. Have to stay in touch with Momma and you. That phone was vital, man." I glanced around at the ground beneath our feet, frustrated that darkness and the lack of time wouldn't permit me to give a thorough look. The thing was the only bridge keeping me connected with my ol' girl. I figured if I couldn't be with her twenty-four-seven, I could at least hear her voice.

"Jordan?" Rico asked.

"Got away. That's how I reinjured my friggin' knee. Fell over some wino."

Rico pointed to my head. "Do you know you're bleeding?"

The streetlights were shining above highlighted the crimson blood flowing down my fingers after I gently touched the wound.

"Looks like you're gonna have to drive, Rico."

Rico helped me into the passenger side. "No problem. Can you continue?"

"Have to. My family's at stake. I'm gonna finish what I started. Even if I have to crawl." Tears swelled into my eyes. The strength of my manhood stopped them from falling. We left The Cemetery. I had a knee full of pain. The heat inside the van blew lukewarm as usual. I hated to admit it, but I was going to miss this van. My mail route. Bribing my potbellied supervisor, Stanley Focus, with Wendy's burgers and fries.

We drove in silence. I didn't know what Rico was thinking. My mind, on the other hand, was backlogged by worries, plotting strategies, praying for my mother, and thinking about the private, violent torture session Highnoon had planned.

"Stop by the ATM," I told Rico.

We stopped at the ATM. The machine happily spat out the remaining money I had in the whole world. It wasn't much. A portion of the eighty dollars would be used for sports tape and a knee brace. Walmart provided the things I needed: tape, brace, flashlight and spray paint.

"What's the spray paint for?" Rico asked.

"You'll see."

Rico drove me to one of his connects. Being his friend was enough to land a huge discount on a bootleg cell joint. One of those cell phones that provided illegal, unlimited minutes with no monthly bill. The homeboy hookup. The 'hood special. I usually didn't partake in illegal devices, but desperate times bred even more desperate measures. I would have to beg God for His forgiveness before Highnoon put my lights out.

And speaking of Highnoon, I called him to inform him that he should call Rico's phone if he needed to get in touch with me. Rico didn't like the idea of Highnoon having his number but he never verbalized it. My bootleg joint couldn't receive any incoming calls.

"Wisdom, my man, you have a couple of days left," Satan reminded me. The visualization of a smelly cigar stuck in his mouth made me nauseous.

"I think I know how that whole calendar thing works," I said, keeping it short and unpleasant.

He laughed arrogantly. "Same time, too. Friday. Midnight. How's your—"

I hung up without further words. There was no need for chitchat. Same time and place was all I needed to know. Damn the rest. Skip the gold-tooth-wearing roach.

The time was now nine o'clock.

We had a little time to kill, so we posted up at a little hole-in-the-wall bar.

Think-n-Drink came to be named such because of an overwhelming, economically challenged country that turned so many to the bottle. The owner wanted to create an environment where people could come in and temporarily lose themselves in a bottle of something hard.

We didn't wanna get sloppy, so Rico and I sipped beer. Over a couple of cold ones, we regaled each other with hood survival tales.

"It's 'bout time," Rico stated, pointing at the clock on the wall. I gently touched the bandage on my forehead. It was a lesson on how not to break a fall by using my face.

"Let's go get my sister, man."

Inside the van, my face and knee both complained about abuse. But I could only take one complaint at a time.

While Rico drove, I slid on a Tandem X-Factor brace over my aching knee—the swollen joint hot-mouthed me the whole while. I felt a minor bit of relief. Just enough to be mobile. A confrontation would be another story.

We made it out to Southfield within thirty minutes. Traffic on the Lodge Freeway at eleven-thirty at night was a breeze compared to rush hour.

Rico's eyes sparkled with mischief, tapered by a hint of concern. "How we gonna do this, Wiz?"

"I'd be lying if I said I had a plan," I said honestly. "Just follow my lead. Whatever play I make, you just back me."

The truth of the matter was that I was operating on fumes. I hadn't had a decent meal since I started this operation. Sleep had been a couple of winks far and few between. Not to mention all the rough stuff I'd been engaging in lately. I really didn't have much left.

Maria had to be blowing my cell up. The thing had to have been lying somewhere in the wet alley. My MetroPCS had undoubtedly fallen into the hands of a crackhead that had probably traded it for drugs by now. I thought about it. Maybe losing the phone had been a good thing. This meant I'd have no distractions.

"Yo', Wiz. We comin' in, man."

Geechie was living out here like a king. His enormous ranch rested on about four acres of land. We found out on one ride by that Geechie's closest neighbors weren't within earshot. Nobody would hear us if we had to break glass. Another slow roll-by revealed no cars in the driveway. No lights were on. And the streets were shadowy dark.

Out in suburban America, the residents didn't park on the streets like their city-dwelling counterparts. It would make stashing the van harder than a first-time author receiving a book deal from a top-shelf publishing house.

"Rico, I know you're not going to like this, but I gotta go in alone." I disclosed it at the last minute while tightening the knee brace.

"Man, damn," Rico said in disgust. "Ain't no way I'm gonna let yo' cripple ass go in there like that." He gestured at my knee.

We drove around the block again.

"Rico, you don't have a choice. We can't stash the van. The locals won't hesitate to the call cops around here. We can't take the risk."

"Look at you. Man, you can barely walk."

"I'll make do. Remember how you showed up, caving that CIA cat's skull in?"

He said nothing.

"If you had gone with me, the cat would've had all three of us buried out there. I need you to hang back, baby. I'll be fine."

"I don't like this, Wiz."

"Our mothers used to give us castor oil when we were shorties. We didn't like that crap either, but it was good for us." Light split the shadows every time we drove under streetlights.

"Are you retarded, Wiz? This ain't castor oil, guy. You get caught up in Geechie's crib, you won't make it to see Highnoon." A stupid look cut across Rico's grill. He couldn't believe that he'd made reference to the contract that would take his best friend away from him. "Wiz, I'm so— "

"Don't even worry about it." I patted his shoulder. "We're brothers, man. Nothing's gonna stop that. Not even death. Rico, man, I love you."

"Why you doin' this, man?" He wiped at his eyes.

"What?"

"This soap opera moment. You know I'm no good with words."

"I know. Now drive up in front Geechie's crib, bitch!" A Kool-Aid smile replaced his melancholy one.

"Whatever, nigga. I got yo' bitch hanging."

"Hangin' no lower than a poodle's."

Our laughter was short lived when we pulled in front of the house. Rico reached into his waistband. "Here, man. Take this." He handed me his pistol.

"If you got God in your corner, He's all you need." With that said, I opened the door, limping badly into the Antarctic blast. Cold. Just plain cold. My sister was in this house. I could feel her. And there was no way I was gonna leave without her.

Whoops!

I forgot something. I limped back to the van and Rico handed me the bag.

"Get lost. But stay tight," I told him. I tried not to put too much weight on my right leg. When I did, excruciating pain made my chest hairs grow that much longer.

The cold was on my face. My knee was full of pain. I stepped into the mouth of the shadows. Not much to lose, but so much to gain.

TEMPEST

was so weak from dehydration. Couldn't remember the last time I'd had something to drink—or eat for that matter. I didn't know how much longer I could put up with his hellish torture. Since I wasn't permitted to wash my ass, the smell between my legs and armpits emitted a pungent odor. It seemed like he only let me out of my dungeon at night to pee—and God…forcing himself on me. Tears ran down both cheeks mixing with the snot from my nose. I was surrounded by darkness. All four sides. Closing in like wicked walls wielded by a deranged whacko.

The cliché about not being able to see my hands in front of my face was an understatement. I couldn't see a damn thing. The murky darkness didn't permit it, and neither did the restraints. My hands were tightly bound behind my back. My every movement caused the phone cord to cut into my flesh. I wanted to yell, but the gag over my mouth cut short my cries. Wanted to stand, but those same phone cords restrained my feet as well. I'd been raped repeatedly and thrown naked into a walk-in closet. Terrified, I shivered in the shadows. My back to the door. Imagination running wild. We stared face-to-face, darkness and I. Two familiar enemies. Old foes reacquainted with each other—Geechie's foul ass acting as common ground.

The very same darkness I feared as a child was now trying to have its way with my fears. It was strange how sitting in a dark closet could refuel those childhood urban legends, the ones about how hands could reach through a sinister dark pocket of the closet and pull me through.

My imagination brushed across my naked flesh. I cried into the makeshift gag made from my panties. But right about now, I had to put my own fears on the back burner. I'd lost track of time. Didn't know what time it had been when Geechie was last on top and forcing himself in me while bragging into my ear about how he'd gone to the shop and hurt my husband. I cried as he feverishly pumped, yelling out as he climaxed at how my husband had begged him to stop beating him.

I can't remember the last time I'd prayed so much. Was wondering if God was listening. I prayed for my husband. My mother. I prayed for my brothers, but most of all I prayed for my father. If God could get a hold to him one good time, Poppa Jones could be used as the cornerstone to get our family back together.

All of my hope was quickly overshadowed by reality. Geechie was my new master. And unless I could get him off my back, I would never feel the many pleasures of a close, loving family. How could I be happy, running drugs into the prison for Geechie? Tears flowed like Niagara Falls. I cried and prayed until I developed a splitting head-ache. My husband. How could God forgive me for what I'd done? My husband was probably lying in the hospital right now because of my inability to keep my legs closed.

I promised myself life without strife if I would ever see the light of day again. So many things I'd do differently. My marriage was probably over, though. Geechie had made sure of it. I couldn't blame it all on him. It took two to tango.

The surge of energy rushing through my body was unexplainable. Desperate energy. I had to get away. I wanted out. And right now! I took advantage of nobody being home. I banged my head, shoulder and whatever else I could use to tear the door down. I wasn't going out like this. Had just made up with Wisdom.

I wanted out!

Out!

Out!

"Out!" I cried into my panties. I bumped harder.

Eventually somebody would hear me.

WISDOM

What in the blue hell, I thought listening to the loud, intense bumping resonating from the inside of the house.

The old mental light bulb popped on. There were no motion detectors on the inside. That meant that the alarm hadn't been activated. Po-Po would've been out by now if the alarm had been tripped.

I limped around back. Couldn't believe my eyes. This schmuck had a full basketball court, tennis court and a covered, Olympic-size swimming pool. All this from selling drugs to his own people. This fool was only adding to the yoke that had been placed on black folks four hundred years ago.

From the looks of things, I'd say nobody was home. I still didn't know what the bumping noise was, but at this point, I didn't care. It was a page from my own book. I put down the bag, grabbing a cold, hard brick from his garden; put some hip into it and threw with all my might.

I watched the brick sail through the air, smashing, crumbling up as it hit the patio glass doors. Nothing. I guessed the brick had been victimized by Old Man Winter, or this fool was into bootlegging bricks. Don't know, but wasn't gonna stand there scratching my head.

The heavy aluminum lawn chair caught my eyes. I picked the thing up, straining a wee-bit, and tried to put some hip into it. Absentmindedly, I stepped down hard on the wrong leg and dropped like I'd been hit by Mike Tyson. Had fallen so fast the chair seemed to hang in the air, defying gravity, suspended in animation. When gravity regained composure, the chair came crashing down on my body. I didn't even scream. Just lay there holding my knee. I was on the ground again. A very familiar place. It was cold and could be harshly cruel upon impact. Before this mission, I'd never laid on the ground so much.

I prayed for a Vicodin, one million milligrams of it. An overdose was welcomed right now. The bumping coming from inside the house had picked up since the brick had been effectively smashed into the window.

Curiosity drove me to my feet. Rose up like a creature from the Black Lagoon. I hobbled and picked the chair up. This time I summoned all the power my upper body could generate, swinging it and standing back. I watched as the chair coasted through the air, but this time striking pay dirt. The window shattered, and pieces fell to the ground like diamonds raining from heaven. I quickly scanned the yard to see if the screaming glass merited curious neighbors.

None that I could see. The thumping was pretty urgent now. Almost like an SOS. It could've been a cry for help, but I wasn't gonna let my guard down. That thump could be anything: a carpenter trying to finish up a job—not really hearing the glass—or it was just possible that some goon of a jacker could've been inside working over Geechie's spot. I didn't know. Had no clue.

I grabbed my bag of goodies and entered the violated threshold. Inside was as dark as a harlot's heart. This was my second time breaking and entering. The first had prompted me to pack a flashlight this time. Slowly but surely, my criminal instincts were resurfacing. I'd done a lot of things as a teen that I wasn't proud of. Those things were now tapping me on the shoulder. I couldn't remember the name of the song or the singer, but it seemed fitting for my reemergence with my dark side: "Hello, darkness, my old friend."

I snickered, bringing up the beam of light.

The knocking was starting to lose bite. Fading like a haircut. I was in the living room. The beam of light revealed the room's very expensive contents. The schmuck's living room reminded me of the homes on *MTV Cribs*. The enormous flat-screen mounted to the wall was pretty sweet. I could've had a crib like this if that jerk Pogo hadn't busted my knee. But that dog didn't hunt anymore. Especially behind the ass whooping I'd laid on him at the ball court a week ago.

I went into the bag and brought out the ski mask. I slipped it on, looking like an extremely large cat burglar.

I limped through the darkness following behind the

beam of light. All sorts of thoughts tried to blindfold my senses. I had to put those demons to rest right now. I was in unfamiliar territory. Anything could happen. The darkness could grow arms and attack me.

The bright beam of light melted the darkness, blazing a pathway through the thick forest of gloom.

Maria was trying to dance my mind away from the task, but I had to switch dance partners. I started dancing with the lady of focus, stanky-legging with concentration.

My beam swept across the contents of the kitchen. I assumed the door near the pantry let out into the garage. Two sets of car keys hung from the rack on the wall near a nice-sized stainless steel refrigerator. I took both pairs, opening the door. The door led to the garage all right. An *NCIS: Los Angeles*, LL Cool J-style black Dodge Challenger and a Yukon Denali sat in the three-car garage. A covered motorcycle sat in the third bay.

Bump, bump, bump.

The sound pulled me back on the pathway with destiny.

A long hallway stretched from the kitchen. I was assuming that the four closed doors—two on each side— belonged to bedrooms. The thumping came from the last one. No doubt the master suite. My knee was blazing with pain, a four-alarm fire of agony. I hobbled to the door, slowly opening it.

The master bedroom. Something bumped behind me. I was ready to swing the flashlight. I inwardly laughed as the big, furry cat came to me, meowing and licking my boot. This fool was supposed to be a big dog. How could a big dog keep company with a cat?

Punk!

I swept the light through the room. So far there were no signs of my sister. The knocking was coming from the closet. Loud and clear. My heart skipped beats, praying for my thoughts to be heard. I painfully limped over the threshold. The master bedroom was laid out. A lair fit for royalty. The California King looked like it could sleep ten. Another huge flat-screen was mounted on the wall in front of the bed. The punk had a player's pad. The golden stripper's pole off in the corner was a proven fact.

Bump...thump...bump.

Directly in front of the closet door, I inhaled deeply. My pulse pounded like that of a Triple Crown thoroughbred.

I dropped the bag and placed a sweaty palm on the door knob. I could hear my heart beating savagely in my ears. I slowly turned the knob, not knowing what to expect. As a naked body rolled out, I stepped down hard on the wrong leg, trying to get the hell out of the way. The flashlight flew from my hand.

The light hit the carpet, spinning a few times, the beam coming to rest on my sister's terrified face. She was gagged by panties and hogtied with phone cord like a wild animal. Tears mixed with her snot—but the body odor—damn! She smelled like Ody-yu-di-day. Her long, black hair was matted to her face by sweat and tears.

The bruises on her mug angered me to new heights. I considered a man to be a coward if he put his hands on a woman. It really got my goat when guys roughed up dames. Especially when that dame happened to be my sister.

Tempest was scared. Shaking. Trembling. She didn't know what to make of me.

I gathered the light, trying hard to steady my voice.

"Don't be afraid of me," I said in the same deep voice I'd used on my father. "I'm here to help."

Tempest stopped trembling, but her eyes still held a frightened look. I could tell it would take more than mere words to gain her trust. After all, I did have a ski mask on, and I wasn't the average-size jacker. Removing my jacket, I covered her nakedness.

I gently removed the gag.

"Who are you?" she asked, tears still streaming down her face. I could tell that she'd been through a lot. Her loud, musky scent told me that Geechie hadn't allowed her to shower. Right then and there, Geechie's fate had been sealed. The bruises on her face alerted me. They had all the signs of rape. Oh yeah, Geechie had to leave this earth. If not by my hands, then by someone else's. This goon couldn't continue to terrorize my sister, or any other woman for that matter.

"Who I am is not important," I said, untying her restraints, growing angrier by the moment. "I've been sent here to help you."

"Thank you. I thought you were another one of Geechie's thugs come to…" Her voice trailed off with humiliation, her eyes dropped to the floor. "I'm hungry and terribly thirsty. Can I have some water?"

It took a lot of grunting and foul words under my breath but I accomplished a normal stride. To really sell this line of jive, I really wanted to come off like God had sent me. And I couldn't do this if I showed weakness. So I sucked it up, walking into the master bathroom.

This punk even had Dixie cups in his potpourri-scented bathroom.

What a vicious killer, I thought.

I backed out, handing my sister the water. Ol' girl drained it like she'd just been rescued from floating for weeks on the ocean in a life raft.

"Thank you."

"No thanks needed," I said. "I've been sent here by God. You've been saved this time. God has a plan for you. But you need to stay out of trouble. That means no more adultery."

She made the face of someone that thought they were the only ones holding a secret.

"Yes, the Boss sees everything. Straighten your ways. Try and work things out with your husband. Live a decent life." I removed a pair of car keys from my pocket and handed them to her. "Because if you don't, the next time I see you, it will be for punishment."

Tempest took the keys. To my surprise she hugged my

waist. That threw me. I didn't know what to think. My mind clicked with different scenarios. Had she been able to sense that the masked man standing before her was her brother? I didn't know but her eyes held confirmation that she'd gotten the message. Whether the message carrier was immortal or mortal.

"Quickly," I said and broke the embrace, still disguising my voice. "There's a Dodge these keys belong to. Take it and get out of here."

She moved to leave.

"By the way, don't go to the police about this. Geechie will be punished."

I followed behind her, my beam ushering her to the garage. No more words were passed. My sister stepped behind the door. Seconds later I heard the garage door go up, followed by the engine humming to life.

I was limping back in the direction of the bag when I heard the Dodge roar out of the garage. My sister was on her way to a brand new life in Christ. Of that I was sure.

Geechie had violated my sister. He deserved to die. Plain and simple. And since I didn't have the right to take another man's life, I removed the spray paint can from the bag. I sprayed the master bedroom walls, spraying with my right, holding the light with my left. I repeated the same task in the living room, kitchen and garage.

When I finally limped out of the broken patio doors, I made sure that Geechie knew that Highnoon owned the Detroit Underworld.

The biting, cold winds outside let me know I had an equipment problem. My generosity had cost me a coat. And thanks to Malisa, I didn't have another. I had no business thinking the thought, but I hoped that she would get caught in the middle of a Crips and Blood war and receive a cap in the caboose.

I limped from the patio, removed the mask, then left all that other crap inside. I figured when Geechie found out that Highnoon had been behind the break-in, he wouldn't involve cops. There would be no fingerprinting. I chuckled as the little gray cat stepped out on the patio, glass crunching underneath its tiny little paws.

"Bring it on," I quietly spoke into the cell.

Within seconds, Rico pulled the mail van up like he was a valet.

Limping, I crawled into the van and the night swallowed us.

Tick, tock. I could feel death coming in the air—yeah, getting closer.

Two down, two more trifling souls to go.

TIME TO PAY THE PIPER

After the incident with the Rottweiler, Jordan should've never wanted to see another dog again. The dog attack had completely torn open his left hand and was responsible for Jordan having to receive fifty-three stitches to close him up. Aside from a tetanus shot and a painful round of rabies injections, the canine had come within a tooth away from severing a major nerve that would've rendered Jordan's left hand useless.

With all of the pain that he was experiencing, the hand might as well have been useless because he couldn't go out and get his hustle on. Every time he tried, the pain was immense and throbbed with every beat of his heart. The doctor at Beaumont Hospital had given him a prescription for Vicodin. But it was useless as well. The prescription took money to fill and the last time he'd checked, a crack addict was a full-time, sweatshop occupation that didn't offer a 401k or a health benefits package. Having every workable body part on deck was the only benefits package that a guy like him could depend on. Crack would be the alternate pain medication. Being down one hand, there was no way in hell that he was going out into the snow and cold to attempt a robbery to get some. The lick hadn't gone down so well the last time, and he had been working with two good hands that night. If the bitch hadn't had the dog with her, Jordan wouldn't be sitting in Monique's apartment in severe pain.

His cracked-out girlfriend, Monique, hadn't been the same since Popeye had turned his rage loose on her to extract Jordan's whereabouts. The detective had beaten her face into hamburger. It was the closest that she had ever come to death, and it frightened her—frightened her to the point where she had reconciled the crumbling relationship with her mother and enrolled in a drug treatment program. For support, Monique chose to move in with her mother until she completed the program. But she still kept her apartment. She'd sustained some serious injuries during the beating. They had been so extensive that she was receiving a monthly disability check. It was enough to pay the rent and keep the lights on.

With Popeye banging on every door in the ghetto trying to catch him, Jordan was running out of places to hide. It wasn't the smartest move in using Monique's crib to escape the below zero temperatures, but it was the only chance he had to avoid frostbite. Jordan had keys to her place and was free to come and go as he pleased. Besides, Monique was at her mother's house in Romulus, Michigan, and wouldn't be home for a couple of days. He wasn't a fool; Jordan knew that Popeye had around-the-clock surveillance on the apartment. That's why he'd crept up to the third floor by using the back stairway. Yeah, he was playing it close, but Jordan had plans to vacate the premises before morning light.

The dog attack had come with brutalizing paranoia and a burning curiosity to know a little bit more about the nature of man's best friend. The raggedy twenty-seven-inch color TV sitting on a stack of yellow pages in the middle of a semi-empty living room was tuned to the Nat Geo Wild channel. *Dog Whisperer with Cesar Millan* was on, but Jordan's hand had him in far too much agony to pay attention. The pain had started a couple of days ago and now was unbearable. The swelling was a dangerous indication that infection had set in. Without immediate medical attention, the doctors had explained to him that the potential for losing his hand greatly increased. There was nothing he could do about it tonight.

Jordan sat uncomfortably in a mangy, moth-eaten armchair, wishing that he had a package of his little white god to dull the raw pains from the troubling siblings of physical and mental reality. His plan, once he'd stepped foot out of the emergency ward after the dog attack, was to score a Greyhound ticket and head to New York. He hadn't counted on the debilitating condition of his hand getting in the way at putting in his brand of work to acquire funding for purchase.

Jordan was sitting bent at the waist with his head between his knees, right hand locked around the left wrist and rocking side-to-side to cope with the pain—when the front door of the apartment exploded into flying wood splinter projectiles. Jordan nearly shitted himself when he saw Popeye step through what was left of the door. He thawed from the fear long enough to make a break for the bedroom, not even seeing five other plainclothes cops file in behind Popeye. Jordan would rather jump from a third-floor window and risk sudden death than face the worst that the detective had to offer.

"Come back here, you fucking crackhead!" Popeye yelled at Jordan's fleeing back. "I'll make sure you never touch anybody's mother again, you piece of shit!"

Jordan had the window raised, the cold air blowing in, with one foot dangling from the ledge, when it felt like he was pulled back inside by a million pairs of hands. He felt the first punch, but everything after that was nothing but numbness.

WISDOM

FRIDAY, DAY FIVE...

"Ouch," I yelled, "not so hard."

"It looks pretty bad—all big and swollen." Rico examined us from his chair.

"Do this hurt?" Maria looked up at me with a smirk on her face.

"Actually, that feels good."

"Papi, you should be more careful." Maria advised.

"If he let his boy help in some of this mess," Rico butted in, shoving a forkful of pancakes in his pie hole, "he wouldn't be so banged up."

"Aw, here we go again. Listen, you short, light-skinned Floyd 'Money' Mayweather wannabe. I told you why it had to go down like that."

"Pacquiao will dust Mayweather—call me the Pacman, chump." Rico blazed back.

"Wisdom, relax." Maria ordered calmly. She was massaging my bruised and swollen knee. I sat in a chair in her kitchen. She sat on the floor, rubbing away with that green rubbing alcohol.

"How's your head?" she asked with an angelic smile on her face.

I tenderly rubbed the bandage on my forehead.

"Hurts a little."

"It should hurt, too." Rico cut loose again. "Should serve as a reminder that you do have friends who want to help!" The punk was sipping on a glass of orange juice and started choking.

"Uh huh—now, down the wrong pipe. Bet you'll shut up now," I ribbed, smiling.

Rico was coughing so hard, juice exploded from his nose.

"Wisdom, you just going to let him choke to death?" Maria walked over to Rico and asked, lightly patting him on the back. She handed him some Kleenex.

We'd come to Maria's in the dead of morning. Even though her voice had been slumbering with sleep, she didn't resist. She'd welcomed us with open arms.

After I'd gotten a stern five-minutes worth of scolding, Maria drew me a bath and washed my clothes. The girl knew no strangers. She treated Rico like he was family. Her house was small, but she made room. Maria had fixed the couch up for my homeboy. She only had two bedrooms—one being an office.

I hadn't objected to her sleeping in the king with me. The lady was classy. I liked that about her. She slept at the head of the bed and me at the foot. The size of the bed kept us from touching. I had to fight back the impulse to grab her, hold on for dear life. It had been a while since I'd made love to a woman, a real woman for that matter.

Not a Malisa, but a Maria.

About an hour ago, when I was in the bathroom brushing my teeth, Rico had stuck his head through the door and gave me the old thumbs up sign on Maria. But who couldn't like a woman like her: considerate, kind, caring and understanding. Pretty easy to handle. So much unlike that broad who had exhaled while barbecuing my rags. Malisa had been the complete opposite: gold-digger, ungrateful, liar—a deceitful, backstabbing Jezebel. I had more, but why go on. Maria had awakened extra early this morning. She ironed my clothes and fixed a breakfast fit for a king.

The instinct to fall in love with this lady was put in check by the cold reality of a future without me.

I could love her. Oh, God—how I could love her. In just a short time, she'd awakened something in me that had been lying dormant ever since Caliba.

Robbery. It was highway robbery. I was a little bitter at God for allowing this lady to come into my life at the wrong time. But one thing I did get from Poppa Jones' Sunday sermon was that everything happened for a reason. I was curious to see how this would turn out.

"Maria, I want to thank you for this wonderful breakfast." Rico complimented her. "Unlike my lifelong pal over there, you really know how to make a person feel wanted."

Maria smiled pleasantly. "Thank you." She playfully sat on my lap. "Any friend of Wisdom's is a friend of mine."

Maria was wearing a thick, navy blue housecoat and fuzzy bunny slippers. Her silky hair was pulled back in a ponytail. The girl was a natural woman. No makeup. Definitely not one of those that had to rush in the bathroom to throw on a face before anybody could gaze at them first thing in the morning.

"Yeah. Thank you, Maria. Don't know where I'd be without you," I said, hugging her. She felt good inside my embrace. Baby oil scented her hair.

"Alright." Rico barked, sipping orange juice. "Cut that crap out. What I wanna know is where do we go from here? I mean, reforming Zoo and trying to catch Jordan is gonna be a tall order. The boy got moves. He left your ass in the dust."

I rubbed my knee. "Left in the dust is an understatement."

"Wisdom," Maria said, kissing me on the cheek. "Do you have everything you want? I'm gonna go make the beds."

She popped up from my lap.

"Yes, mommie, I'm cool."

"You boys behave while I'm gone."

Rico watched Maria walk out the kitchen, a sneaky smile on his light-skinned grill. He looked back at me and then craned his neck around the corner to see if she was out of earshot.

"Nice," he said while laughing. "I like her, Wiz." He picked up his glass of juice. "Besides our mamas, I ain't never seen one of these modern day women go out for a guy like this." He pointed at the feast spread over the table.

"Yeah. She is special." I was trying to eat something, but knowing when and where I was due to be executed made eating was the last thing on my mind.

"You think Tempest gonna go straight?" he asked.

"We did our part, man. That's up to her, but the look in her eyes said that she was gonna taking her wedding vows more seriously. I just hope Geechie bites the bait."

"Did you really spray paint a message from Highnoon on Geechie's wall, giving him the actual address of where Highnoon will be?" My boy's voice dropped a little with heavy emotion. The thought of me going through with it had him almost in tears.

"Yep. Among other things."

"Like what?"

"I want to pit one against the other. Get 'em paranoid. Like one is trying to move in on the other. Make it look like Highnoon is trying to rub out all competition. Set up a meeting so they could talk things over. No reason why they can't split the city down the middle to coexist. But they would need to meet to iron out details."

"Same place, huh?"

"Yup. Same place Highnoon has arranged my farewell party. I also warned Geechie that he had a snake in his family."

"Snake?" Rico asked, but really not liking where the plan was going.

"I told Geechie that Yazoo was the serpent in his garden.

Played it up like Yazoo was a hired gun sent in to penetrate Geechie's family. But instead of going along with the hit, he fell in love with the riches and defected."

Rico stood up so fast the chair rocked on its hind legs, making a screeching sound. "What the hell is wrong with you? Did that bump on the head give you brain damage?"

"Sit down," I said, waiting for this clown to take his seat. "Hear me out first before you go off on the deep end."

He took his seat, looking at me like my head was spinning and I was spewing vomit.

"I don't know, Wiz. That's playing it awfully close. If you ask me, I think that's pretty risky, puttin' Zoo's life at stake. How do you know Geechie won't just rock Zoo's cradle before the meeting?"

"Left it like Highnoon would pay big dollars to have his top operative back. Now Geechie's a businessman before anything—won't pass up no loot. Of course, Zoo would have to be present at the meeting before they could start discussing business."

"Still risky."

"Geechie is gonna kill my brother. And if you got any ideas, let me hear 'em. If you don't, then it's going down," I said, playing in my eggs. The pain in my knee had downgraded to a level four. Still difficult to walk on, but tolerable.

"Wisdom." Maria called from in the living room.

I looked at Rico. "I'll be back."

Maria's living room was decorated. Couch, loveseat, end

tables. Her most prized possession was an old piano parked in the corner.

Black and white photos of her relatives hung on walls and shelves. A huge portrait of a blond-haired, blue-eyed Jesus hung over the fireplace.

Maria was sitting on the arm of the loveseat, looking out the window.

"It's not easy for me to stand by and let somebody I care about die," she said, still peeping out.

I walked behind her and placed my hand on her shoulder. My nose began to run.

"That's a nice picture." I pointed to the portrait over the fireplace. I wasn't caught up on color, but my race, for many decades had been fed a steady diet of Jesus Christ being a blond, blue-eyed Messiah.

"How's your faith?" I asked.

"My faith?"

"Yep."

"I have faith." She still gazed out of the window.

"Let God do His will," I said, sniffling.

"It's not fair," she said, finally turning from the window. Her angelic face was engrossed by worry.

I pulled her to her feet and sat her on the sofa. I parked my big butt on a wooden end table directly across from her. The slight tingling inside my throat was the last thing I needed right now.

"I've been thinking. I believe I have a way out of this mess."

I saw her face lift with relief.

"But it would be just as dangerous as me honoring Highnoon's contract."

It pained me to watch her hopes and dreams burn.

"My plan is to pit the dealers against each other. Fool both. Get Highnoon thinking that Geechie is planning a massive take over on his city. Make Geechie believe that Highnoon is eliminating threats, and future rivals. And his name just so happens to be next on Highnoon's hit list." The sudden rush of heat made me itch. I looked back at the thermostat on the wall to see if Maria had the heat on *Hell*.

"You okay?" she asked.

"Fine"—I was still looking back at the thermostat, scratching—"What do you have the heat on?"

"Seventy-five," she answered. "Why?"

"Gettin' a little hot in here." I coughed just as Maria felt my forehead.

"You're burning up," she revealed. I heard the side door open and slam. Guessed Rico had gone to the van.

"I'm serious." I tried to front. "I'm fine."

"You don't feel fine," Maria replied. She got up quickly and left the room, her fuzzy slippers hopping down the bunny trail.

Pictures on the mantle caught my attention, and so did a hot chill through my flesh. I picked up the picture. The photo of Paco and his gang needed no special introduction. It was probably a good thing that I would have no future with Maria. Mexicans were hard-pressed on revenge. If I could somehow survive this mess, somewhere down the line Paco and his punks would come for retribution. I knew I would, after the beating I'd laid on them in the parking lot that night. I laughed as sweat beaded my forehead, thinking about how Paco would come for me on our wedding day. Picture it: me bucking with one of the groomsmen. That would be a sight to behold.

"Sit down," Maria ordered.

I was starting to become infatuated at this little honey bossing me around.

"Stick this under your tongue." Maria shoved the thermometer under my tongue before I could object. "Hold it there for a moment."

The side door opened and slammed urgently this time. Rico stood in the archway. A very frightened, stupid look strained his face. He was holding my old cell.

"We don't have to find Jordan," he mentioned.

"Why not?" I asked, but not really wanting to know the answer.

He looked me straight in the eyes. "Because Popeye did."

The thermometer fell from my lips.

My frying pan-sized hands gripped the steering wheel so intensely my knuckles were turning different shades.

Had my foot so far off in the gas, my ankle was acting an ass. Hot chills surged through my body. My head still ached from being formally introduced to that dumpster I'd run into chasing Jordan. My clothes had gone up in flames, and I was developing a nasty cough.

But my ultimate humiliation came as I stared down at my flooding wrist. Maria—God bless her soul—felt sorry for me and let me wear one of Paco's coats. Paco was a fat bastard who had never missed a sit-down meal at the dinner table, and the sucka had short arms. His coat on me made it look like I was wearing a short sleeve jacket. Fruity colors atrociously decorated the thing. It wasn't a good look.

"Man, you look like a box of crayons," Rico joked after I'd first slipped on the jacket.

My friend sat in the passenger seat of the mail van with a silent look of horror on his mug. No doubt thinking about Jordan. Rico had been Jordan's favorite. As a kid, instead of following behind me, Jordan would cry if he couldn't follow Rico. The two had remained almost inseparable until Jordan had found out the special purpose for his third leg. The discovery led to the immediate dismissal of the super, skin-tight bond the two shared.

Divine intervention was the only way I could describe Rico finding the cell I thought I'd lost while chasing Jordan in the van. If he hadn't found it, Poppa Jones wouldn't have gotten through to leave a text and voice-mail message. He wouldn't say how badly Jordan was hurt.

Just said that it wasn't good. And before Jordan had passed out, he'd mumbled a cell number. Guess that so happened to be the old man's.

I could only think the worst. Just remembering how Popeye had done a number on Jordan's girlfriend, Monique, sent shockwaves of terror tingling up my spine.

The freeway was one big blur. Hadn't remembered taking it. The only thing I could remember was turning up into the entrance of Mercy General Hospital. A place of horror stories, horrible health care, limited funds, thin staff, very little security, and the highest emergency room death rate of any in the nation. Junkies prowled the lobbies and thieving nurses went through the pockets of the comatose.

I barked a dry cough and limped across the parking lot. I wasn't feeling good at all. I had a too-little coat on with nothing on my head. I'd learned that valuable heat escaped through an uncovered head in the wintertime. Didn't have time to think about myself. I'd have plenty time to sleep when I was dead. With that in mind, I limped on, Rico at my side. He still hadn't broken his code of silence. Worry lines were embedded deeply on his forehead. If I knew Rico, the kid had painful punishment in mind for the Pig who'd perpetrated a fiendish act of police brutality. Popeye had laid his hands on the wrong one.

We entered through the emergency room doors. And right into a warzone of a lobby. The place was crammed.

Sick people everywhere. Chairs were limited. People lay out on the floor. Stab victims held pressure on their wounds. Gunshot victims lay on gurneys lining the ward walls like they were being mass produced from an assembly line of violence.

Who in the city could be this damn mad?

"Jordan Jones?" I asked a big walrus of a nurse at the nurse's station. The sister was working on the computer, ignoring the hell out of me, popping the hell out of some gum.

That's when the little bulldog by my side went off; pounding the desk so hard her computer shook.

"Bitch, you heard the man," Rico growled, showing teeth.

She cut her eyes at Rico and popped her gum extra loud. The fat broad grabbed a clipboard and flipped through pages.

"No need to get nasty. He's in three"—she popped her gum—"C."

"Get some real help in this dump," Rico yelled over his shoulder.

"Whatever," she remarked sarcastically.

In a hospital with minimal security, the fat broad knew she didn't want any part of a pissed off Rico.

Pops had been the first to arrive. He was standing outside the room with a black leather Bible in hand. He was wearing a warm-up suit, sneakers and a heavy coat. The old man shook his head like Jordan was in bad shape.

"Son, it doesn't look good," he warned.

"Who?" I tried to ask.

"Before he passed out, the nurse said he mumbled my phone number and kept calling out Popeye."

"Tempest come down yet?"

"Nope. Just me."

I bit down on my lip hard to suppress the urge to kill.

"Don't go looking for trouble. I have Sharpton on speed dial. I can have a protest underway within a few hours. This detective is not gonna get away with this. I know the police chief and we—"

I pushed past him. "You do it your way and I will handle it mine," I said over my shoulder, taking a seat in a chair a few wards down. I looked at Rico. "You go in before me, brah."

Rico acknowledged Pops before walking in.

I couldn't bear to look at Jordan first. As Rico stepped inside, I scanned the hallways. The sounds of the sick and dying haunted the corridors. Dim lighting picked up faint traces of dried blood droplets on the floor.

Rico stumbled out not minutes before going in, almost in tears.

"Popeye's gonna die behind this," he said to nobody in particular, his eyes glossy, glazed over with murder. I don't think he even noticed me.

I slowly rose from the chair. It was my time to go in. I walked by Pops and he immediately dropped his head and started praying.

Butterflies flew through my stomach with every forced step. I pushed myself inside. Upon seeing him, I wished I hadn't. Jordan was clinging to life on some machine that was breathing for him. Tubes ran out of him like he was some kind of switchboard. IVs hung overhead. Machines beeped, monitored and dispensed.

I'd seen a few pictures of Emmett Till; Jordan's head was just as swollen. My brother's head was twice its normal size. White bandages circled the top of his cranium. Both eyes were swollen shut. Lips looked like chopped liver. His chin had been bandaged as well. Tears entered my eyes. Anger moved into my heart. Revenge just down the block. Rage around the corner.

How could this stuff keep on happening? How could God continue to keep this carousel of madness going? The more I put in, the less I was getting out.

"I was supposed to be there to protect you," I whispered. Tears started falling like the first signs of rain. Light at first, and then the eventual downpour.

I coughed into my hand, away from the bed. My brother had enough problems. He didn't need what bug that was now resting and rooting inside my body.

I'm not lying. If the bed chart at the foot of the bed didn't have my brother's name on it, I probably would've gone back down to the nurse's station and beaten some pounds off the whale for sending me to the room of a circus freak. This didn't look nowhere near the dude I'd chased through the ghetto last night.

Denial had me seeking out a childhood scar on Jordan's chest for confirmation. I didn't want to, but I gently pulled the covers back. I cried more because he didn't even flinch. No sensory activity. Zero reflexes. He looked like a stuffed dummy lying up here.

Why?

I kind of got confused when I saw a king-sized bandage covering his entire chest. Tears of curiosity pushed me to explore. Carefully peeling back the bandage, I cupped my hands over my mouth in horror. With one hand, I continued removing. Cuts were everywhere. It wasn't until I had the entire bandage pulled down that I noticed his chest had been used as a message board. The raw cuts made a statement. Served as a warning to all those who opposed the crooked cop.

Through the antibiotic lubricant glistening on Jordan's wounds, I read the fleshy message. "Finally got you" had been carved into his chest. Despite the pain in my knee, and my straight jacket of a coat, I dropped to my knees.

Finally found you!

Poor Jordan. He'd undergone extensive pain. The kind of pain nobody should ever have to endure. I hadn't approved of him smoking crack, but I only hoped that he was high at the time of this happening.

Finally found you!

I wiped my running nose with the back of my hand. My flesh was so hot that it felt like brimstone was attached to my back.

It took a real sicko to hold another man down while a psycho whacked away like he was cutting up raw chicken. The idea of more than one attacker came clearly to my mind. A few people had to have held my brother in order for this maniac to accomplish this—probably other dirty cops. I wanted them all—I coughed dramatically into my hands. Everybody who was involved would pay.

Vengeance is mine, says the Lord. God forgive me, but I'm sending these psychos to You ahead of time for Judgment.

Finally found you!

Tears dripped until my eyes were dry. I felt helpless. My brother didn't have any money or insurance. Mercy General was nowhere to be with severe injuries like these. I'd been in this room for at least thirty minutes and hadn't seen hide nor hair of a nurse or anyone remotely close to resembling a doctor. To give my brother a fighting chance, I had to get him moved to another hospital. And the only man with that kind of cheese and power, I'd saved a couple of nights ago.

I walked out into the hallway to have that discussion with Poppa Jones. My dad didn't put up any resistance. He'd been at Momma's bedside when the nurse had called him. Poppa Jones said that she was sleeping. He didn't wake her. Just crept out. I was impressed. The reverend had been at Momma's bedside after almost getting the business from the business-end of the former CIA goon's Glock. We didn't have time for chitchat. The man made a few phone calls, getting the ball rolling.

Pops was outraged, screaming that the mayor would hear about this latest act of police brutality.

Yeah, I thought. Mayor Thomas would hear about this all right. But instead of the good reverend being the vessel carrying the news, I intended for *The Detroit News* to bear the news, front page, big bold letters, too: "Police Officer Found Slain." Kind of hoped that the mayor would be drinking his morning coffee when this headline hit him in the cranium.

After I collected Rico, cussed out a few of the hospital doctors, and one inebriated ambulance driver, Jordan was on his way to Mount Saint Helens. The hospital that still held Tempest's husband, Darrius.

Finally found you!

Just one week had taken a toll on my family members. The list ran like that of a church list for the sick and shut in: My momma—My Lady Memorial. Darrius—Mount Saint Helens. Jordan—Mount Saint Helens. And eventually: Geechie, Popeye and Highnoon—Cape Hope Cemetery.

The doctors at Mount Saint Helens didn't waste any time. Jordan had an extensive battery of tests done. Bloodwork, CT scan. The knife wound to his left side—which I didn't see at the other hospital, required a trip to the operating table. They immediately put him on an IV antibiotic for an infection that had set up in his left hand from a wound of some kind.

Surprisingly, Jordan's CT scan had come back negative. The blood in his stool would need further examination.

I left when Pops' prayer warriors started filing into the room and surrounded my brother's bed.

Not much more I could do, so Rico and I went down to see how Darrius was making out. Tempest was at his bedside. Darrius looked the worse for wear. You could tell that he'd been given a good beating. His left arm was in a long-arm cast, but he seemed to be in a jovial mood.

"I can't go up to see him, Wisdom," Tempest explained, crying, burying her face into my chest.

"He's gonna pull through." I comforted her, not even believing myself. "You'll see."

Rico played the background. Tempest didn't like him that much. But it wasn't painfully obvious. The two still spoke and greeted each other like long lost siblings. My sister used to blame Rico for all the crap I used to get into.

"How you feeling, Darrius?" I asked.

"Not bad, brother-in-law. Could be better, but not bad." He winced in pain before making an attempt to sit up in the bed. "Doctor says I'm going home today."

"Cool," I responded.

"Wisdom, you don't look too good," Tempest said. "You should go home and get some sleep."

I hated to tell her that I had no home. No clothes, either. I guess she was trying to be polite. I caught her examining my loaner coat throughout our little visit. At some point, Rico excused himself to go make some phone calls.

I stood to say my goodbyes when Tempest asked if she could speak in private.

"Take care of yourself, brother-in-law," I said as Tempest and I headed for the door. We both excused ourselves from the room, resuming the conversation in the hallway.

"Big brother, what's wrong with you?" Tempest asked, sounding more like Momma than herself.

"I wish I could get some sleep," I admitted, coughing into my hands. Could feel my chest tightening. My voice was getting hoarse, too. "How's everything between you and Darrius?"

Her eyes dropped to my boots. "Could be better. We'll get it together, though. He's been through a lot."

"Where'd you disappear to? I'd been calling you," I asked. Even though I knew the answer, I just wanted to examine her face. Any signs of fear.

"Aw...I...I was out of town on some business. That's it." As she stumbled and fumbled over one lie after another, I could see stark terror in her eyes. All the confirmation I needed to see. Job well done.

Finally found you!

"Wisdom, I'm scared. Jordan's close to death. And I..." Her voice trailed off.

"What?" I pushed.

"I'm scared." Tears ran down her chocolate cheeks. "Momma, Jordan, and now you don't look so hot." She felt my forehead. "You feel hot. Maybe you should—"

I waved her off. "I'll take a few aspirin. I'll be cool. But right now I need to go."

Tempest examined the coat once more. But this time, she said, "Wisdom, you need some money?" I was praying like mad that she didn't make the connection. "You know, I have a coat that just so happens to be your size. It's in my truck. This guy left it at my shop. He was just about your build, too."

Sure, I thought—the irony behind her wanting to offer my coat back. I offered a smile. "I'll get it later. I'll see you, sis."

"Take care of yourself, Wisdom," Tempest said to my parting back.

Finally found you!

One of Rico's connections had come through. Operation "Get at Popeye" was in full swing. We'd gotten his home address and paid a shortie to deliver an envelope. From a safe distance, we watched one of Rico's little thugs-in-training ring Popeye's doorbell, drop the envelope and run like greased lightning. The one-eyed son of a bitch stuck his head out of a rancher on Littlefield Street in Detroit, looking around before coming to rest on the envelope. He picked it up and opened it. Through binoculars I could see the punk smile, shaking his head. The stupid expression on his face and the greedy look in his eyes confirmed that the chump would be at the little party I was throwing.

"See you soon, Punkeye," I mumbled.

Finally found you!

"No. I've finally found you, you son of a bitch," I said aloud.

I was laid up over Maria's crib.

"Papi, please take yourself to the hospital," Maria pleaded, but I was too pigheaded to go anywhere. "Your fever is high and you're shaking."

It was now eleven o'clock Friday night. Two days before my so-called agreement would be fulfilled. I bet'cha Highnoon was licking his chops. Sharpening his sword. I had all the pieces in place. All the major players had invitations. This thing was up to the Man upstairs, who would live and who would die.

My coughing was almost nonstop. Full-blown barking, a nasty hoarse, hacking, dry cough. Sweat poured down my head and forehead. Chills freezing me to the bone. My body was seriously aching.

"Just give me a couple of aspirins, some Theraflu and a little rest. I'll be fine."

"Wisdom, you sound like you have pneumonia. Listen to your cough."

After we'd delivered Popeye the party invitation, Rico and I went back to be with Jordan. I'd called Momma from there. She sounded like I was feeling. But if High-noon honored his part of the agreement, she would be up and performing the dance of the Holy Ghost in no time.

"Maria, do you honestly think I really care right about now." I hacked, almost coughing up a lung. "My brother's lying in the hospital with his"—cough—"head almost the size of a car tire. Sunday night could be"—cough—"my last night on this earth. I really don't give a fuck anymore."

"Wisdom, you might be the savior of your family and a first-class saint in my eyes, but don't you use that language in my presence again," Maria said firmly.

I coughed. "I'm sorry, baby. Just got much pressure on my shoulders."

We were lying in Maria's bedroom, my head on her lap. The TV was on but we weren't watching. An old episode of *The Fresh Prince of Bel-Air*. Wasn't paying attention to the juvenile antics of Will and Carlton. Maria was rubbing my head and jaws with tender strokes of passion.

"Okay," she said, smiling again. For a minute there, I thought I'd earned myself a trip to the curb. "I forgive you. And I understand that you have a lot of pressure on you. But I do believe everything will be all right." She tenderly took the back of her hand down my face. I felt like I was about to die, but her caress was giving me a reason to live.

"Baby, I hope my brother makes it. Jordan has to. The kid has a lot of life left. This entire thing is my fault. I could've caught him that day. I could've—"

"Worn your red cape? Papi, you're not Superman. You've been doing your best. Tell you the truth; you've done more than many in this unique situation of yours. I'm sad, but proud of you."

I grabbed her hand, caressing it with mine. "Maria, you've shown me nothing but kindness since I've met you. You have to be the last woman in this world who would deal with a condemned man. Thank you for caring.

And if I get out of this okay, I have plans for rehabbing my knee"—I lifted my left leg—"and getting a tryout with an NBA team. I would like to take you far away from this place."

She blushed, looking around her room. "Nothing's wrong with this place. I think it's the fever talking."

"It's my promise to you."

"How can you talk about playing basketball with this Highnoon person waiting to get"—she swallowed hard—"his revenge?"

I rose up and coughed into my hand. This time I hacked up something yellowish.

"Here," Maria said, handing me some tissue.

"The dream is the only thing I have. Don't take it," I said as I wiped away the slime. I examined it. "This doesn't look good."

"You need to go to the emergency room."

"Don't have time. Where's Rico?"

"Took him home while you were napping. He needed fresh clothes, a shower...sex—his words. He's all torn up over Jordan." Maria touched my cheek. "I'm gonna make you some tea. You could use it." She went to move but I stopped her.

"Maria, I'm sorry."

"For what?"

"Coming into your life so late."

"What makes you think this?"

"I could fall in love with you."

She kissed my hot forehead. "I'll take your temperature."

"Don't worry about that. I don't wanna know. Can't be thinking about that Sunday night." I gently pulled her down on my hot flesh. "Maria, I just want to lay here with you, without thinking about nobody. Can I do that?"

And we did. We held each other until the birds started chirping.

Outside the bedroom window, the sunrise was magnificent. The girl sleeping in my arms was beautiful. She'd been up half the night, trying to nurse me back to health. The Theraflu was helping. I'd sweated a little of the cold out of my chest. My fever had broken, but I still had a cough. The girl had skills. Skills to take care of her man. I kissed her on the forehead. She stirred a little, settling closer to me.

If this was the last morning I had to spend on Earth— I gazed at Maria's beauty—this was how I wanted to spend it.

I whispered, "I like you."

"I like you, too," Maria whispered back without opening her eyes.

I'd finally found you!

WISDOM

SATURDAY, DAY SIX...

The moment came for me to leave. Maria was strong at first, but quickly disintegrated into an emotional outburst of tears.

"Girl…" I caught her face with both hands. "You have to trust me. Be strong. I can't leave you like this."

Maria's tears slowed. She shook her head, holding on to my waist.

"I'll be back. Trust me. We're going to the NBA, mommie. You trust me?" I asked, trying to offer reassurance.

"Yes," she whimpered. "Yes. I believe you."

"Listen. If you don't hear from me, take this." I handed her a piece of paper with the address of the warehouse. "Call the police." She started crying again. I left before chickening out.

Mount Saint Helens was my first stop. Jordan still hadn't awakened. I walked up to his bedside. It was still pretty early. He had no visitors. Poppa Jones was probably posted up in Momma's room. This gave me a little time for a soul-cleansing confession. My knee was still tender, but starting to loosen up. I pulled up a chair and leaned in.

"How's it going, baby boy?"

Heavy machinery beeped and lights flickered. The absence of the ventilator meant that Jordan was breathing by himself.

"I know you can hear me, Jordan. Just wanted to tell you that you're the best little brother a guy could ever have. I know we had our moments, but I never stopped loving you, man." I coughed, hearing the mucus break up in my chest. I wiped my eyes on the sleeves of my too-tight coat.

"Don't let this beat you, lil' bro. Everybody's entitled to screw up. Just look at me. It ain't like I'm where I wanna be. Don't leave us. Come back. Don't leave." I glanced around to see if we were still alone. Leaning in closer, I whispered, "He's gonna pay, Jordan. He's gonna pay for what he's done to you. On my soul, man, that schmuck's gonna pay." I coughed. "Get well. I'll see you soon." I stood and leaned in even closer to kiss his forehead.

Oh my God! Movement! Jordan's right arm twitched.

My brother had heard everything I said. His right arm twitched again.

"That's right. Fight it. Fight. The next time I see you; you'd better be talking." My cell rang.

"Wisdom, I'm with you." Maria professed in a strong voice. "I'll be waiting, Papi." I ended the call.

Momma wasn't doing so hot, either. I stepped up to her bed and kissed her like Prince Charming by laying a big wet one on Sleeping Beauty.

"Hey, Wiz," Momma said weakly. "How's Momma's boy?"

"Alright, ol' lady."

"Where's that little brother of yours?"

Poppa Jones walked up behind her. Momma's eyes were closed, so she missed him putting a finger to his lips for me to keep quiet.

"We haven't told her about Jordan," he whispered into my ear.

Pops smelled good. Expensive suite. Trademark Gucci loafers, holding a large Starbucks coffee container.

"Look, Wiz, look what the cat done dragged back in," Momma said, half-smiling, pointing at Pops.

I was about to comment but a rather chunky black lady entered the room, dragging a pretty nice-sized machine on wheels.

"Dialysis," the nurse announced. "I'm gonna need you gentlemen to step out the room, please."

"Momma, I'm gonna see you later." I kissed her on the cheek.

"Where you going, boy?"

"To get you a gift. How would you like to be dialysis free?"

"What you gonna do, boy, knock off a kidney donor truck?" She giggled a little.

"You just keep living, ol' woman. Help is on the way."
I kissed her cheek again.

"Son, what are you up to?" Dad asked me after we
stepped out the room. I didn't even mind him calling
me *son*.

"Nothing, Pops. How's everything going?" I leaned
against the wall Maria was heavy on my mind. I hacked
up some mucus. Held that slime in my mouth. My fever
had picked back up.

Dad gave me his hanky. "Everything's fine. I'm not
going back to the pulpit until all of this is over…with
Jordan and all."

I turned my head and released the gucky stuff. "You
tell Momma yet?"

A blank expression crossed his face. "Yes. Let's just say
if God's will be for her to live, then I'll be sleeping in
the guest bedroom for a long time."

"I hear that," I said. "Be prepared to be lonely."

Pops turned up his nose at my leather straight jacket.

"What's with the coat?" he asked. That was the one trait
I admired about my father: his ability to speak his mind.

"Malisa burned my clothes."

"Son, about Malisa…"

"Pops, you don't have to keep apologizing for that. It's
all right. If Jesus can forgive his crucifiers, then who am
I not to forgive you?"

"Thank you, son. And about those clothes, I'll—"

"Don't worry about it, Dad. I don't have much time."

"What do you mean?"

"Don't worry about that. I just need you to promise that you will get our family back together."

"Son, are you in some kind of trouble?"

"Pops, just promise me."

"Okay, but—"

"You think Jordan's gonna pull through?" I coughed.

"God's will, son. God's will."

"I've always admired the man you are. Everybody falls short, but not everybody takes the opportunity to get back up and follow. From what I see"—I shook his hand firmly—"I'm impressed. The job that you have is a hard one, a shepherd. Guard the sheep well. I've got faith in you." I pulled the old man into my embrace. "I've got faith in you."

"Wisdom, what's going on?" Poppa Jones asked concernedly. "You look like you're about to pass out."

"Love my momma the way Jesus loves you." With that said, I let go and walked away.

McDonald's was off the hook. The way people were lined up, I would've thought that the world was coming to an end and all the Big Mac diehards were about to get their end-of-the-world grub on.

I looked around.

"The afternoon crowd, huh?" I held up my double cheeseburger. "You know how health conscious I am. I don't usually eat this crap, but since this might be my last meal, might as well swallow this crap." I took a couple of bites. "Rico, this is what we gonna do."

The cheeseburger had his attention.

"Rico?"

"Yeah. Go ahead. I'm listening." Rico was dressed in a Sean John winter coat with one of those furry brimmed hoods. His black pants and Tims matched the coat. The boy had to have had a million pairs of Timberland boots. Every color.

"You're gonna meet me at the warehouse. We're going in together. I'm gonna get Highnoon to give you the contract. Make sure you get it to my father."

"What if Highnoon doesn't honor it? Ain't no honor among thieves," Rico said.

"Trust me. He will. Make sure my momma gets that kidney. Either way, that schmuck is not walking away with both kidneys."

"On my grandmomma, nigga," Rico said, giving me dap.

I loved his flavor. An old school cat sprinkled with tons of ghetto seasoning.

"I ain't got a problem with it, dog. But you know I can't let Punkeye slide with what he did. He's gonna get tightened up. Straight twisted."

You couldn't buy Rico's loyalty.

"I ain't trying to be a party crasher," I said, drinking Sprite. "What if he doesn't show?"

"Then the hunt is on, dog. That fool's gonna get it wherever."

"What about your boxing career?" I asked.

"Fool, when I drop Punkeye, ain't nobody gonna find his foul body."

Rico's threat was as promising as the actions he took. The dude was about his business. The skeletons in his closet belonged to pushers, women beaters and knuckleheads.

"Well, for your sake, we hope that doesn't happen. If everybody shows who we gave invitations to, this thing will be the mother of all parties. Just keep your ass low."

Outside in the parking lot, a white Ford Bronco pulled up to the drive-thru window. My top lip quivered and the nerves in my stomach were tripping. I gazed deeply through the tinted windows, almost coming out of my seat. I couldn't see him, but I knew it was the white man I'd chased a few nights ago. It had to be him. Before I knew it, I was up and dodging other customers in getting to the exit. There, I got a better look at the vehicle. Relief washed over my body. The SUV sitting in line didn't have any front-end damage. The Bronco I'd pursued had slid and taken out a large section of wrought iron fence that surrounded the cemetery. The last time I'd seen the SUV, the truck's front end was pushed up toward the windshield. Unless this guy owned a body repair shop, there was no way the Ford in line was his.

What the hell is happening to me? I asked myself, walking back to the table. There were so many standing in line for a piece of my ass it was ridiculous. Seemed the closer I was to carrying out the mission, the more hostile the opposition became that was coming out of the woodwork. I wanted to know if I'd stepped on the white dude's toes in some kind of way. Mister Buzz Cut wearing Ray Bans had been stalking me for a few weeks now. I wished I had more time to find out why this moron was sniffing around.

Rico looked at me like I'd lost my damn mind. "You want to tell me what that shit was about?"

I sat down and pinched the bridge of my nose. "My friend, I'm afraid that's a story for another day—whoops, I forget—there might not be another day."

"You need to stop with the jokes."

"Serious, man, it was nothing."

"Didn't look that way."

"Forget about it. We have bigger fish to fry."

"Maria's a good woman," Rico said and changed the subject. "Compared to the last broad, she's Mother Teresa. How'd she take it?"

"Not so good. But she's a trooper." I coughed loud and hard. "She's a good reason for me to stick around." Felt like my nose had become a flamethrower. My throat was itchy and my body rocked with aches and chills.

"I hear you," Rico said. "One day I'll run up on a dime like that."

"I'm sure you will. Listen, Rico"— Rico waved me off.

"No. Not one of those Hallmark card moments. Too corny. Let's just go and do the damn thing."

I smiled. "One love," I said.

"One world." Rico came back with the last half of our old school's 'get pumped up' mantra. We used to use that one before we served up serious nastiness on a rival.

Finally found you!

One could argue and say that I was taking one for the team. But that wouldn't be the truth. In fact, I was merely doing what a guy filled with unconditional love would do. The idea was to save my mother's life and save the souls of my family members. Saving three birds with one sacrifice.

I'd set myself up to bite the bullet. I knew my idea sounded crazy, but what could I do? A wise man once told me, "Corral all your problems inside one room and they'll take care of themselves." My family was being terrorized by a three-headed monster: Highnoon, Geechie and Popeye. Three heads, three problems, one warehouse.

Finally found you!

One helluva recipe for a party.

WISDOM

SUNDAY NIGHT, LAST NIGHT...

To the nocturnal creature, nighttime brings about feeding time, but for some, the dark hatches out deep dark fears of a sleepless, slumbering humanity. A world only known to those who prey on the possessions of others by using shadowy curtains to camouflage their heinous activities.

Two minutes past midnight, I rolled into the parking lot of my last breath. Rico was still by my side. Faithful until the bitter end.

He stayed in the van. It was starting to snow as I made my way up the walkway leading to two enormous steel doors of the warehouse, hobbling all the way. The bitter cold winds were beginning to stiffen my knee. The doors ascended upward as the rattling, creeping chain worked its magic.

As the doors slowly rose, the first things I saw were two enormous tan-colored Timberland boots. It didn't take a detective to figure out whom the boots belong to. The door slowly rose, revealing the rest of Highnoon's Frankenstein of a bodyguard.

"You're late. The man's waitin' on you," he barked.

Unlike the last time, there were no floodlights. Just darkness behind the monster.

"What?" I asked. Much attitude. "That fool's gonna penalize me or sumptin'?"

The monster looked down on me, scowling. "Don't make me take you out right here." He caressed the butt of a pretty impressive weapon sticking from the front of his pants. "Get it movin'."

"It ain't that easy. I'ma need that contract before this crap goes down." I folded my arms defiantly, my dime-store leather cracking because of the super cold temperatures. "Business is business."

The monster disappeared for a couple of minutes, and then returned holding a briefcase.

"Like I said"—he handed me the briefcase—"he don't have all night."

I checked the contents. Everything seemed to be in order. Signatures were in place. I signaled toward the van. Rico walked up. The monster pulled his pistol.

"What's this?" he said, pointing at me. "This a double cross?"

I wasn't worried about the big idiot using the hand cannon. He might've been a few table legs short of a dinette set, but he knew that his boss had a low tolerance for incompetence.

"Hold your water," I said, holding a hand up. "Just a messenger."

Rico stood a measly five-ten, standing as a mere child in the shadows of giants. Hell, I was six-six and the monster still made me look like a midget. But my boy held his ground. Rico glared up at the big lug with loads of contempt.

I handed Rico the briefcase.

"You know what to do," I said.

Rico slowly backed away, keeping an eye on the armed giant. After seeing Rico safely into the van, I sadly watched my friend drive away for what could be the last time.

The mail van seemed to be mourning too, as it moped through the darkness.

"This way," the monster said, but it was more of an order.

As we stepped inside, I could see track lighting split the darkness into groups of light and shadows. I followed the monster's movie theater screen-sized back through a few twists and turns, wondering how this whole thing would play out.

I'd taken a big risk ratting out my brother to his boss. As the saliva slid over the lump in my throat, I prayed that everything turned out for the best. Geechie could be brutally barbaric. I'd seen that in the form of a badly beaten Darrius. If anything, Yazoo would probably receive a slapping around. But nothing more. I kept telling myself that Geechie was a businessman. He wouldn't do anything to cross Highnoon.

We entered into a part of the warehouse that resembled

the size of a football stadium, completely gutted. The roar of generators could be heard throughout. Compared to the rest of the place, this part glistened like expensive diamonds. I gave up figuring why Highnoon had gone through all of this in the first place, but I was sure glad. This situation was perfect for the plan I'd outlined.

We rounded a wall. The four, high-powered Dodge Ram pickup trucks bewildered me. They were all black, all facing in different directions.

"Wisdom, Wisdom, Wisdom," Highnoon's sickening voice sang out. "Welcome. I trust you've had an impact on the heavenly direction of your family."

"Save it." I nodded in the direction of all four trucks. "I know this ain't some *Fear Factor* stunt, so why don't you explain yourself?"

The creep stepped from behind one of the trucks.

I nodded at the getup he was wearing.

He smiled at me, looking down at his outfit. "Oh. This old thing. As a kid, race cars fascinated me. Always wanted to drive one." He patted the tailgate of the truck facing South. "I guess this'll have to do."

"You're not making any sense."

"Not supposed to." He lit a cigar, blowing smoke.

"Tonight you're going to die, my friend. And in the most horrible way."

Keep smoking, punk. Keep smoking. Cancer'll be your karma.

"You see, I'm kinda glad you didn't go through with the first way I had planned. I started thinking of a more

painful way the moment you left. Took me a few minutes to come up with a suitable method. And thanks to
The History Channel, I've modernized a primitive form
of torture. Instead of some medieval torturing device,
these trucks will serve as your painful one-way ticket to
the great beyond."

I didn't understand how he did it, but immediately
following his last words, his gorillas appeared from behind
the other trucks grabbing me by the limbs.

"What the hell?" I said, struggling against the goon
squad.

"Settle down, Wisdom. No need to prolong this thing.
Just relax and let it be."

Highnoon gave the signal, dispensing a man to the cock-
pit of every truck. On command, the engines started.

"Truck drivers," Highnoon ordered, "move up a couple
of feet."

They obeyed.

When I looked back from the trucks, standing behind
Highnoon was a small army. The men were dressed in
black. Highnoon arrogantly eyed the questions in my
eyes, staring back at his soldiers.

"You know how I roll, Wisdom. Can't go nowhere
without having my back watched. Ain't no telling what
might you have planned." He played with the cigar in
his mouth. "Plus, the boys were curious to see how this
was gonna turn out."

His laughter was sick. I felt weak at the knees. Almost

came close to passing out a few times, but I wasn't gonna give the chump the satisfaction.

The place was cold. Chills chased my flesh. I coughed. A couple of times. While butterflies danced around in my stomach. The goons physically ushered me into the circle made by the truck beds after they'd been moved up.

The monster appeared, holding chains. Not little dorky chains, but thick, industrial-strength types. Now I saw where this was going. But I shuddered to imagine the pain.

"How can you be so cruel, man?" I asked, shaking my head in a disapproving, disgusted manner.

"Ask yo' cousin—oops you can't, because the weak fuck took himself out in jail. Ask yourself, what would you do if somebody took away everything you had in this world?"

The monster went around, fastening the hooks of the chains to the strong, sturdy tailgate hitches.

"Your cousin, Smoke, tore my whole world apart." Highnoon stared as the monster connected the last chain. "It's only fitting that I return the favor, don't you agree?" Highnoon threw the cigar to the ground, heeling it out. "Do it," he ordered his flunkies.

Two held me, while the monster fastened chains to my legs. I was about to be pulled apart like a chicken wing stashed away at a weight loss camp for extremely obese people.

After the monster finished, my legs had been hooked up to the tailgate hitch of the truck pointed in the South direction. Right arm anchored by the truck pointed

West—left arm secured by the East truck and the chain leading up to my neck was attached to the North. With my body heavily chained, I felt like a slave foot-shuffling up the stairs to the trading block.

The drivers gunned their idling engines as if waiting for the starting flag to fly, signaling the beginning of my imminent body dismemberment. My mind tumbled with hope. Hope that something or someone would stop this. Faith that God would be generous and spare me a miracle. The whole last week of my life had gone into putting my body on the line in saving folks, my folks—time, talent. And all I wanted out of life was just peace. Serenity. Tranquility. This was a degrading, unfitting end for such a noble, finely tuned, athletic body.

I watched Highnoon light up another cigar, smiling at me. Taunting me. Sweating me. Pleasuring himself at the life and death power he possessed.

One word—all it took was one word from him and my body parts would be dragged in all different compass points. What he would do with my severed head was a chilling thought.

"Wisdom, Wisdom, Wisdom. The week I gave you seemed like an eternity to me. Didn't think I was gonna make it through. But now, time's here. This is so beautiful. I wish that this little foreplay moment could last forever, the pleasurable crescendo to a much-needed euphoric release."

I looked over the trucks. The entire goon squad was

cracking up with hysterical laughter. But I also saw something else. Moving swiftly through the shadows. Lurking in the darkness. I closed my eyes, praying for my miracle.

Highnoon cracked one joke after another. His crew was bent over, chuckling like hyenas on steroids. Due to the bulk of the light concentrating on this area, the Negro ninjas lurked from the shadows unnoticed by Highnoon and his soldiers.

"Alright"—Highnoon chuckled—"let's get on with it." He twirled his cigar around in his lips. "Now, I would ask you if you had any last words, but the last time I ended up giving you a week"—he looked at my stone face—"Okay, damn. Last words, you have the floor."

I almost laughed in Highnoon's face as Geechie and his crew broke through the shadows.

"Yeah…I've got a question." I pointed to Geechie. The gorillas behind him matched the number of Highnoon's. "They don't look like they came with popcorn to enjoy the show."

Highnoon almost choked on his smoke. His soldiers stopped laughing and stiffened up, trying to look as intimidating as possible. Highnoon walked over, stopping any further advancement, his soldiers in tow.

"Gentlemen, to what do I owe the nature of this intrusion?" Highnoon asked, disrespectfully blowing smoke in Geechie's direction. Even though the two men were separated by four or five feet, the smoke managed to reach Geechie.

He waved off the cloud. "You invited me here, 'member? Yo' old ass must be goin' senile. When a man violates another man's home. Spray paints an invitation to this little party of yours on his fine walls. A nigga gets to thinkin': Either you want me to see something, or yo' arrogant ass trying to wage a war."

"…hell you talkin' 'bout, crack pusher? Didn't nobody break into your trailer home and spray nothin', punk," Highnoon said, blowing smoke again.

Geechie sarcastically laughed off the insult. Kingpins were exceptionally sensitive about their titles. And to be called the lowest forms of the hustle was considered a supreme insult.

"Oh, that's pretty low." This was the first time Geechie had paid me any attention. He was bugging over the chains. "What he do?"

"He was my friend," said Highnoon.

"Remind me to never make that mistake. But I'm here because of you and me," Geechie said.

"Stop talkin' in riddles."

"In so many words, you told me that if I didn't come to this meeting, my organization would be wiped out," Geechie concluded.

The statement made the drivers exit the trucks and stand behind Highnoon. Like chess pieces on a board, the monster moved to his king's side. Some black-burnt, gigantic cat moved to Geechie's. I'm assuming the mountain with legs was Geechie's bodyguard.

"Toy, nigga," Highnoon spat. "You ain't even on my level for me to be sending you messages like that, but I heard that your little weak ass was looking to take me out and make a come up."

Nobody was paying me any mind. My miracle was here. But my biggest concern was Yazoo. Where was he? It was at this moment that I cursed myself for shallow planning. I seemed to have underestimated Geechie's savage nature. I prayed for Yazoo's safety.

"I was told that this nigga was my ticket in here. I would be collecting some kind of finder's fee for producing this fool," Geechie said, snapping his fingers, producing a badly beaten Yazoo. My brother looked whipped but no worse for wear. His face was bruised, his spirit broken. No eye contact. He just kept his bruised peepers to the ground, not noticing me.

Highnoon looked a little confused. "What—"

Nobody was looking. They were so distracted; no one had seen me remove the chains. I still had no idea how I was going to free my brother, but the voice speaking from the shadows froze everybody.

"Freeze!" the gruff command rang out." Nobody move. You're surrounded."

"That yo' man, kingpin?" Geechie asked Highnoon.

Highnoon ignored Geechie and my brother.

"Show yourself!" he demanded.

Popeye was right on time. He strolled from the shadows, six guys in tow. All police officers. Bright gold badges dangled from black cords around their necks, guns in hand.

"What we got here?" Popeye asked, following behind with his Glock. The tension in the air was uneasy and hostile. All it would take was an itchy trigger finger to bring about a bloodbath.

"Popeye—" Highnoon said.

"Kill that Popeye shit," the pig blazed, taking exception to being called the character of a cartoon. Drug dealers never referred to him by the nickname, but Highnoon was a heavy exception to the rule. Popeye was on the payroll.

"This Pontiac," Highnoon said, gesturing around the building with his cigar. "You're out of jurisdiction. What brings you up here?"

"The big payday, boys. I heard you boys were throwing a party fit for the makings of a millionaire." The cop nodded to his boys. "We want a piece."

"What you talkin' 'bout, cop?" Geechie asked, still staring at Highnoon. "Ain't nothin' goin' on up in here except murder."

"You got the wrong department." Popeye spat. "I'm a narcotics cop, dumb ass. So now that I've given you a crash course on divisions, where the hell is the money and drugs?"

"Don't I pay you enough?" Highnoon asked. He looked at my mangled brother. "Greedy cops are a disgrace to this way of life. That's why they end up retired before retirement."

"Is that a threat?" one of the cops yelled from behind.

"What you want it to be?" the monster answered from Highnoon's side. Popeye, Highnoon and Geechie all stood in a triangle, facing each other, their crews in tow. It looked like one big United Nations gathering of thugs, hooligans and corrupt bacon boys in blue, ambassadors from different walks of filth.

Popeye smirked arrogantly. It took everything I had not to go bananas on that bum, but my brother stood in the middle of that mess. I had to find a way to get him before the drama began.

"Gentlemen," Highnoon said, blowing smoke, "this is my place. All of you are trespassing. I could get you all tossed in jail. The police up here are on the payroll."

"What you gonna tell 'em?" Geechie cut in, glancing in my direction. "That we were keeping you from cutting down one of your homeboys?"

"Enough of this crap," Popeye jumped in, his closed eyelid looking gross. "Give up the cash or my boys start shooting."

The gunshot was so loud and sudden, nobody worried about *who*, but we all scrambled for safety.

One of the cops lay dead. Looked like the loud mouth one. A bullet had replaced his right eyeball. The ensuing silence was louder than a library. Nobody said nothing for a few seconds. My guess was that cats were taking inventory of body parts and trying to get a hold on bodily functions.

"Larry's dead!" I heard Popeye scream from the shadows. I took refuge behind one of the pickups.

"You fuckas!" Popeye shouted. Automatic gunfire followed, igniting blaze from every inch of the large area.

Crackles of gunshots popped off all around me, lighting the shadows up like a Fourth of July night.

"I'm hit, dammit!" someone yelled out in pain.

"Tony, where you at?" some schmuck called out over the gunfire, giving away his position. He never got an answer. At least not the one he was expecting.

"I'm right here," a different voice answered, laced by pure venom.

"Shit"—was the last thing I heard from the "Tony" dude before his cries were cut short by automatic blasts. These fools were playing for keeps.

"Yazoo!" I screamed. "Yazoo!" I called out. Getting no answer pushed me to look around the truck bed.

Pure chaos. Bodies lay on the floor, gunfire crackled overhead and guys were engaged in the physical. The whole scene reminded me of one of those war movies. Men doing battle in every fashion.

"Yazoo!" I called out again, wondering where the hell Highnoon had gotten off to. I didn't really give a flying rat's behind about him. I just didn't want nothing to happen to the kidney he was carrying.

I had to find my brother. I got down, staying low to the ground. As I moved through the violence, a real stupid thought seem to percolate through my mind: *I'd planned for all this to happen and now that it was going on, how the hell was I going to keep Highnoon to his word?* Especially when I hadn't kept mine.

I'd screwed up royally. Didn't factor any of these equations in. It would take a massive miracle now to save Momma. About fifteen minutes after the first blast, most of the gunfire had stopped. Brothers were now scrapping the old-fashioned way. I hadn't run into Geechie or Highnoon, but their bodyguards were ten feet away, clashing like gladiators in a Roman coliseum. The monster looked to be losing. Geechie's bodyguard was a mountain with legs, but the monster eclipsed him. The keen-edged Rambo blade the mountain slashed with was the difference–maker. Judging by how the monster was attacking, he didn't give a damn about the mountain's little equalizer. It seemed that the more his ass was cut, the harder he fought.

I left the monster slapping the blade from the mountain's hands. The mountain was now struggling to breathe in the monster's death grip of a headlock. I stumbled over a body. Checked it. Nope, not Yazoo's—thank God. But whoever he used to be, his next of kin would be in for a rough time, trying to identify the body without the head.

"Yazoo!" I continued to call. A bullet whistled past my head. It missed me, but unexpectedly struck somebody behind me.

"My God!" I heard the victim cry out in agonizing

pain. I crawled to the far end of the building. Bodies were lying around as if waiting to be called by number into the coroner's lab. The sounds of the sick and dying filled the air.

I figured Geechie was long gone. The police would be coming shortly. This much gunfire under one roof couldn't and wouldn't go unnoticed much longer. My heart sank. If one of the stray bullets didn't get Yazoo, Geechie would. And if my brother wasn't one of the dead or dying, he would be soon.

This was a bullshittin' plan, filled with holes. Now, my brother's blood poured through. I'd played myself into thinking that I could save 'em all. But all I'd accomplished was destruction. All around. My pity party would have to wait. Whoever had snatched me up by my shoulders was inhumanely strong. I couldn't see who I was battling because some of the lights had been shot out. But I could smell his breath, though. Smelled like hell wrapped up in the stench of a backed-up septic tank.

I could hear the cheap leather of my loaner coat tear as I freed myself, snapping out a haymaker of a right cross.

"Awwwww," the creep yelped, stumbling backward. His jaw had to be broken: I'd caught him flush. Had to get to the light, so I could put this bum out of his misery. Tried to break and run, but I stumbled over another body. I didn't have any light, so I couldn't make any IDs. I identified the pain in my knee. Had felt that on the way to the ground. I'd twisted my knee again. I couldn't see the sissy, but I felt his boot connect with my head. It wasn't quite the light I was hoping to reach. This light was accompanied by stars and more stars. How this cat saw me was a mystery. It was like the schmuck had on a pair of night vision goggles.

With one powerful surge, I pushed off the floor, hobbling for the light. Had a little help getting there by a boot in my ass. Off balance, I flipped headfirst into the light.

Crumpled up on the ground, I saw him—or rather—them. The huge Timberland boots were standing in front of me.

"Let's see how much mouth you got now," the monster said, his face bloody, and his hands held knife slashes from his battle with Geechie's bodyguard. The monster standing here only meant that the mountain had been reduced to rubble.

Somehow, I knew that this beast and I were destined to tangle. This was Highnoon's boy. Right-hand man. Down the way, I could still hear gunfire and screaming. I stood up, balancing the majority of my weight on my good leg. The monster peeped out my weakness, smiling.

"I'm gonna enjoy squeezing the life out of you," he said, cracking his knuckles.

My thoughts were of my brother. But in order to find him, the road went through this wall of a man standing in front of me. I flexed my neck like the actors did in those action movies. I guessed they did it to look macho in front of the cameras.

"Don't sweat this, homes," a familiar voice spoke from behind, "we take care of the small work." I knew the voice. It was dripping with a Spanish accent. But why was its owner here? I'd find out later, but for now I reveled in the help. Didn't give a damn if it came from Paco or the Pope. Paco stepped from behind.

Paco was wide, but he would be no match for the monster. He answered the question in my curious eyes. "Any friend of my sister is a friend of mine." The monster looked confused.

"No thanks, Paco," I said. "This fool's twice your size." Paco smirked.

"Pride, huh? I can dig it, but I wasn't talking about me, or you fighting the Votal." Paco called out to the shadows. Mexicans came from everywhere, but the last one stood eye level with the monster, and just as wide.

"Like I said, *ese*." Paco shook my hand. "Any amigo of my sister's is a friend of mine. Now go find your brother."

I limped off right after the big Mexican, with the green bandana tied around his melon, khakis kicked up to his Adam's apple, fingerless, leather driving gloves, green flannel shirt and black Chuck Taylor All-Stars picked the monster up like a loaf of bread and deposited his ass to the cold, hard floor.

Even after I was halfway to the other end, I could hear the voices of my brown brothers laughing and speaking their native tongue. I could hear no more gunfire—only wounded souls, crying out from the turf. The lights that hadn't been shot out revealed a few skirmishes here and there, but most of the fighting had stopped. I stumbled through the way I'd entered.

Geechie and Highnoon were unaccounted for, but the lights ahead shone brightly on Popeye's body. He'd taken one through the forehead. Dead center!

His empty eyes revealed an even emptier head. The bullet had made a tiny entrance but exploded through the back of his skull. *Ashes to ashes, dust to dust*, I thought. I pushed on, knee hurting, and soul crying.

My eyes blurred. Tears slid down my face. A poorly devised plan could've cost my brother his life, and probably my mother's, too.

I leaned up against the wall, trying to take the weight off my bad knee. The voices were muffled at first, but the more I strained my hearing, they became clearer. Somewhere in one of the rooms ahead, I could hear Highnoon and Geechie. They seem to be calmly talking at first, but then Highnoon started raising his voice. The scuffle was instantaneous. The closer I limped, the better I could hear the sounds of furniture being moved around by a brawl shaping up. I was careful as I stared into the room. I was right. Highnoon was manhandling Geechie. We were in the front office part of the old warehouse. The chair that Highnoon threw Geechie over had confirmed their private war.

"I'm the king, young nigga," Highnoon yelled as he approached Geechie's body, kicking furniture out of his way. "If you want the crown, come and get it."

He pulled Geechie to his feet. Geechie must've been playing possum because he came to life and caught Highnoon in the throat with some kind of karate chop.

The big man hit the floor, holding his throat, gasping for air. Because of his vast street-fighting experience, Highnoon was my personal favorite to win. That didn't mean that I was going to count Geechie out. The fool was a feisty scrapper.

Slight moaning caught my attention. Over in the corner, my brother lay sprawled out on the floor. Highnoon and Geechie were so into their private fight for the championship to be the undisputed drug kingpin of Detroit that they didn't see me limp in. Yazoo had a lump on the side of his head. One of them had probably laid him out with the butt of a gun.

"When I get through with you," Highnoon said, his ashy hands wrapped around Geechie's throat, straining, gritting teeth, choking the crap out of him. "I'm gonna go out and show that slut you call a baby's momma a real man." The insult seemed to energize Geechie. His hands searched the floor, finding a metal pipe.

Whack!

Highnoon loosened his grip. Blood splattered from the open head wound. My only hope was that nothing happened to damage Highnoon's kidneys.

"Yazoo," I spoke, "Come on, get up."

I scooped him up, draping his arm around my neck. He moaned louder. We were outside the room when two gunshots popped off. The unmistakable sound of a body hitting the floor broke the pursuing silence, then the struggle to get up. Highnoon stumbled out first, holding his side.

The shots were probably the exchange of fire, with Geechie receiving the worst end. And judging by the surprised look on Highnoon's gold-tooth grill, I thought the schmuck had taken care of his business, and our friend, Geechie, would be front-page gossip over morning cups of coffee.

Without as much as a grunt, Highnoon fell—face-first—to the floor. I thought the bullet to the side had been enough to chop the big, black, gold-teeth oak tree down. But the orange-size hole between the shoulder blades had done the job.

The barrel of the pistol was still smoking when Geechie walked out of the office behind it. Yazoo moaned in pain.

"Hey, has-been," Geechie called out to our fleeing backs. With me assisting Yazoo, we weren't exactly fleet of foot.

"Face me." I turned us slowly. "Can't believe I'm about to put a cap in the ass of the best collegiate player—I think—since M.J. skied out of North Carolina," Geechie stated. "Even though you a has-been now."

I said nothing as he babbled. Yazoo was whispering, mumbling something that sounded like a disoriented version of the 23rd Psalm. His eyes still closed, he sounded like his conscious mind was struggling to merge, trying to win gloriously over his nearly unconscious state.

"Yeah, I thought I recognized you. The stupid nigga who blew his whole career and millions on a pick-up game. I followed your college career." He pointed the pistol at Yazoo. "Didn't know this trash was yo' brother, though." Foolishly, the moron slightly tapped his noggin with the barrel sights as if to beat out a thought. "Highnoon let me in on the surprise party he had in store for you." He slowly backpedaled while keeping us in check. He kicked the crap out of Highnoon's head. "Mister Kingpin here wasn't gonna honor the contract. Said that once he was finished with you, he was gonna put contracts on the heads of yo' entire family. Called it his little escape clause."

"What's your plan?" I asked in a no-nonsense voice. "I mean, should we be thanking you, or...." My eyes fell down toward Highnoon's body.

"Looks like you missed the whole web and fell right into the lap of the spider, superstar. No witnesses. You know how the game goes. I took out Highnoon. Even dead, this nigga still has the power to ice me. I can't take any chances. I gotta kill Zoo anyway. The nigga killed my dog. You...you were just in the wrong place at the wrong time."

He raised the firearm to tighten up loose ends. The barrel of death looked sinister. It was as if I could see deeply into the dark chamber of the weapon. Could see the small bulldozer preparing, digging up the earth. Two plots. Two caskets dropping. Crying, sniffling. Then the dirt falling back into the graves. And just before my face was completely covered, I heard the thunderous blast from a gun.

A stupid look of pain gripped Geechie's thuggish mug. He fell to his knees, his finger still threaded through the trigger guard, the weapon hanging lifelessly. Behind him, Highnoon had somehow come back from hell, Satan giving him one last mission: to bring him another wretched soul. The barrel of Highnoon's weapon smoked like Satan was about to come through and make a guest appearance. Highnoon had made the kill, lying on his back. He offered one last gold-toothed grin before ushering Geechie's pathetic soul to his seat in Hell. The pistol fell from Highnoon's large hand clattered to the ground. Simultaneously, Geechie's body fell—face-first–his eyes holding the shock of death.

The nature of what I'd done tugged at the heartstrings of my morality. But I couldn't think about that. My mother needed Highnoon's offerings.

The two parasites lay across from each other. Cancelled like bad checks of society. For what I'd done, I felt no better than them. No matter how purposeful the deed seemed. Wheeling around, I struggled to balance all our weight on one good leg.

"I'll be in church Sunday," Yazoo weakly stated.

"Me too, brother, me too."

It was funny how some people didn't reach out for the Maker until their time of need. My brother had spent years rebelling against God. He swore he'd never step foot inside church again. Now, here he was...bruised, misused and torn-down, talking about God. I just smiled as we struggled toward the front. The red and blue police lights flooded the inside of the building, mixing red and blue with the shadows.

I could only imagine the chaos going on outside in the parking lot. Police. Dogs. Paramedics. Macho, over-zealous SWAT guys who were probably waiting to make their bones by plugging the first schmuck who was retarded enough to get caught up in the crosshairs. I stopped at the door to catch a steadied breath. Yazoo looked like he was barely hanging on.

Besides getting Highnoon's carcass to the hospital, my only other priority was not getting shot after we limped into the cold night air.

"Wounded man coming out," I shouted, cracking the door. "Please...don't...shoot."

I gave it to the count of three, and then I fully opened the door, my brother draped around my neck, stumbling out into the smog of red, blue and white lights.

FIVE MONTHS LATER

Maria was decked all out in her Sunday best, a plain-looking, fruity-colored skirt and white blouse. A cute little Sunday hat capped her beautiful head. My baby didn't really have taste when it came to clothing but neither did I. A corny-looking sports jacket, button down shirt and slacks hugged my six-six frame. Mama's ordeal had taught me that life was too short to be concerned with materialism. God, health and a very good woman were all I needed. The rest of that monkey mess would take care of itself.

We were running a little behind schedule for Sunday night service at my father's church. Thanks to Rico's first professional debut, the boxing contest had lasted one minute and twenty-seven seconds. A new world's middleweight record. The match was over from the opening bell. Rico had beat on his opponent like a drum. His prediction for a knockout was on the money. He kind of reminded me of the old Muhammad Ali days. Rico ran his mouth just like the champ, too. But he'd backed up his game.

The post-match interview was nothing short of hilarious. He'd made fun of the interviewer's receding hairline. Said that the white man's head looked like an egg wearing a mink bomber and cracked a couple of jokes about the current middleweight champion's wife.

We'd chatted for a couple of minutes in the locker room. I'd hugged him, telling him how proud I was. To knock out schmucks until he was undeniably the undisputed middleweight champion of the world. From there I went and retrieved Maria and was pulling up in the parking lot of Infinite Baptist. After two warm, loving smiles, we hustled into the building. No words were passed until we stepped into the sanctuary. One of the handsome-looking ushers handed us two programs and hugged me until I almost coughed up a lung. Jordan kissed Maria on the cheek.

"Thank you for not giving up on me, brother," he whispered.

"That's what big brothers are for." I teased. I stepped back. "Nice usher uniform." I think I chuckled a little too loud.

"Shhh," Monique, the other usher, gestured with her finger to her lips. Jordan's ex-crackhead girlfriend looked vivacious. I was in church and had no business examining Monique's revitalized figure, but damn. Whoever would've known that girlfriend was stacked in the back like that? I'm just glad it wasn't too late to save and restore a body like hers. And, oh my God, the girl's hair and skin resembled the stuff of runway models. My brother looked healthy as well. Fat cheeks, radiant and glowing skin. He'd gained all of his weight back and then some.

Part of his healing didn't include rehabbing old memories of the heartless cop who'd put his stamp on Jordan's life, soul and face. My brother would live with the fleshly scarring of "Finally found you" that had been carved into his chest. Although the plastic surgeons were quite skilled in their jobs, they were unsuccessful at totally eradicating substantial scarring. Monique was also left with a scar above her right eyebrow, too. Jordan hadn't bothered to bring up the deadly night in the warehouse and I didn't see fit to force any information on him. Foolish, but we just lived like that night was a fable in a far away land. A bedtime story for hardened criminals locked down, living out basketball score-type prison sentences. Jordan ushered us to our seats. I firmly gripped Maria's slender hand as though expecting this dream to fade any moment, leaving me all alone in my bed of horrific nightmares.

We sat noticing that the church was more packed than usual. Church hats were out in full force, hovering over our heads like flowery, but very colorful flying saucers. The mistress of ceremonies even adorned one. Her brim was a lovely summer yellow with flowers sprouting out all over. The sanctuary lighting made love to the brilliance of the rhinestones until the courtship produced a gleaming, almost blinding spectacle, causing me to shield my eyes. The lady that lived under the huge hat was lovely. In every way one could possibly imagine. A true warrior. A gift from God. The only gift I knew that kept on giving.

The mistress of ceremonies—my mother—smiled at me as she introduced the choir for two selections. They stood to their feet in unison. Men and women draped in red rose-colored robes. But one face outshined them all. She took her position in front of the microphone. She opened her mouth and we were blessed with the most amazing voice I'd ever heard. I had no clue that my sister's voice sounded so angelic.

Tempest smoothly harmonized about how amazing God's grace was. She was once lost but now found. Once blind but now her eyes were open to obey the Master and be more of a wife to her husband.

Darrius seemed to be enjoying the spectacular performance his wife was rendering as he sat on the far side of the church. But to me, I think he was not only hypnotized by her singing, but fixated on her perfectly round, very noticeable, protruding belly. That's right. My sister and her husband were going to be proud parents in five more months. It would be ludicrous for me to believe that countless sessions of marriage counseling with my father was what kick-started their marriage. This was God's work. Well, maybe some of it. A cold chill crept down my spine. My hands moistened and my mouth tasted like a fresh sheet of sandpaper. My mother swayed along with the music, clapping her hands and gazing up at her daughter. So sweet. So innocent.

I did what I had to do. I had lied my ass off at how her name was pumped up the donor's list. If my confession wouldn't be enough to kill her; knowing what her son had perpetrated to save her life would be enough to worry her away from the land of the living. Only five people in this whole world knew: Rico, Maria, Pops, myself, and his attorney. The night of the warehouse, Rico had delivered the documents to Pops. Pops had a hard time believing what I'd done, but he called up his attorney and rushed over to the hospital where Highnoon's body lay. From there, wheels were set in motion. The kidney had reached my mother within hours. The surgery was a success. Recovery was touch-and-go for awhile, but with the help of medication, my mother had made a full recovery. My heart had sunken into a slim pit of self-loathing when my momma's eyes opened in recovery. The first thing out of her mouth was: "Thank you, Jesus, for the miracle."

I felt like an abomination. I had indirectly planned the murders of all those parasites who'd plagued my family. Highnoon, Geechie, Popeye—the three-headed monster that was looking to decimate my people.

Had blood on my hands. Didn't know how God would forgive me for totally erasing the sixth commandment from my heart. For all I knew, I could step outside of the church and get mowed down by gunfire. Couldn't say it wouldn't be deserving. Eye for an eye. Tooth for a tooth. Geechie's confession. How Highnoon had planned to go out on my family after he disposed of me. The schmuck was gonna totally go back on his word. A wee-tiny spot in my soul made me burn with satisfaction in taking part in his demise. Nobody threatened my family. I would have to do a lot of praying for God to remove the destructive stain from my heart.

"You okay?" Maria asked, smiling, squeezing my thigh. I smiled back.

"Just fine." I wanted to kiss her full lips, but my pops rising to walk to the podium stalled the thought. After all, we were in the Lord's house, a place that didn't tolerate any premarital hanky-panky—or hanky-panky of any kind.

A loving look in Mom's direction and Pops was off to do his thing. His warrior robe made him look taller than usual. His face was a picture of spiritual maturity. A leader. Finally, a true man of the cloth. No nonsense. Pop's spiritual transformation had been incredible. The man went from taking from his flock to leading and encouraging them all to live Godly lives.

Sister Walker was noticeably absent from the sanctuary. The sister had disappeared right after her husband went haywire, trying to plant my father in the cold, hard ground. I still remembered the crazed look in his eyes. One thing I learned was that some men handled adultery better than others. Some cried, while others pretended like nothing was going on. I'd been dreadfully introduced to the side that didn't fare too well. Had been in the presence of a man who'd studied—dissected his wife's infidelities, and then premeditated a heartless plan to correct his failing marriage by disposing of my pops. Murder in the form of marital counseling.

Wellington Walker was now serving a life sentence for killing the police chief. The news hounds had been all over it. The bastard had made national headlines. His sinister face had graced the front page of every newspaper, magazine and news channel. A media field day.

What did the moron think: he had the green light to whack every Tom, Dick and Harry who slid between his wife's trifling thighs? But despite all my efforts, my greatest achievement was sitting up front with a very dignified crop of clean-cut, well-dressed young men. My Pops stood and read scriptures from the Gospel of John. He delivered his text, launching right off into the body of the message.

"Amen," a few responded.

"Say that, Rev!" the congregation shouted and praised.

Pops delivered the closing with the death, burial and resurrection of Christ. It was now time for the part of the service that I was ultimately going to enjoy: the installation of the young deacons sitting up front. My heart skipped beats as Yazoo rose at the calling of his name, and didn't stop until his installation was complete. Kinda felt like a proud parent at a high school graduation.

Yazoo was the most surprising. The man had done a complete one-eighty. My brother went from hating the Lord to feverishly going to church every time the doors opened. My pops was proud. From the look of them at the altar, hugging, it was almost impossible to believe that Pops was Zoo's stepdad.

The pregnant lady holding the camcorder was the most shocking surprise. Samantha Jones was the newest addition to our family. She'd been with Yazoo years before his pretty brief rise to power on the streets. Come to find out that his aloofness prevented us from knowing about her.

I found out that he'd met Sam at a frat party. She liked his braids. He loved her smile. The rest was history. Light-skinned, thick sister with cute freckles. She complemented my brother very well. They were expecting their first. Three months away. Of course, Tempest and Sam were inseparable, shopping for baby clothes and whatnot.

My focus rested on Yazoo's head, though. Samantha was going to have to get used to the new look. Zoo had cut his braids off. They'd been the first things to go after rebuilding his relationship with God. The love in the sanctuary was thick. My family was growing, learning and bonding. I didn't think this kind of love was possible. Thought that this type of stuff only happened only on *The Cosby Show*. The good could always be subtracted from the bad. How this whole kidney thing went down. Good was pulled from Moses murdering the Egyptian and then fleeing. The hardening of Pharaoh's heart, and the crucifixion of Jesus Christ.

I'll forever have to live with the treacherous stain on my conscience. We serve a forgiving God, but I'll have a dandy of a time trying to forgive myself. I know one thing—all things are possible if I let go and let God.

EPILOGUE

With all the turbulence in my rearview mirror, I was now able to focus on my brand new family. Maria was my queen. My wife. My entire earthly life. I'd do anything to keep a smile on baby girl's face—which wasn't hard. All my cupcake craved was my love. Attention. Affection. I was more than happy to keep her heart's shelves stocked with the stuff until our graying days.

I still couldn't believe how she'd hung around, even when the chips were down. At times when most women would've hot-footed it to the next player with the Cadillac and a life's supply of dead presidents. My cupcake stayed faithfully by her man's side. Never doubting. Never complaining. In fact, Maria never did anything except shower me with love. Encouraging me to shoot for my dreams. Her belief in me manifested when she held down two jobs to support us, while I rehabbed my knee and got my body into basketball shape. I'd promised her the moon. I wasn't gonna disappoint.

Rico's manager put me in touch with Tony Lagrosser, a premier sports agent out in Los Angeles. Tony flew to

Detroit to meet me. The chemistry was off the charts. He was impressed. Lagrosser liked what he saw. And I liked what I heard. I had busted my ass to get in shape. Worked harder than I'd ever worked in my life. Lagrosser had lined up a tryout in the Lakers training camp. Competition was cutthroat, a ton of guys fighting for a few measly spots on the roster. Heart, desire and the willingness to out-work all the others had earned me a pretty cool nickname. The Machine—I was affectionately called by players and the coaching staff.

I married Maria a week after training camp when I got the good news. I'd done the impossible and had become a professional player. Maria threw me a celebration picnic in Belle Isle Park. Family, friends. Paco, my brother-in-law, and his posse arrived late. A fleet of low-rider cars bounced into the parking lot. After a few beers, my brother-in-law and I laughed about our first run-in. I even rolled my pants leg up, showing off the knife wound that was left by his late partner, Julio, drawing a couple of laughs. Julio had been killed in a drive-by a week before our wedding.

Everybody was having a great time until that damn white Ford Bronco pulled onto the grass next to our shelter. Most of the laughter stopped as the white man, sporting the shades, a serious look, and a buzz cut stepped out. Like the jerk had been invited, he strolled up to where I was sitting—Maria was sitting on my lap. Paco must've sensed trouble because my brother-in-law stood, his friends doing the same. Tension mounted as the white man removed his shades and placed them into his shirt pocket. I thought this was surely the end of my party when Mr. Buzz Cut smiled, then started congratulating me on my success.

The guy had turned out to be Caliba's half-brother. He kept it real. Said that he had wanted to get revenge for a number of years now. He'd blamed me for the death of his sister. Said he'd thought about killing me since Caliba's funeral. My ex's brother, Lucas Downing, and I must've talked for hours. I was deeply sorry for his sister. She'd deserved better. He forgave me and we shared a few brews.

A year later Maria gave birth to a cute little boy. We named him Chance. Don't ask. Don't know where she came up with the name. Chance Jones was born in a hospital in Beverly Hills, California. Our home was probably bigger than the hospital's entire West wing. Yes, my contract was phat. The end of the first season saw a scoring title and an All-Star nod. OKC eliminated us in the second round of the playoffs. It was cool—next year, right?

One day on my drive to the Staples Center, I thought I saw Malisa pushing a shopping cart filled with cardboard. Couldn't tell for sure. I was running late for work. Just knew karma was a bitch. I came from tragedy. I thank God every single day for His mercy. Dreams do come true. I'm living proof that the collection plate is only as corrupted as the hand reaching in.

ABOUT THE AUTHOR

Thomas Slater is a native of Detroit, MI. He is the author of *Show Stoppah* and *No More Time-Outs*, and under the pen name, Tecori Sheldon, he is the author of *When Truth is Gangsta*. He hopes to create a footprint by stepping off into the cement of literary greatness. Visit the author at www.slaterboyfiction.com, facebook.com/thomaseslater and Twitter @EarlWrites.